I0523924

Henry Frederic Reddall

Henry M. Stanley

A record of his early life and struggles; his career in the Confederate army, in the

United States navy, and as a war correspondent in Abyssinia

Henry Frederic Reddall

Henry M. Stanley
A record of his early life and struggles; his career in the Confederate army, in the United States navy, and as a war correspondent in Abyssinia

ISBN/EAN: 9783337240073

Printed in Europe, USA, Canada, Australia, Japan

Cover: Foto ©Raphael Reischuk / pixelio.de

More available books at **www.hansebooks.com**

HENRY M. STANLEY

HENRY M. STANLEY

A RECORD OF

His Early Life and Struggles; His Career in the Confederate Army, in the United States Navy, and as a War Correspondent in Abyssinia; How He Found Livingstone, Traced the Course of the Congo, and Founded the Congo Free State

WITH A FULL ACCOUNT OF

HIS LATEST AND GREATEST ACHIEVEMENT,

THE

RESCUE OF EMIN BEY.

COMPILED FROM STANLEY'S NARRATIVES AND OTHER AUTHENTIC RECORDS

By HENRY FREDERIC REDDALL.

———

NEW YORK:

ROBERT BONNER'S SONS,

PUBLISHERS,

PRESS OF
THE NEW YORK LEDGER.

CONTENTS.

HENRY M. STANLEY.

CHAPTER I.

BOYHOOD AND EARLY MANHOOD.

The true story of the life of Henry Morton Stanley reads like a romance, and is another example of that truth which is more interesting than fiction. The man known the world over as Stanley was born in 1840, at Denbigh, Wales. His real name is John Rowland. His parents were so poor that when the boy was three years old he was taken in charge by the parish of St. Asaph, and was reared in an almshouse. He remained in the almshouse until he had received as good an

education as that institution could give, which
having awakened a desire to know still more, he
accepted a situation as a school-teacher at Mold,
in Flintshire, hoping that circumstances would
so shape themselves that, at a later period, he
might be able to finish his education. He
remained at Mold one year, at the end of which
time he felt that he was not called to be a school-
teacher. Having received the amount due him,
and succeeding in obtaining a situation as cabin-
boy on board a ship bound for New Orleans, he
embarked for the New World, in which he hoped
to earn a better living than that which he could
obtain at home, and at the same time gratify the
strong instincts of his nature. Soon after his
arrival he was fortunate in obtaining the friend-
ship of a gentleman named Stanley, who, having
been drawn toward the frank Welsh boy, gave
him employment. As days resolved themselves
into weeks and months, and his employer and
friend found that his confidence had not been
misplaced, he adopted young Rowland, and

bestowed upon him his own name. With plenty
of means to be had for the asking, the youth
tramped around the Southwest, and spent considerable time among the Indians. Doubtless he
gained some ideas about savages there which
were of great use to him in after years. His
foster-father died without making a will, and this
left the young man poor again.

Says one of his many biographers, Professor
Packard : "While thus engaged in schooling
himself, though unconsciously, to his great
work, the civil war broke out in the United
States. Here a new field presented itself to him.
The South had for a long time been his home,
and he had been educated among circumstances
which would naturally lead him to accept the
views of the South. To a certain extent he did
believe them ; and as the life of a soldier was in
keeping with his nature, he enlisted in the Confederate army. The roaming life of the army he
loved ; and instead of shrinking from danger
when it presented itself, he rather courted it, and

the story of his connection with the 'Lost Cause'
was one of courage and daring. In addition to
these, he possessed those qualities which lead to
success and fame. In carrying out one of his
bold projects, he was taken prisoner by the Union
troops, and the South lost him forever. His
prison was the iron-clad *Ticonderoga*. His
manliness and courage won the admiration of
the commander of the vessel, who after a time
released him upon the condition that he should
join the American navy. A sailor's life was not
exactly suited to his nature, and consequently he
was not adapted to it ; yet, nevertheless, his conduct was such that he was soon raised to the
position of acting ensign.

"When at last the war was over, and peace
came again to our beloved land, he was discharged
from service, and as his nature demanded something to do, he began to look about for some
congenial field of labor. At this time the Cretans
were struggling for independence, determined to
throw off the yoke of Turkish oppression, and be

free from its tyrannical rule. Having by chance learned the fact, Stanley resolved to join the Cretans, and assist them in their efforts to become a nation.

"Securing a situation as correspondent of *The New York Herald*, in company with two Americans, he sailed for the island of Crete. Having reached his destination, he first sought to learn 'the lay of the land,' and, in so doing, became so disgusted with the leaders of the rebellion, their mode of conducting it, and their treatment of prisoners, that he abandoned his original intention, and resolved to travel in the East. The commission which he had received from Mr. Bennett, the proprietor of the *Herald*, allowed him to roam wherever his inclinations led him. Under this broad license he had a wide field of adventure and travel before him.

"At this time, Stanley had passed through more, and witnessed more, than most men do in a lifetime ; and yet he had seen but little more than twenty-five years. In 1867 he returned to

the United States, where he was warmly received
by Mr. Bennett. Soon after this the English
government sent out an expedition against the
king of Abyssinia, who had committed grievous
wrongs upon the subjects and representatives
of Her Majesty. Here again Stanley saw a field
of usefulness, the nature of which was congenial
to his tastes. He therefore joined the expedition,
retaining his situation as correspondent of the
Herald. His letters, as published in the *Herald*,
present a succinct account of the campaign, its
battles, and the final victory. One of the peculiar
traits of Stanley's character is his ability to overcome seeming impossibilities ; and where many
men would have paused, he has pushed onward.

"When the final battle had been fought, and
the British troops had succeeded in winning the
victory—when peace was at last restored, and the
forces of Britain were triumphant—he at once
sent the glad news to one of the dailies of London, where it was received and published before
the arrival of the official dispatches. Stanley's

letters are considered the best history of the campaign which has as yet been written.

"After the absence of one year, Stanley returned to the United States in 1868. Mr. Bennett was one of those men who recognize talent wherever they see it. When, therefore, he saw the ability and the peculiar characteristic of Stanley, he felt sure that he had found just the man that he had been seeking for a long time; and the letters which Stanley sent from time to time to the *Herald*, confirmed this opinion. Having need of a correspondent in Spain, which was at this time convulsed with a civil war, he at once sent Stanley to that country. In his new situation he displayed that same promptness, energy, and faithfulness which had previously marked his career. Being constantly upon the field, his letters always contained the latest news; and the papers containing them were eagerly sought after, since they presented a correct aspect of the situation of Spanish affairs."

His successful performance of all that had been

entrusted to him thus far disclosed his fitness
for the greater work to which he was soon to be
appointed.

David Livingstone, a Scotch missionary and
explorer, had been engaged for thirty years in
opening Central Africa to the light. His success
had placed his name among the most famous in
the record of the present century. But in 1870
he had been for two years buried in the heart of
the African continent, and the world had come
to think that he was dead. In that year the
enterprise of the editor of *The New York Herald*
suggested a search expedition. Young Stanley
—then thirty years of age—was placed in command, and after nine months of vigorous and
perilous research came upon the brave explorer
on the shores of Lake Tanganika.

"Henry M. Stanley," says a recent writer,
"could say in all modesty the other day that he
believed the mantle of Livingstone had fallen
upon his shoulders. These two names will be
forever linked in the story of the awakening of

Africa from her sleep of ages. It can be said in
general of Stanley's books that though his earliest
ventures in the literature of exploration are full
of graphic power, his writings have shown a
steady and rapid advance in felicity of description
and in fulness and accuracy of statement. In
the intervals between his journeys in Africa,
Stanley put forth every effort to acquire the
scientific equipment which would impart to his
labors in the field an enduring value. The result
is that he became one of the most competent geographers as well as the greatest explorer of the
age. It was a remarkable feat he achieved when,
chased by thousands of enemies down the Congo,
he mapped the course of the great river for 1500
miles so accurately, that his delineation of its
channel in *Through the Dark Continent* is, to
all intents and purposes, the map of the Congo
to-day. The longitudes he was able to take were
not quite accurate, but his map, considering the
circumstances under which it was made, has been
more and more the wonder of geographers as our

knowledge of the Congo has grown ; and what a
prince of explorers that famous work shows
Stanley to be! *Through the Dark Continent* is the
Odyssey of African travel. No intelligent person
can afford to say that he has not read it, for it is
the book that first revealed to the world a vast
continent from sea to sea, with the greatest of its
lovely lakes ; with its myriads of princes, powerful and puny ; with its jumble of tongues and
races ; its vast variety of habitations and modes
of living ; its greatest river now tumbling to
lower levels over cataracts, now crowded with
verdant islands, sea-like in breadth, and navigable
for over a thousand miles at a stretch. Livingstone prepared the way, but Stanley opened the
door through which the world saw millions of
people in the Congo Valley of whom it had never
heard."

The records of his first journey to the heart
of Africa are contained in the book entitled, *How
I Found Livingstone*, and this episode in his

career appropriately forms the second chapter of this biography.

One cannot read the actions of the heroes, Henry M. Stanley and Charles Gordon, without feeling that they belong to a type of men which is sometimes mourned as extinct. They are not unlike the noblest ·of the early navigators and explorers, who confronted peril, not for glory, nor entirely because they were born with the thirst for heroic enterprise, but largely to extend the domain of faith and pure worship. The religious idea has been modified in the last three or four centuries, but some of the characteristics are the same. It still embraces belief in an Invisible Power, which works unceasingly in the world it created.

The development of Henry M. Stanley from an adventurer into a hero, remains the grand feature of his last and greatest journey. The explorer was compelled to meet entirely new obstacles, and defeated them all. It must be remembered, of course, that he is his own historiographer ; but there is no reason to suspect his perfect veracity, and he obviously places strong restraint upon himself to keep down his natural bitterness of feeling.

A very curious letter, says Mr. Theodore Child, in which Henry M. Stanley gives his views on love and the ladies generally, has fallen into my hands. The letter is dated from Jermyn Street, London, where Stanley lived before his departure for his last trip into the heart of the Dark Continent, and it is dated August 1, 1884. He says:

"For the life of me I cannot sit still a moment when anything approaching to love comes upon the tapis. I have lived with men, not women, and it is the man's intense ruggedness, plainness, directness, that I have contracted by sheer force of circumstances.

"Poets and women appear to me to be so soft, so very unlike (at least, what I have seen,) the rude type of mankind, that one soon feels by talking to them that he must soften his speech, and drawl, or affect a singular articulation, lest offence be taken when none was intended. Hence men are seldom sincere to women or poets. Have you ever thought of how you looked when speaking to a woman? If my recollection serves me right, I have seen you talk with such an affected softness that I cannot compare the manner of it to anything better than that of a strong man handling a baby—tenderly, gingerly. So! But my pen is carrying me away. I wish to say, my dear friend, that I am absolutely uncomfortable when speaking to a woman, unless she is such a rare one that she will let me hear some common sense. The fact is, I can't talk to women. In their presence I am just as much of a hypocrite as any other man, and it galls me that I must act and be affected, and parody myself for no earthly reason but because I think, with other men, that to speak or act otherwise would not be appreciated. It is such a false position that I do not care to put myself into it."

Stanley then goes on to qualify his strictures by saying that there is one lady, a friend of the

poet to whom he writes, to whom he can speak,
because "after the first few minutes of strange-
ness have gone she soon lets you know that
chaff won't do. Therefore," he adds, "please
say a hearty friend wishes her daily enjoyment
of her life."

As we have seen, before Stanley was known
as an explorer he served as the *Herald* correspondent in two British campaigns, directed,
one against the Ashantees, and the other against
King Theodore of Abyssinia. He brilliantly
improved this opportunity to record two grand
successes gained by British soldiers in East and
West Africa, and the volume in which he told
the story is called *Coomassie and Magdala : the
Story of Two British Campaigns in Africa.*
With stern eloquence and graphic power he describes that memorable march when the unsea-
soned British army waded for one hundred and
forty miles through deadly swamps, or scrambled
through the thick jungly forests on their way to
attack Coomassie. General Fever and General

Forest, the Malagasy say, are the commanders who defend their capital. It was much the same with the chief town of Ashantee, and the strongest fell victims to the malaria that brooded everywhere. At length the fever-stricken column reached Coomassie, and the town was theirs after five days' hard frighting. Stanley describes the alacrity with which the British, their work accomplished and Coomassie in ashes, fled for their lives to the sea.

The scene and conduct of the other campaign affords a stricking contrast—a lofty and salubrious region of wonderful wildness and grandeur, a march into the heart of Abyssinia that bristled with interesting incidents, the storming of Magdala, a town planted on a crag 10,000 feet above the sea. The book presents a brilliant picture of these two campaigns, and Stanley's humor breaks forth upon the smallest provocation—a quality he does not display in such abundant measure in his later writings.

In the peaceful conquest of Africa now in

progress, says a writer in the *Fortnightly Review,*
Great Britain has borne the greater part of the
burden—her sons were among the first to enter
the Unknown. Of Scotsmen alone, we may mention James Bruce, the Abyssinian traveler; Mun-
go Park, the discoverer of the Niger ; Colonel
James Augustus Grant, the discoverer (with
Speke) of the Victoria Nyanza ; Joseph Thomson
and Keith Johnston ; and, the greatest of all
African travelers, Dr. Livingstone, who, between
1840 and 1873, discovered the great Lakes Nyassa,
Tanganika, Bangweolo, and the Lualaba (Upper
Congo). Dr. Robert Moffat, Livingstone's father-
in-law, also deserves mention in the same honor-
able field of missionary enterprise. Dr. Livingstone showed us how Africa was to be overcome
and civilized, and Christian missions have sprung
up in his track. But Dr. Livingstone's method
has latterly been discarded in favor of an easier
and more profitable " Plan of Campaign." We
no longer care so much for the spiritual awakening of Africa, or, if we have awakened its semi-

barbarian inhabitants, it is only to lay upon them the curse of Adam—toil; not toil to evolve the higher capacities of the natives, but toil to enrich the taskmaster. Their confidence in Europeans has first been gained by the work and example of our missionaries, who have taught them to trade, to till the soil, to gather the fruits of the earth, and to live in peace and contentment. Close on the heels of the missionary—if we omit the explorer, who penetrates everywhere, but rests nowhere—comes the irresponsible, individual trader. To him the native is an instrument for his special use; he is his carrier in a land where no other beast of burden can be employed, his laborer where no other laborers can be introduced. With gin and gunpowder the individual trader buys the land, if not the souls, of its native owners. Wherever he settles the native degenerates. On the West Coast of Africa this degeneration, arising out of contact with Europeans, is specially observable. The great trading companies, on the other hand, rigidly restrict or entirely prohibit the

sale of ardent liquors to the natives, with the most
beneficial results.   It is these trading companies
which now are bent upon the partition of Africa
into " spheres of interest," just as two or more
doctors may divide off a village or town into districts for their special practice ; their Governments
do not always go with them, and, unless committed to a course of protection, are very unwilling
to accept responsibility.   On the West Coast we
have the Royal Niger Company, which for years
has been steadily, though quietly, establishing itself on the Niger and Benue ; in 1886 it obtained
a royal charter, conveying sovereign rights over
the whole of the Niger from Timbuktu, and of
the Benue from Yola, extending on both banks
for thirty miles inland.   On the great lakes and in
the Zambesi zone, we have the African Lakes
Company ; and only the other day two new companies were formed ; the British and the German
East African Associations.   It is now proposed to
form a new (British) Trading Company to tap the

riches of the Eastern Soudan, from the Red Sea littoral.

Spain and Portugal, in the beginning of the sixteenth century, divided the world between them—at least on paper ; the Pope, to whom the matter was referreed as arbitrator, drew the dividing line on the other side of the world, somewhere in the longitude of the Philippines. In spite of this convenient arrangement, however, the United States, Australia, and India belong to neither Power ; it clearly was not binding on *third* parties. We have mentioned this case to illustrate a principle that is entirely overlooked by those who wish to gain something in the " scramble " for Africa. The rightful owners of the land, being for the most part barbarians, are treated unjustly ; they sign away their birthright for a mess of pottage ; too often they lay their necks under the Juggernaut car of Commercial Progress. The " spheres of influence " are delimitated in too hopeful a spirit ; they in some places clash with the interests of third parties. The

map of Central and Southern Africa is now neatly
partitioned off into British, French, German,
Portuguese, and Congo Independent State spheres
of influence. It is a paper warfare, and it is
wonderful what "a scrap of paper" can do.

Let us briefly consider the position of affairs.
Africa, as we all know, is a vast plateau continent, with an area of over eleven million English
square miles in extent. Its general elevation
varies from 1000 to 4000 feet above the sea level ;
the higher lands and mountains (roughly speaking) fringe the seaboard, and on the Red Sea and
at the Cape they fall in sheer heights close to the
water's edge. There are ports all round the coast,
but the only proper access to the interior is by the
great water-ways. The continent, from the point
of view of commerce, can therefore best be
divided into basins or zones : (1) The Niger ; (2)
the Chad and Shari ; (3) the Zambesi ; (4) the
Nile ; (5) the Congo ; (6) remaining area. We
leave altogether out of account the Mediterranean
coast.

Of these, the Niger zone appears to be the most important. The Royal Niger Company have, it is true, the French and Germans to compete against; but they are so firmly established that they may now safely be left to their own resources: they tap the rich, populous and civilized States of the Central Soudan, and have concluded treaties by which an immense area is placed under their sovereignty. The Chad-Shari zone may, for these reasons, also be left out of account. Were the other commercial companies as firmly established as the Royal Niger Company, there would be no Central African question to day; they could be left to safeguard their own interests without calling for Government protection.

In the Zambesi zone a very different state of affairs exists. The Portuguese authorities have been established on the Sofala and Mozambique coasts for centuries. The only access to the great lakes is by way of the Zambesi, and the Zambesi mouths are in the hands of the Portuguese, who

sit at the receipt of custom, and collect all the
dues they can impose upon merchandise. Their
prohibitive tariffs, political inaction, destroy trade.
From Cape Delgado to Delagoa Bay they hold
undisputed sway. Their colonial policy has been
to gather where they have not sowed, and instead
of developing the country and elevating its
inhabitants, it has had quite a contrary effect;
foreign enterprise and native emancipation have
been crippled by its exactions and immorality.
In spite of this, the African Lakes Company, of
Glasgow, have established a trade-route from the
mouths of the Zambesi to the head of Lake
Tanganika. They have a steamer running
regularly on the Nyassa Lake, and a portage (the
Stevenson road) from the latter to the former
lake. If a steamer were placed upon Tanganika,
one of the best and quickest routes into Central
Africa would be established. The missionaries
on the lakes give constant work to the company,
and its trade could be immensely increased if
only the country were under a settled and active

government. At the present moment this trade-route is closed. The Arab slave-raiders have swept the shores of Tanganika, blocked the Stevensou road, and occupied the country to the north of the Nyassa. They have destroyed the villages of the Wa-Nkonde, killed or captured hundreds of men, women and children, and have given out that in future they intend to occupy the land, and exact tribute (which is their idea of occupation) from all who return there, even from Europeans.

This, then, was the region to be conquered for civilization by the indomitable energy of one white man. "It is safe to say that no other ex-plorer of Africa, America, or any other part of the world, has ever accumulated on a single jour-ney such wealth of materials, enriching at once so many fields of science, and so replete with roman-tic, picturesque, and thrilling incidents as fell to Stanley's lot on the memorable journey he has described in *Through the Dark Continent.*

"It was his good fortune to see at its best the

powerful kingdom of Uganda, and few parts of
Africa were more interesting or more worthy of
Stanley's brilliant pen-pictures than M'Tesa's
domain on the shores of Lake Victoria before all
the miseries of a prolonged civil war had befallen
its once happy people. How full of strange and
even tragical adventures were the long boat voy-
ages around the wooded shores of Lakes Victoria
and Tanganika, and how full of life and variety
were the scenes and people the explorer met
among the ten tribes who dwell along Tanganika's nine hundred miles of coast line ! It is
in this book that Stanley makes us well
acquainted with Tippoo Tib, whom he regarded
as the most remarkable man he had met in
Africa, and who has since become so rich and
powerful. Tippoo Tib and two hundred of his
men helped Stanley start down the unknown
Congo from Nyangwé, where both Livingstone
and Cameron were defeated in their purpose to
descend the mysterious river. Twenty of the
dusky favorites of the great trader's harem went

with him on this journey, his first trip down the river, which he was soon after to bring completely under his control for a distance of three hundred and fifty miles. The Arabs and half-castes from Zanzibar had been long deterred by stories of cannibals and fierce dwarfs from venturing further down the river, and their descent to Stanley Falls would perhaps have been delayed several years if Stanley had not pioneered the way."

It is extremely interesting after reading some of Stanley's powerful descriptions of fights for life with Congo cannibals to compare with them the native versions of the same occurrences, which they are very glad to give to all who wish to hear them. Take, for instance, Stanley's account of his thirty-first fight on the terrible river, the last but one, and the hardest battle of all, when a fleet of sixty-three great Bengala war-canoes came out to exterminate the strangers, who numbered only forty-four guns. It was two hours before the Snider muskets won the victory, and three hearty cheers rang over the flood as the foe

retreated to the shore. Here is a part of the
description of this battle given by Chief Muéle to
Captain Coquilhat awhile ago.

"We had not the slightest idea that such
beings as white people existed. One day, when
the sun stood right above our heads, we saw a
fleet of strangely formed canoes quietly passing
in front of our villages. We were astonished to
see that the men were covered with white cloths,
and it seemed very singular, for the richest men
we knew wore only a little rag of banana fiber,
and we saw two men as white as our pottery clay,
who seemed to be chiefs. Our alarm drums
sounded, and we crowded the canoes, and started
out for a fight. As we approached them, we saw
that one man had straight gray hair, and his eyes
were the color of the water. He stood up, and
held toward us a red cloth and some brass wire.
The other white man aimed his weapon at us,
and the older man talked to him rapidly in a
language we did not understand. We thought
their actions boded us no good, and so we opened

the battle, and it was the most terrible we ever fought.

"Our spears fell fast among them, and we killed some, and their bodies lay half over the sides of their canoes. But, oh, what fetich gave their weapons such wonderful power? Their bullets, made of a gray metal we had never seen before, hit women and old men who were following the combat from the shore. The walls of our huts were pierced, and goats in the fields dropped dead of their wounds. As for us, who were on the water, our shields were pierced as though they had been bananas. Many of us were killed and wounded, and others were drowned, for holes were knocked in some canoes, which filled and sank. Still we fought desperately, and followed the white beings some distance below our villages, but they finally escaped us, and raised loud cries of triumph as we ended the pursuit."

An insight into the character and influence of Stanley is revealed by an incident which occurred during the descent of the Congo. He had had

much trouble with his men, on account of their
inherent propensity to steal, the results of which
brought upon the expedition much actual disaster. At last Stanley doomed the next man
caught stealing to death. His grief and distress
were unbounded when the next thief, detected in
a case of peculiar flagrancy, was found to be
Uledi, the bravest, truest, noblest of his dusky
followers. Uledi had saved one hundred lives,
his own among the number. He had performed
acts of the most brilliant daring, always successful, always daring, always kind. Must Uledi die?
He called all his men around him in a council.
He explained to them the gravity of Uledi's
crime. He reminded them of his stern decree,
but said he was not hard enough to enforce it
against Uledi. His arm was not strong enough
to lift the gun that would kill Uledi, and he would
not bid one of them to do what he could not do
himself. But some punishment, and a hard one,
had to be meted out. What should it be? The

council must decide. They took a vote. Uledi must be flogged.

When the decision was reached, Stanley standing, Uledi crouching at his feet, and the solemn circle drawn closely around them, one man, whose life Uledi had saved under circumstances of frightful peril, stood forth, and said : "Give me half the blows, master." Then another said in the faintest accents, while tears fell from his eyes : "Will the master give his slave leave to speak?"

"Yes," said Stanley.

The Arab came slowly forward and knelt by Uledi's side. His words came slowly, and now and then a sob broke them.

"The master is wise," he said. "He knows all that has been, for he writes them in a book. I am black, and know not. Nor can I remember what is past. What we saw yesterday is to-day forgotten. But the master forgets nothing. He puts it all in the book. Each day something is written. Let your slave fetch the book, master, and turn its leaves. May-be you will find some words there about Uledi. May-be there is something that tells how he saved Zaidi from the white waters of the cataract; how he saved many men—how many, I forget. Bin Ali, Mabruki, Koni Kusi—others, too; how he is worthier than any three of us, how he always listens when the master speaks, and then flies forth at his word. Look, master, at the book. Then, if the blows must be struck, Shumari will take half and I the other half. The master will do what is right. Saywa has spoken."

And Saywa's speech deserves to live forever. Stanley threw away his whip. "Uledi is free," he said. "Shumari and Saywa are pardoned."

"At this moment," says an editorial writer in *Harper's Weekly*, "the most conspicuous man in the world is 'Stanley Africanus.' Every newspaper in Europe and America simultaneously announced his arrival upon the eastern coast of Africa. Europe spoke by the German Emperor offering him a war ship to carry him from Zanzi-

bar, and welcoming him to the triumph of a hero.
He is honored as the chief of travelers, as a hero
of romance ; and his comrade, Mr. Joseph Thomson, who thought him hopelessly lost, now
hastens to celebrate his Homeric exploits and his
Napoleonic energy. Germany and England prepare for him an unprecedented reception, in
which practically every country and the intelligence of the world will join. The newspaper
reporter has scaled the heights of distinction, and
written his name by those of the greatest of
explorers.

"The secret of such renown is not hidden. It
is the instinctive delight of men in heroism, in
personal courage, in perilous adventure happily
surmounted. It is a career which implies an undaunted spirit, immense resource, complete self-
possession, and prompt seizure and wise improve-
ment of opportunity. They are the qualities
which in other spheres of activity found States,
baffle apparently resistless forces, and change the
course of history. Stanley has confronted the

almost boundless and unknown forests and jungles, the morasses and waters and mountains of
a continent swarming with savage hostility, with
pestilence, and a myriad nameless obstructions,
in an impenetrable silence and absolute separation
from the rest of the world and from all hope of
communication or succor. And upon him alone,
upon his health, strength, intelligence, spirit,
nerve, and persistence, not only his own life, but
the lives of hundreds, the welfare of thousands,
increased knowledge, and the progress of civilization depended. He has not failed. He has overcome. It is not a picnic from which he emerges,
but he comes a conqueror from a tremendous and
prolonged conflict with what seemed invincible
forces.

" When Dr. Kane returned from his great voyage to the north pole—a small, quiet, refined, and
modest man—Thackeray, who was then in this
country, met him one day at dinner, and heard
his simple and thrilling story. When Kane
paused, Thackeray arose to his full height, and

gravely asked to be permitted to kneel and kiss his foot. It was a humorous form of the instinctive homage of the hardy English race to indomitable pluck and persistence. It is the same feeling which will bring Germany and England to receive Stanley as a conqueror—not from battle-fields or bloody decks, but from the long contest with savage nature, which, whether at the icy North or the burning equator, has always had the profoundest fascination from the night, three centuries ago, when Sir Humphrey Gilbert's light suddenly vanished upon the ocean, to the happy morning, just now, when Stanley was known to have arrived at Zanzibar. 'Heaven is as near by sea as by land,' said the unconquerable Sir Humphrey, and Stanley's letter is in the same high strain."

CHAPTER II.

THE LIVINGSTONE QUEST.

"On the sixteenth day of October, in the year
of our Lord one thousand eight hundred and
sixty-nine, I am in Madrid, fresh from the carnage at Valencia.   At 10 A. M. Jacopo, at No. ——
Calle de la Cruz, hands me a telegram : on opening it I find it reads, ' Come to Paris on important business.'   The telegram is from James Gordon Bennett, jun., the young manager of *The
New York Herald.*

" Down come my pictures from the wall of my
apartments on the second floor ; into my trunks
go my books and souvenirs, my clothes are
hastily collected, some half washed, some from
the clothes-lines half dry, and after a couple of
hours of hasty hard work my portmanteaus are
strapped up and labelled ' Paris.'

DAVID LIVINGSTONE.

"The express-train leaves Madrid for Hendaye at 3 P. M. I have yet time to say farewell to my friends. I have one at No. 6 Calle Goya, fourth floor, who happens to be a contributor to several London dailies. He has several children, in whom I have taken a warm interest. Little Charlie and Willie are fast friends of mine ; they love to hear of my adventures, and it has been a pleasure to me to talk to them. But now I must say farewell.

"Then I have friends at the United States Legation whose conversation I admire—there has come a sudden ending of it all. ' I hope you will write to us, we shall always be glad to hear of your welfare.' How often have I not during my feverish life as a flying journalist heard the very same words, and how often have I not suffered the same pang at parting from friends just as warm as these !

"But a journalist in my position must need suffer. Like a gladiator in the arena, he must be prepared for the combat. Any flinching, any

cowardice, and he is lost. The gladiator meets
the sword that is sharpened for his bosom—the
flying journalist or roving correspondent meets
the command that may send him to his doom.
To the battle or the banquet it is ever the same—
'Get ready and go.'

"At 3 P. M. I was on my way, and being
obliged to stop at Bayonne a few hours, did not
arrive at Paris until the following night. I went
straight to the 'Grand Hotel,' and knocked at the
door of Mr. Bennett's room.

"'Come in,' I heard a voice say.

"Entering, I found Mr. Bennett in bed.

"'Who are you?' he asked.

"'My name is Stanley!' I answered.

"'Ah, yes! sit down; I have important business on hand for you.'

"After throwing over his shoulders his robe-
de-chambre, Mr. Bennett asked, 'Where do you
think Livingstone is?'

"'I really do not know, sir!'

"'Do you think he is alive?'

"'He may be, and he may not be!' I answered.

"'Well, I think he is alive, and that he can be found, and I am going to send you to find him.'

"'What!' said I, 'do you really think I can find Dr. Livingstone? Do you mean me to go to Central Africa?'

"'Yes; I mean that you shall go, and find him wherever you may hear that he is, and to get what news you can of him, and perhaps'—delivering himself thoughtfully and deliberately— 'the old man may be in want—take enough with you to help him should he require it. Of course, you will act according to your own plans, and do what you think best--BUT FIND LIVINGSTONE!'

"Said I, wondering at the cool order of sending one to Central Africa to search for a man whom I, in common with almost all other men, believed to be dead, 'Have you considered seriously the great expense you are likely to incur on account of this little journey?'

"' What will it cost?' he asked, abruptly.

"' Burton and Speke's journey to Central Africa cost between £3,000 and £5,000, and I fear it cannot be done under £2,500.'

"' Well, I will tell you what you will do. Draw a thousand pounds now; and when you have gone through that, draw another thousand, and when that is spent, draw another thousand, and when you have finished that, draw another thousand, and so on; but FIND LIVINGSTONE.'

"Surprised but not confused at the order, for I knew that Mr. Bennett when once he had made up his mind was not easily drawn aside from his purpose, I yet thought, seeing it was such a gigantic scheme, that he had not quite considered in his own mind the pros and cons of the case; I said, 'I have heard that should your father die you would sell the *Herald* and retire from business.'

"' Whoever told you that is wrong, for there is not money enough in New York city to buy *The New York Herald*. My father has made it a

great paper, but I mean to make it greater. I
mean that it shall be a newspaper in the true
sense of the word. I mean that it shall publish
whatever news will be interesting to the world,
at no matter what cost.'

"'After that,' said I, 'I have nothing more to
say. Do you mean me to go straight on to Africa
to search for Dr. Livingstone?'

"'No; I wish you to go to the inauguration of
the Suez Canal first and then proceed up the Nile.
I hear Baker is about starting for Upper Egypt.
Find out what you can about this expedition, and
as you go up describe as well as possible whatever is interesting for tourists ; and then write up
a guide—a practical one—for Lower Egypt, tell us
about whatever is worth seeing and how to see it.

"'Then you might as well go to Jerusalem ; I
hear Captain Warren is making some interesting
discoveries there. Then visit Constantinople, and
find out about that trouble between the Khedive
and the Sultan.

"'Then—let me see—you might as well visit

the Crimea and those old battle-grounds.   Then go
across the Caucasus to the Caspian Sea ; I hear
there is a Russian expedition bound for Khiva.
From thence you may get through Persia to India ;
you could write an interesting letter from Persep-
olis.

" ' Bagdad will be close on your way to India ;
suppose you go there, and write up something
about the Euphrates Valley Railway.   Then, when
you have come to India, you can go after Living·
stone.   Probably you will hear by that time that
Livingstone is on his way to Zanzibar ; but, if
not, go into the interior and find him, if alive.
Get what news of his discoveries you can ; and,
if you find he is dead, bring all possible proofs of
his being dead.   That is all.   Good-night, and
God be with you.'

" ' Good-night, sir,' I said ; ' what it is in the
power of human nature to do I will do ; and on
such an errand as I go upon, God will be with
me.'

"I lodged with young Edward King, who is

making such a name in New England. He was just the man who would have delighted to tell the journal he was engaged upon what young Mr. Bennett was doing, and what errand I was bound upon.

" I should have liked to exchange opinions with him upon the probable results of my journey, but I dared not do so. Though oppressed with the great task before me, I had to appear as if only going to be present at the Suez Canal. Young King followed me to the express train bound for Marseilles, and at the station we parted —he to go and read the newspapers at Bowles' Reading room—I to Central Africa and—who knows ?

" There is no need to recapitulate what I did before going to Central Africa.

" I went up the Nile, and saw Mr. Higginbotham, chief-engineer in Baker's expedition, at Philae, and was the means of preventing a duel between him and a mad young Frenchman, who wanted to fight Mr. Higginbotham with pistols,

because that gentleman resented the idea of being
taken for an Egyptian, through wearing a fez cap.
I had a talk with Captain Warren at Jerusalem,
and descended one of the pits with a sergeant of
engineers to see the marks of the Tyrian work-
men on the foundation stones of the Temple of
Solomon.   I visited the mosques of Stamboul
with the Minister Resident of the United States
and the American Consul General.   I traveled
over the Crimean battle-grounds with Kinglake's
glorious books for reference in my hand.   I dined
with the widow of General Liprandi at Odessa.
I saw the Arabian traveler, Palgrave, at Trebi-
zond, and Baron Nicolay, the Civil Governor of
the Caucasus, at Tiflis.   I lived with the Russian
Ambassador while at Teheran, and wherever I
went through Persia I received the most hospit-
able welcome from the gentlemen of the Indo-
European Telegraph Company; and following
the example of many illustrious men, I wrote
my name upon one of the Persepolitan monu-
ments.   In the month of August, 1870, I arrived
in India.

"On the twelfth of October, I sailed on the barque *Polly* from Bombay to Mauritius. As the *Polly* was a slow sailer, the passage lasted thirty-seven days. On board this barque was a William Lawrence Farquhar—hailing from Leith, Scotland—in the capacity of first mate. He was an excellent navigator, and, thinking he might be useful to me, I employed him ; his pay to begin from the date we should leave Zanzibar for Bagamoyo. As there was no opportunity of getting to Zanzibar direct, I took ship to Seychelles. Three or four days after arriving at Mahe, one of the Seychelles group, I was fortunate enough to get a passage for myself, William Lawrence Farquhar, and Selim—a Christian Arab boy of Jerusalem, who was to act as interpreter—on board an American whaling vessel, bound for Zanzibar, at which port we arrived on the sixth of January, 1871."

The foregoing is Stanley's memorable introduction to *How I Found Livingstone*, in which he tells, better than any one else could tell it, of the

inception and formation of what was regarded at
the time as the most quixotic enterprise since the
days of the good knight of La Mancha.

"Zanzibar," says Professor Drummond, " is the
focus of all East African exploration. No matter
where you are going in the interior, you must
begin at Zanzibar. Oriental in its appearance,
Mohammedan in its religion, Arabian in its
morals, this cesspool of wickedness is a fit capital
for the Dark Continent. But Zanzibar is Zanzibar simply because it is the only apology for a
town on the whole coast. An immense outfit is
required to penetrate this shopless and foodless
land, and here only can the traveler make up his
caravan. The ivory and slave trades have made
caravaning a profession, and everything the
explorer wants is to be had in these bazars, from
a tin of sardines to a repeating rifle. Here these
black villians, the porters,—the necessity and
the despair of travelers, the scum of old slave
gangs, and the fugitives from justice from every
tribe,—congregate for hire. And if there is one

thing on which African travelers are for once
agreed, it is that for laziness, ugliness, stupidness
and wickedness, these men are not to be matched
on any continent in the world. Their one strong
point is that they will engage themselves for the
Victoria Nyanza or for the Grand Tour of the
Tanganika with as little ado as Chamounix guides
volunteer for the Jardin ; but this singular avid-
ity is mainly due to the fact that each man cher-
ishes the hope of running away at the earliest
opportunity. Were it only to avoid requiring to
employ these gentlemen, having them for one's
sole company month after month, seeing them
transgress every commandment in turn before
your eyes—you yourself being powerless to check
them except by a wholesale breach of the sixth—
it would be worth while to seek another route
into the heart of Africa.

"But there is a much graver objection to the
Zanzibar route to the interior. Stanley started
by this route on his search for Livingstone, two
white men with him ; he came back without

them. Cameron set out by the same path to
cross Africa with two companions ; before he got
to Tanganika he was alone. The Geographical
Society's late expedition, under Mr. Keith John-
stone, started from Zanzibar with two Europeans ;
the hardy and accomplished leader fell within a
couple of months. These expeditions have all
gone into the interior by this one fatal way, and
probably every second man, by fever or by accident, has left his bones to bleach along the road.
Hitherto there has been no help for it. The great
malarious coast belt must be crossed, and one has
simply to take his life in his hands and go
through with it."

In view of these facts the wisdom of Stanley's
choice of the Congo route in his last journey
would seem to be amply vindicated, even had
there been no other reason to influence his choice.

The same mode of commerce obtains here as
in all Mohammedan countries—nay, the mode
was in vogue long before Moses was born. The
Arab never changes. He brought the customs of

his forefathers with him when he came to live
in Zanzibar. He is as much of an Arab here
as at Muscat or Bagdad ; wherever he goes to
live, he carries with him his harem, his religion,
his long robe, his shirt, his watta, and his dagger.
If he penetrates Africa, not all the ridicule of the
negroes can make him change his modes of life."
So the Arab, who dominates the trade of the
entire region, travels by caravan.

Naturally Stanley's first inquiry at Zanzibar
was if any tidings of Dr. Livingstone had been
lately received. There was one man of all others
resident there who was by all accounts the most
likely to be the depositary of any such intelligence. This was Dr. Kirk, the British consul.

" I felt quite a curiosity to see this gentleman,
from the fact of his name being so often coupled
with the object of my search—Dr. David Livingstone. In almost all newspapers he was mentioned as the 'former companion of Dr. Livingstone.' I imagined, from the tone of the articles
that I saw published, and from his own letters to

the Indian Government, that if I could obtain
any positive information from any person regard-
ing the whereabouts of Dr. Livingstone, I should
be able to procure it from Dr. Kirk. It was with
feelings of no small impatience, therefore, that I
awaited the honor of an introduction to him.

"On the second morning after my arrival at
Zanzibar, according to the demands of Zanzibar
etiquette, the American Consul and myself sallied
out into the street, and in a few moments I was
in the presence of this much-famed man. To a
man of rather slim figure, dressed plainly, slightly round-shouldered, hair black, face thin, cheeks
rather sunk and bearded, Captain Webb said,
'Dr. Kirk, permit me to introduce Mr. Stanley, of
The New York Herald.'

"I fancied at the moment that he lifted his
eyelids perceptibly, disclosing the full circle of the
eyes. If I were to define such a look, I would
call it a broad stare. During the conversation,
which ranged over several subjects, though
watching his face intently, I never saw it kindle

or become animated but once, and that was while relating some of his hunting feats to us. As the subject nearest my heart was not entered upon, I promised myself I would ask him about Dr. Livingstone the next time I called upon him, which was at a sort of weekly reception.

" The entertainment which the British consul and his lady provided for the visitors on their 'evening' consists of a kind of mild wine and cigars ; not because they have nothing else in the house—no decoction of bohea, or hyson, with a few cakes—but I suppose because it is the normal and accustomed habit of a free Zanzibarized European to indulge in something of this sort, mixed with a little soda or seltzer-water, as a stimulant to the bits of refined gossip, generally promulgated under the vinous influence to sympathizing, interested, and eager listeners.

"It was all very fine, I dare say, but I thought it was the dreariest evening I ever passed, until Dr. Kirk, pitying the wearisomeness under which I was laboring, called me aside to submit to my inspection a magnificent elephant rifle, which he said was a present from a governor of Bombay. Then I heard eulogies upon its deadly powers and its fatal accuracy ; I heard anecdotes of jungle life, adventures experienced while hunting, and incidents of his travels with Livingstone.

" 'Ah, yes, Dr. Kirk,' I asked carelessly, 'about Livingstone—where is he, do you think, now ?'

" 'Well, really,' he replied, 'you know that is very difficult to answer ; he may be dead ; there is nothing positive whereon we can base sufficient reliance. Of one thing I am sure, nobody has heard anything definite of him for over two years. I should fancy, though, he must be alive. We are continually sending something up for him. There is a small expedition now at Baga moyo to start shortly. I really think the old man should come home now ; he is growing old, you know, and if he died, the world would lose the benefit of his discoveries. He keeps neither notes nor journals ; it is very seldom he takes observa- tions. He simply makes a note or dot, or something, on a map, which nobody could understand but himself. Oh, yes, by all means if he is alive he should come home, and let a younger man take his place.'

" ' What kind of a man is he to get along with, Doctor ?' I asked, feeling now quite interested in his conversation.

" ' Well, I think he is a very difficult man to deal with generally. Personally, I have never had a quarrel with him, but I have seen him in hot water with fellows so often, and that is principally the reason, I think, he hates to have any one with him.'

" 'I am told he is a very modest man ; is he ?' I asked.

" ' Oh, he knows the value of his own discoveries ; no man better. He is not quite an angel,' said he, with a laugh.

" 'Well, now, supposing I met him in my travels —I might possibly stumble across him if he travels anywhere in the direction I am going— how would he conduct himself towards me ?'

" ' To tell you the truth,' said he, ' I do not think he would like it very well. I know if Burton, or Grant, or Baker, or any of those fellows were going after him, and he heard of their coming, Livingstone would put a hundred miles of swamp, in a very short time, between himself and them. I do, upon my word, I do.'

" This was the tenor of the interview I held with Dr. Kirk—former companion of Livingstone —as well as my journal and memory can recall it to me.

" Need I say this information, from a gentleman known to be well acquainted with Dr. Livingstone, rather had the effect of damping my ardor for the search, than adding vigor to it. I felt very much depressed, and would willingly have resigned my commission ; but then, the order was, ' GO AND FIND LIVINGSTONE.' Besides, I did not suppose, though I had so readily consented to search for the Doctor, that the path to Central Africa was strewn with roses. What though I were rebuked as an impertinent interloper in the domain of Discovery, as a meddler in things that concerned not myself, as one whose absence would be far more acceptable to him than my presence—had I not been commanded to find him? Well, find him I would, if he were above ground; if not, then I would bring what concerned people to know, and keep."

Stanley was totally ignorant of the interior, and it was difficult at first to know what he needed in order to take an expedition into Central Africa. Time was precious, also, and much of it could not be devoted to inquiry and investigation. In a case like this, he says, it would have been a godsend had either of the three gentlemen, Captains Burton, Speke, or Grant given some information on these points; had they devoted a chapter upon How to Get Ready an Expedition for Central Africa.

"These are some of the questions I asked myself, as I tossed on my bed at night:

" ' How much money is required?'

" ' How many pagazis, or carriers?'

" 'How many soldiers ?'

" 'How much cloth ?'

" 'How many beads ?'

" 'How much wire ?'

" 'What kinds of cloth are required for the dif ferent tribes ?'

" Ever so many questions to myself brought me no nearer the exact point I wished to arrive at. I scribbled over scores of sheets of paper, making estimates, drawing out lists of material, calculating the cost of keeping one hundred men for one year, at so many yards of different kinds of cloth, etc. I studied Burton, Speke and Grant in vain. A good deal of geographical, ethnological, and other information appertaining to the study of Inner Africa was obtainable, but information respecting the organization of an expedition requisite before proceeding to Africa. was not in any book. I threw the books from me in disgust. The Europeans at Zanzibar knew as little as possible about this particular point. There was not one white man at Zanzibar who could tell how many dotis a day a force of one hundred men required for food on the road. Neither, in-deed, was it their business to know. But what should I do at all, at all? This was a grand question.

"I decided it were best to hunt up an Arab merchant who had been engaged in the ivory trade ; or who was fresh from the interior."

The reader must bear in mind that a traveler requires only that which is sufficient for travel and exploration; that a superfluity of goods or means will prove as fatal to him as poverty of supplies. It is on this question of quality and quantity that the traveler has first to exercise his judgment and discretion.

Stanley's informants gave him to understand that for the subsistence of one hundred men for two years would require 4000 doti=16,000 yards of American sheeting ; 2,000 doti=8,000 yards of kaniki ; 1,300 doti=5,200 yards of mixed colored cloths. This was definite and valuable informa-tion. Second in importance to the amount of cloth required was the quantity and quality of the beads necessary. One tribe preferred white to black beads, brown to yellow, red to green, green to white, and so on.

" After the beads came the wire question. I discovered, after considerable trouble, that Nos. 5 and 6—almost of the thickness of telegraph wire—were considered the best numbers for trading purposes. While beads stand for copper coins in Africa, cloth measures for silver ; wire is reckoned as gold in the countries beyond the Tanganika. Three hundred and fifty pounds of brass-wire, the Arab adviser thought, would be ample."

Having purchased the cloth, the beads, and the wire, it was no little pride that Stanley surveyed the comely bales and packages lying piled up, row above row, in Captain Webb's capacious store room. Yet there were provisions, cooking-utensils, boats, rope, twine, tents, donkeys, saddles, bagging, canvas, tar, needles, tools, ammunition, guns, equipments, hatchets, medicines, bedding,

presents for chiefs—in short, a thousand things
not yet purchased.

"The next thing was to enlist, arm and equip
a faithful escort of twenty men for the road.
With the aid of the dragoman, Johari, I secured
in a few hours the services of Uledi, Ulimengo,
Baruiti, Ambari, Mabruki, five of Speke's ' Faith-
fuls.' When I asked them if they were willing
to join another white man's expedition to Ujiji,
they replied very readily that they were willing to
join any brother of ' Speke's.'

"When my purchases were completed, and I
beheld them piled up, tier after tier, row upon
row, here a mass of cooking utensils, there
bundles of rope, tents, saddles, a pile of portmanteaus and boxes, containing every imaginable
thing, I confess I was rather abashed at my own
temerity. Here were at least six tons of material.

"The traveler, with a lake in the centre of
that broad African continent before him, must
needs make his way there after a fashion very
different from that to which he has been accus-

tomed in other countries. He requires to take with him just what a ship must have when about to sail on a long voyage. He must have his slop chest, his little store of canned dainties, and his medicines, beside which, he must have enough guns, powder and ball to be able to make a series of good fights if necessary. He must have men to convey these miscellaneous articles ; and as a man's maximum load does not exceed seventy pounds, to convey 11,000 pounds requires nearly one hundred and sixty men.

"The African traveler can hire neither wagons nor camels, neither horses nor mules to proceed with him into the interior. His means of convey- ance are limited to black and naked men, who demand at least $15 a head for every seventy pounds weight carried only as far as Unyany- embe."

At length the weary preparations were com- pleted, and the expedition left Zanzibar to cross to Bagamoyo on the mainland, twenty miles away. Here the pagazis, or bearers, were to be engaged, and another dreary time of haggling set in. But within a month enough men had been hired, and three relays or sections of the expedition had been sent forward. Here is Stanley's memorandum of the progress made up to this time :

1871. *Feb.* 6.—Expedition arrived at Bagamoyo.

1871. *Feb.* 18.—First caravan departs with twenty-four pagazis and three soldiers.

1871. *Feb.* 21.—Second caravan departs with twenty-eight pagazis, two chiefs, and two soldiers.

1871. *Feb.* 25.—Third caravan departs with twenty-two pagazis, ten donkeys, one white man, one cook, and three soldiers.

1871. *March* 11.—Fourth caravan departs with fifty-five pagazis, two chiefs, and three soldiers.

1871. *March* 21.—Fifth caravan departs with twenty-eight pagazis, twelve soldiers, two white men, one tailor, one cook, one interpreter, one gun-bearer, seventeen asses, two horses and one dog.

Total number, inclusive of all souls, comprised

in caravans connected with the "New York Herald Expedition," 192.

"On the twenty-first of March," says Stanley, "exactly seventy-three days after my arrival at Zanzibar, the fifth caravan, led by myself, left the town of Bagamoyo for our first journey westward with 'Forward!' for its *mot du guet*. As the kirangozi unrolled the American flag, and put himself at the head of the caravan, and the pagazis, animals, soldiers, and idlers were lined for the march, we bade a long farewell to the *dolce far niente* of civilized life, to the blue ocean and to its open road to home, to the hundreds of dusky spectators who were there to celebrate our departure with repeated salvoes of musketry.

"Our caravan is composed of twenty-eight pagazis, including the kirangozi, or guide ; twelve soldiers under Captain Mbarak Bombay, in charge of seventeen donkeys and their loads ; Selim, my boy interpreter, in charge of the donkey and cart with its load ; one cook and sub, who is also to be tailor and ready hand for all, and leads the

gray horse ; Shaw, once mate, of a ship, now
transformed into rearguard and overseer for the
caravan, who is mounted on a good riding-don-
key, and wearing a canoe-like topee and sea-
boots ; and lastly, on a splendid bay horse (presented to me by Mr. Goodhue, an American gentleman, long resident at Zanzibar), myself, called
' Bana Mkuba,' the ' big master,' by my people—
the vanguard, the reporter, the thinker, and
leader of the Expedition."

"We left Bagamoyo the attraction of all the
curious, with much *éclat*, and defiled up a
narrow lane, shaded almost to twilight by the
dense umbrage of two parallel hedges of mimosas.
We were all in the highest spirits. The soldiers
sang, the kirangozi lifted his voice into a loud
bellowing note, and fluttered the American flag,
which told all on-lookers, ' Lo, a Musungu's caravan ;' and my heart, I thought, palpitated much
too quickly for the sober face of a leader. But I
could not check it ; the enthusiasm of youth still
clung to me—despite my travels ; my pulses

bounded with the full glow of staple health;
behind me were the troubles which had harassed
me for over two months. With that dishonest
son of a Hindi, Soor Hadji Palloo, I had said my
last word; of the blatant rabble of Arabs,
Banyans, and Baluches I had taken my last look;
with the Jesuits of the French Mission I had
exchanged farewells, and before me beamed the
sun of promise as he sped towards the Occident.
Loveliness glowed around me. I saw fertile
fields, *riant* vegetation, strange trees—I heard
the cry of cricket and pee-wit, the sibilant sound
of many insects, all of which seemed to tell me,
'At last you are started.' What could I do but
lift my face toward the pure-glowing sky, and
cry, 'God be thanked!'

The next three months were occupied in covering the distance from Bagamoyo to Unyanyembe,
and Stanley had his first real taste of African
travel. Its story was one of struggles with
relentless and savage nature and often still more
savage peoples; of conflicts with refractory

porters ; of disaffection among the subordinate officers of the expedition ; of forced marches amid torrential rains and through miasmatic swamps ; of fightings with fever and dysentery ; of sleepless nights and wearisome days ; of heroic battling and triumph over unseen and unlooked for dangers and difficulties ; yet the indomitable will, courage, and energy of the solitary chief brought order out of chaos, snatched victory out of the very jaws of defeat, and inspired confidence in those weaker than himself.

At Unyanyembe all the parts of the expedition were united, and a prolonged halt was made, partly for recuperation, but rendered doubly necessary by the fact that a war, in progress between the Arabs and some native tribes, for a time barred further progress. But here Stanley was prostrated by a terrible attack of fever. Desertions, sickness, and thefts diminished both men and goods during this period of enforced idleness. Stanley's journal tells the tale more eloquently than any other pen could hope to tell it :

Kwihara, Friday, 11*th August,* 1871.—Arrived
to day from Zimbili, village of Bomboma's.   I am
quite disappointed and almost disheartened.   But
I have one consolation, I have done my duty by
the Arabs, a duty I thought I owed to the kindness they received me with ; now, however, the
duty is discharged, and I am free to pursue my
own course.   I feel happy, for some reasons, that
the duty has been paid at such a slight sacrifice.
Of course if I had lost my life in this enterprise,
I should have been justly punished.   But apart
from my duty to the consideration with which
the Arabs had received me, was the necessity of
trying every method of reaching Livingstone.
This road, which the war with Mirambo has
closed, is only a month's march from this place,
and if the road could be opened with my aid,
sooner than without it, why should I refuse my
aid ?   The attempt has been made for the second
time to Ujiji—both have failed.   I am going to
try another route ; to attempt to go by the north
would be folly.   Mirambo's mother and people,

and the Wasui, are between me and Ujiji, without including the Watuta, who are his allies and
robbers. The southern route seems to be the
most practicable one. Very few people know
anything of the country south ; those whom I
have questioned concerning it speak of "want of
water" and robber Wazavira, as serious obstacles ; they also say that the settlements are few
and far between.

But before I can venture to try this new route,
I have to employ a new set of men, as those
whom I took to Mfuto consider their engagements
at an end, and the fact of five of their number
being killed, rather damps their ardor for traveling. It is useless to hope that Wanyamwezi can
be engaged, because it is against their custom to
go with caravans, as carriers, during war time.
My position is most serious. I have a good
excuse for returning to the coast, but my conscience will not permit me to do so, after so
much money has been expended, and so much

confidence has been placed in me. In fact, I feel
I must die sooner than return.

Saturday, August 12th.—My men, as I supposed they would, have gone ; they said that I
engaged them to go to Ujiji by Mirambo's road.
I have only thirteen left. With this small body
of men, whither can I go? I have over one
hundred loads in the store-room. Livingstone's
caravan is also here ; his goods consist of seventeen bales of cloth, twelve boxes, and six bags of
beads. His men are luxuriating upon the best
the country affords.

If Livingstone is at Ujiji, he is now locked up
with small means of escape. I may consider
myself also locked up at Unyanyembe, and I
suppose cannot go to Ujiji until this war with
Mirambo is settled. Livingstone cannot get his
goods, for they are here with mine. He cannot
return to Zanzibar, and the road to the Nile is
blocked up. He might, if he has men and stores,
possibly reach Baker by traveling northwards,
through Urundi, thence through Ruanda, Karag-

wah, Uganda, Unyoro, and Ubari to Gondokoro.
Pagazis he cannot obtain, for the sources whence
a supply might be obtained, are closed. It is an
erroneous supposition to think that Livingstone,
any more than any other energetic man of his
calibre, can travel through Africa without some
sort of an escort and a durable supply of market-
able cloth and beads.

I was told to-day by a man that when Livingstone was coming from Nyassa Lake towards the
Tanganika (the very time that people thought
him murdered) he was met by Sayd bin Omar's
caravan, which was bound for Ulamba. He was
traveling with Mohammed bin Gharib. This
Arab, who was coming from Urungu, met Livingstone at Chi-cumbi's, or Kwa-chi-kumbi's,
country, and traveled with him afterwards, I
hear, to Manyuema or Manyema. Manyuema is
forty marches from the north of Nyassa. Livingstone was walking ; he was dressed in American
sheeting. He had lost all his cloth in Lake
Liemba while crossing it in a boat. He had three

canoes with him ; in one he put his cloth, another
he loaded with his boxes and some of his men,
into the third he went himself with two servants
and two fishermen.   The boat with his cloth was
upset.   On leaving Nyassa, Livingstone went to
Ubissa, thence to Uemba, thence to Urungu.
Livingstone wore a cap.   He had a breech-load-
ing double barrelled rifle with him, which fired
fulminating balls.   He was also armed with two
revolvers.   The Wahiyow with Livingstone told
this man that their master had many men with
him at first, but that several had deserted him.

August 13*th.*—A caravan came in to-day from
the sea-coast.   They reported that William L.
Farquhar, whom I left sick at Mpwapwa, Usa-
gara, and his cook, were dead.   Farquhar, I was
told, died a few days after I had entered Ugogo,
his cook died a few weeks later.   My first impulse
was for revenge.   I believed that Leukole had
played me false, and had poisoned him, or that he
had been murdered in some other manner ; but a
personal interview with the Msawahili who

brought the news informing me that Farquhar
had succumbed to his dreadful illness had done
away with that suspicion. So far as I could
understand him, Farquhar had in the morning
declared himself well enough to proceed, but in
attempting to rise, had fallen backward and died.
I was also told that the Wasagara, possessing
some superstitious notions respecting the dead,
had ordered Jako to take the body out for burial,
that Jako, not being able to carry it, had dragged
the body to the jungle, and there left it naked
without the slightest covering of earth, or anything else.

"There is one of us gone, Shaw, my boy!
Who will be the next?" I remarked that night
to my companion.

Let us for a moment explain to the uninitiated
the true mode of African travel. "In spite of all
the books that have been lavished upon us by
our great explorers, few people seem to have any
accurate understanding of this most simple pro-

cess. Some have the impression that everything
is done in bullock-wagons—an idea borrowed
from the Cape, but hopelessly inapplicable to Central Africa, where a wheel at present would be as
great a novelty as a polar bear. Others, at the
opposite extreme, suppose that the explorer works
along solely by compass, making a bee line for
his destination, and steering his caravan through
the trackless wilderness like a ship at sea. Now
it may be a surprise to the unenlightened to
learn that probably no explorer in forcing his
passage through Africa has ever, for more than a
few days at a time, been off some beaten track.
Probably no country in the world, civilized or
uncivilized, is better supplied with paths than
this unmapped continent. Every village is connected with some other village, every tribe with
the next tribe, every State with its neighbor, and
therefore with all the rest. The explorer's business is simply to select from this network of
tracks, keep a general direction, and hold on his
way. Let him begin at Zanzibar, plant his foot

on a native footpath, and set his face towards
Tanganika. In eight months he will be there.
He has simply to persevere. From village to village he will be handed on, zigzagging it may be
sometimes to avoid the impassible barriers of
nature or the rarer perils of hostile tribes, but
never taking to the woods, never guided solely by
the stars, never in fact leaving a beaten track,
till hundreds and hundreds of miles are between
him and the sea, and his interminable footpath
ends with a canoe, on the shores of Tanganika.
Crossing the lake, landing near some native village, he picks up the thread once more. Again
he plods on and on, now on foot, now by canoe,
but always keeping his line of villages, until one
day suddenly he sniffs the sea-breeze again, and
his faithful foot-wide guide lands him on the
Atlantic seaboard.

"Nor is there any art in finding out these suc-
cessive villages with their inter-communicating
links. He must find them out. A whole army
of guides, servants, carriers, soldiers and camp-

followers accompany him in his march, and this nondescript regiment must be fed. Indian corn, cassava, mawere beans, and bananas—these do not grow wild even in Africa. Every meal has to be bought and paid for in cloth and beads ; and scarcely three days can pass without a call having to be made at some village where the necessary supplies can be obtained. A caravan, as a rule, must live from hand to mouth, and its march becomes simply a regulated procession through a chain of markets. Not, however, that there are any real markets—there are neither bazars nor stores in native Africa. Thousands of the villages through which the traveler eats his way may never have victualled a caravan before. But, with the chief's consent, which is usually easily purchased for a showy present, the villages unlock their larders, the women flock to the grinding stones, and basketfuls of food are swiftly exchanged for unknown equivalents in beads and calico.

" The native tracks just described are the same

in character all over Africa. They are veritable footpaths, never over a foot in breadth, beaten as hard as adamant, and rutted beneath the level of the forest bed by centuries of native traffic. As a rule these footpaths are marvelously direct. Like the roads of the old Romans, they run straight on through everything, ridge and mountain and valley, never shying at obstacles, nor anywhere turning aside to breathe. Yet within this general straightforwardness there is a singular eccentricity and indirectness in detail. Although the African footpath is on the whole a bee-line, no fifty yards of it are ever straight. And the reason is not far to seek. If a stone is encountered no native will ever think of removing it. Why should he? It is easier to walk round it. The next man who comes that way will do the same. He knows that a hundred men are following him; he looks at the stone; a moment, and it might be unearthed and tossed aside, but no; he also holds on his way. It is not that he resents the trouble, it is the idea that is wanting. It

would no more occur to him that that stone was
a displaceable object, and that for the general
weal he might displace it, than that its feldspar
was of the orthoclase variety. Generations and
generations of men have passed that stone, and it
still waits for a man with an altruistic idea. But
it would be a very stony country indeed—and
Africa is far from stony—that would wholly
account for the aggravating obliqueness and inde-
cision of the African footpath. Probably each
four miles, on an average path, is spun out by an
infinite series of minor sinuosities, to five or six.
Now these deflections are not meaningless. Each
has some history—a history dating back, perhaps,
a thousand years, but all clue to which was lost
centuries ago. The leading cause, probably, is
fallen trees. When a tree falls across a path no
man ever removes it. As in the case of the stone,
the native goes round it. It is too green to burn
in his hut; before it is dry, and the white ants
have eaten it, the new detour has become part

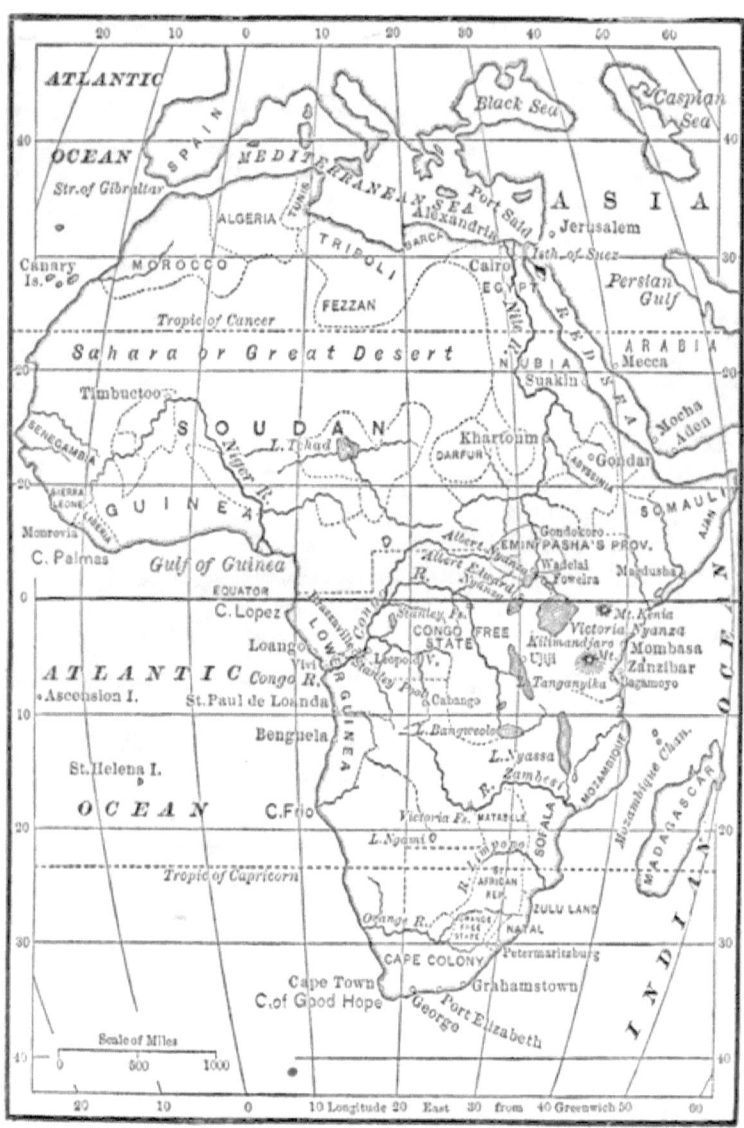

PROFILE MAP OF AFRICA.

and parcel of the path. The smaller irregularities, on the other hand, represent the trees and stumps of the primeval forest where the track was made at first. But whatever the cause, it is certain that for persistent straightforwardness in the general, and utter vacillation and irresolution in the particular, the African roads are unique in engineering ."

Three distinct Africas are known to the modern world—North Africa, where men go for health ; South Africa, where they go for money ; and Central Africa, where they go for adventure. The first, the old Africa of Augustine and Carthage, every one knows from history ; the geography of the second, the Africa of the Zulu and the diamond, has been taught us by two Universal Educators—War and the Stock Exchange ; but our knowledge of the third, the Africa of Livingstone and Stanley, is still fitly symbolized by the vacant look upon our maps which tells how long this mysterious land has kept its secret.

Africa, generally speaking, is a vast, ill-formed triangle. It has no peninsulas ; it has almost no islands or bays or fjords. But three great inlets, three mighty rivers piercing it to the very heart, have been allocated by a kind Nature, one to each of its solid sides. On the north is the Nile, the river of the past, flowing through Egypt, as Leigh Hunt says, "like some grave, mighty thought threading a dream ;" on the west, the river of the future, the not less mysterious Congo ; and on the east, the little known Zambesi.

The physical features of this great continent are easily grasped. From the coast a low scorched plain, reeking with malaria, extends inland in unbroken monotony for two or three hundred miles. This is succeeded by mountains, slowly rising into a plateau, some 2,000 or 3,000 feet high; and this, at some hundreds of miles distance, forms the pedestal for a second plateau as high again. This last plateau, 4000 to 5000 feet high, may be said to occupy the whole of Central Africa. It is only on the large scale, however,

that these are to be reckoned plateaux at all.
When one is upon them he sees nothing but
mountains and valleys and plains of the ordinary
type, covered for the most part with forest.

Nature, says Drummond, has supplied each side
of Africa with one great river. By going some
hundreds of miles southward along the coast from
Zanzibar, the traveler reaches the mouth of the
Zambesi. Livingstone sailed up this river once,
and about a hundred miles from its mouth discovered another river, twisting away northwards
among the mountains. The great explorer was
not the man to lose such a chance of penetrating
the interior. He followed this river up, and after
many wanderings found himself on the shores of
a mighty lake. The river is named the Shiré,
and the lake—the existence of which was quite
unknown before—is Lake Nyassa. Lake Nyassa
is three hundred and fifty miles long ; so that,
with the Zambesi, the Shiré, and this great lake,
we have the one thing required to open up East
Central Africa—a water- route to the interior.

But this is not all. Two hundred and fifty miles
from the end of Lake Nyassa, another lake of still
nobler proportions takes up the thread of communication. Lake Tanganika is four hundred
and fifty miles in length. Between the lake
stands a lofty plateau, cool, healthy, accessible, and
without any physical barrier to interrupt the
explorer's march. By this route the Victoria
Nyanza and the Albert Nyanza may be approached with less fatigue, less risk, and not less
speed, than by the overland trail from Zanzibar.
At one point also, along this line, one is within a
short march of that other great route which must
ever be regarded as the trunk-line of the African
continent. The watershed of the Congo lies on
this Nyassa-Tanganika plateau. This is the
stupendous natural highway on which so much of
the future of East Central Africa must yet
depend.

Drummond says that Africans will do anything
for flesh in whatever form. "Eggs are never
eaten by the natives, but always set; although

if you offer to buy them, the natives will bring you a dozen from a sitting hen, which they assure you were laid that very morning. In the interior, on many occasions afterwards, these protestations were tested, and always proved false. One time, when nearly famished and far from camp, I was brought a few eggs which a chief himself guaranteed had that very hour been laid. With sincere hope that he might be right, but with much misgiving, I ordered the two freshest looking to be boiled. With the despair of a starving man I opened them. They were cock and hen !"

Breakfast and luncheon and dinner are all the same in Africa. "There is no beef, nor mutton, nor bread, nor flour, nor sugar, nor salt, nor anything whatever, except an occasional fowl, which an Englishman can eat. Hence the enormous outfit which he must carry with him. No one has any idea of what can be had in tins till he camps out abroad. Every conceivable digestible and indigestible is to be had tinned, every form

of fish, flesh fowl and game, every species of
vegetable and fruit, every soup, sweet and
entreé ; but after two or three months of this sort
of thing you learn that this tempting semblance
of variety is a gigantic imposition. The sole difference between these various articles lies, like
the Rhine wines, in the label. Plum pudding or
kippered herring taste just the same. Whether
you begin dinner with tinned calves-foot jelly or
end with tinned salmon makes no difference ;
and after six months it is only by a slight feeling
of hardness that you do not swallow the tins
themselves."

About the middle of August the expedition
made its first acquaintance with fever, that
scourge of the white man who essays to travel in
Africa. Shaw and Stanley were both taken sick.

Malarial fever is the one sad certainty which
every African traveler must face. For months
he may escape, but its finger is upon him, and
well for him if he has a friend near when it
finally overtakes him. It is preceded for weeks,

or even for·a month or two, by unaccountable
irritability, depression and weariness. On the
march with his men he has scarcely started when
he sighs for the noon-day rest. Putting it down
to mere laziness, he goads himself on by draughts
from the water-bottle, and totters forward a mile
or two more. Next he finds himself skulking
into the forest on the pretext of looking at a
specimen, and, when his porters are out of sight,
throws himself under a tree in utter limpness and
despair. Roused by mere shame, he staggers
along the trail, and as he nears the midday camp
puts on a spurt to conceal his defeat, which
finishes him for the rest of the day. This is
a good place for specimens he tells the men—the
tent may be pitched for the night. This goes on
day after day till the crash comes—first cold and
pain, then heat and pain, then every kind of pain
and every degree of heat, then delirium, then the
life-and-death struggle. He rises, if he does rise,
a shadow ; and slowly accumulates strength for
the next attack, which he knows too well will

not disappoint him. No one has ever yet got to
the bottom of African fever. Its geographical
distribution is still unmapped, but generally it
prevails over the whole east and west coasts
within the tropical limit, along all the river-
courses, on the shores of the inland lakes, and in
all low-lying and marshy districts. The higher
plateaux, presumably, are comparatively free
from it, but in order to reach these, malarious
districts of greater or smaller area have to be
traversed. There the system becomes saturated
with fever, which often develops long after the
infected region is left behind.

By August 29th Shaw was out of danger,
yet, says Stanley, I am unsuccessful as yet
in procuring soldiers. I almost despair of ever
being able to move from here. It is such a
drowsy, sleepy, slow, dreaming country. Arabs,
Wangwana, Wanyamwezi, are all alike—all care-
less how time flies. Their to-morrow means

sometimes within a month. To me it is simply maddening

August 30th.—Shaw will not work. I cannot get him to stir himself. I have petted him and coaxed him ; I have even cooked little luxuries for him myself. And, while I am straining every nerve to get ready for Ujiji, Shaw is satisfied with looking on listlessly. What a change from the ready-handed bold man he was at Zanzibar.

I sat down by his bedside to day with my palm and needle, in order to encourage him, and to-day for the first time, I told him that I did not care about the geography of the country half as much as I cared about FINDING LIVINGSTONE ! I told him, for the first time, " Now, my dear Shaw, you think probably I have been sent here to find the depth of the Tanganika. Not a bit of it, man ; I was told to find Livingstone. It is to find Livingstone I am here. It is to find Livingstone I am going. Don't you see, old fellow, the importance of the mission ; don't you see what reward you will get from Mr. Bennett, if you will

help me. I am sure if ever you come to New
York, you will never be in want of a fifty-dollar
bill. So shake yourself ; jump about ; look
lively. Say you will not die ; that is half the battle. Snap your fingers at the fever. I will guar-
antee the fever won't kill you. I have medicine
enough for a regiment here !"

Bah ! Bah ! I was talking to a lifeless mum-
my. His eyes lit up a little, but the light that
shone in them shortly faded, and died. I was
quite disheartened. I made some strong punch,
to put fire in his veins, that I might see life in
him. I put sugar and eggs, and seasoned it with
lemon and spice. "Drink, Shaw," said I, "and
forget your miserable infirmities. Don't breathe
in my face, man, as if you were about to die.
Leave off this pantomime. You are not sick,
dear fellow ; it is only *ennui* you are feeling.
Look at Selim, there. Now, I will bet any
amount that he will not die ; that I will carry
him home safe to his friends at Jerusalem ! I
will carry you home also, if you will let me."

Piff-puff at his nasty pipe. Hear him breathe! You would think he was dying; but he is not even sick. He told me, only the other day, that he knew every trick of old sea-salts when they wished to shirk duty at sea. I am sure he is practicing a trick on me. This intermittent fever! I know every stage of it; and I feel convinced he has not got it.

Of one thing, I feel sure, that if I took a stick I could take the nonsense out of him.

September 1st.—According to Thani bin Abdullah, whom I visited to-day at his tembe in Maroro, Mirambo lost two hundred men in the attack upon Tabora, while the Arabs' losses were five Arabs, thirteen freemen and eight slaves, besides three tembes, and over one hundred small huts - burned, two hundred and eighty ivory tusks and sixty cows and bullocks captured.

September 3rd.—Received a packet of letters and newspapers from Captain Webb, at Zanzibar. What a good thing it is that one's friends, even in far America, think of the absent one in Africa!

They tell me that no one dreams of my being in Africa yet.

I applied to Sheikh bin Nasib to-day to permit 'Livingstone's caravan to go under my charge to Ujiji, but he would not listen to it. He says he feels certain I am going to my death.

September 4th.—Shaw is quite well to day, he says. Selim is down with the fever. My force is gradually increasing, though some of my old soldiers are falling off. Umgareza is blind ; Baruti has the small-pox very badly ; Bilali has a strange disease, an ulcer or something, rear ward ; Sadala has the Mukunguru (the intermittent).

September 5th.—Baruti died this morning. He was one of my best soldiers ; and was one of those men who accompanied Speke to Egypt. Baruti is number seven of those who have died since leaving Zanzibar.

To day my ears have been poisoned with the reports of the Arabs about the state of the country I am about to travel through. " The roads are bad ; they are all stopped ; the Ruga-Ruga are out in the forests ; the Wakonongo are coming from the south to help Mirambo ; the Washensi are at war, one tribe against another." My men are getting dispirited, they have imbibed the fears of the Arabs and the Wanyamwezi. Bombay begins to feel that I had better go back to the coast, and try again some other time.

We buried Baruti under the shade of the banyan tree, a few yards west of my tembe. The grave was made four and a-half feet deep and three feet wide. At the bottom, on one side, a narrow trench was excavated, into which the body was rolled, on his side, with his face turned towards Mecca. The body was dressed in a doti and a-half of new American sheeting. After it was properly placed in its narrow bed, a sloping roof of sticks, covered over with matting and old canvas, was made, to prevent the earth from falling over the body. The grave was then filled, the soldiers laughing merrily. On the top of the grave was planted a small shrub, and into a small hole, made with the hand, was poured water, lest he might feel thirsty—they said—on his way to Paradise; water was then sprinkled all over the grave, and the gourd broken. This ceremony being ended, the men recited the Arabic Fat-hah, after which they left the grave of their dead comrade, to think no more of him.

September 7th.—An Arab, named Mohammed, presented me to-day with a little boy slave, called "Ndugu M'Hali" (my brother's wealth). As I did not like the name, I called the chiefs of my caravan together, and asked them to give him a better name. One suggested "Simba" (a lion), another said he thought "Ngombe" (a cow), would suit the boy child; another thought he ought to be called "Mirambo," which raised a loud laugh. Bombay thought "Bombay Mdogo" would suit my black skinned infant very well. Ulimengo, however, after looking at his quick eyes, and noting his celerity of movement, pronounced the name Ka-lu-lu as the best for him, "because," said he. "just look at his eyes, so

bright ! look at his form, so slim ! watch his
movements, how quick ! Yes, Kalulu is his
name." " Yes, bana," said the others, "let it
be Kalulu."

" Kalulu " is a Kisawahili term for the young
of the blue buck (perpusilla) antelope.

" Well, then," said I, water being brought in a
huge tin pan,—Selim, who was willing to stand
godfather, holding him over the water,—" let his
name henceforth be Kalulu, and let no man take
it from him," and thus it was that the little
black boy of Mohammed's came to be called
Kalulu.

The expedition is increasing in numbers ; it is
now composed of two white men, one Arab boy,
one Hindi, twenty-nine Wangwana, one boy
from Londa (Cazembes), one boy from Uganda,
one boy from Liemba or Uwemba. We had
quite an alarm before dark. Much firing was
heard at Tabora, which led us to anticipate an
attack on Kwihara. It turned out, however, to
be a salute fired in honor of the arrival of Sultan

Kitambi to pay a visit to Mkasiwa, Sultan of Unyanyembe.

September 8*th.*—Towards night Sheikh bin Nasib received a letter from an Arab at Mfuto, reporting that an attack was made on that place by Mirambo and his Watuta allies. It also warned him to bid the people of Kwihara hold themselves in readiness, because if Mirambo succeeded in storming Mfuto, he would march direct on Kwihara.

September 9*th.*—Mirambo was defeated with severe loss yesterday in his attack upon Mfuto. He was successful in an assault he made upon a small Wanyanwezi village, but when he attempted ed to storm Mfuto, he was repulsed with severe loss, losing three of his principal men. Upon withdrawing his forces from the attack, the inhabitants sallied out and followed him to the forest of Umanda, where he was again utterly routed, himself ingloriously flying from the field.

The heads of his chief men slain in the attack were brought to Kwihara, the boma of Mkasiwa.

September 11*th*.—Shaw is a sentimental driveller with a large share of the principles of Joseph Surface within his nature. He is able at times to kindle into an eloquent rant about the vices of mankind, particularly those of rich people. His philippics on this topic deserved a better audience than I furnished him.

He has a habit of being self-absorbed—is an oddity quite the reverse of Jack Bunsby. Instead of looking towards the horizon, he regards the ground at his feet with a look which seems to say, there is something wrong somewhere, and I am trying to find out where it can be, and how to rectify it.

He told me to-day his father had been a captain in Her Majesty's navy, that he had been present at four levees of Queen Victoria. This can hardly be, however, as I cannot imagine a naval captain's son being so ignorant of penmanship as scarcely to be able to write his own name, nor can I see how it is possible that he could have been presented to the Queen, for I have always understood that the Court of St. James's is the most aristocratic in Europe.

He is very angry, though, with me, because I laugh at him, and has just opened a sentimental battery on me which makes me almost cry out with vexation that I encumbered myself with such a fool.

September 14*th.*—The Arab boy Selim is delirious from constant fevers. Shaw is sick again, or pretends to be. These two occupy most of my time. I am turned into a regular nurse, for I have no one to assist me in attending upon them. If I try to instruct Abdul Kader in the art of being useful, his head is so befogged with the villainous fumes of Unyamwezi tobacco, that he wanders bewildered about, breaking dishes and upsetting cooked dainties, until I get so exasperated that my peace of mind is broken completely for a full hour. If I ask Ferajji, my now formally constituted cook, to assist, his thick wooden head fails to receive an idea, and I am thus obliged to play the part of *chef de cuisine.*

September 15*th.*—The third month of my residence in Unyanembe is almost finished, and I am
still here, but I hope to be gone before the 23*rd*
inst.

All last night, until 9 A. M. this morning, my
soldiers danced and sang to the means of their
dead comrades, whose bones now bleach in the
forests of Wilyankuru. Two or three huge pots
of pombe failed to satisfy the raging thirst
which the vigorous exercise they were engaged
in created. So, early this morning, I was called
upon to contribute a shukka for another potful of
the potent liquor.

To-day I was busy selecting the loads for each
soldier and pagazi. In order to lighten their
labor as much as possible, I reduced each from
seventy pounds to fifty pounds, by which I hope
to be enabled to make some long marches. I
have been able to engage ten pagazis during the
last two or three days.

I have two or three men still very sick, and it
is almost useless to expect that they will be able

to carry anything, but I am in hope that other
men may be engaged to take their places before
the actual day of departure, which now seems to
be drawing near rapidly.

September 16th.—We have almost finished our
work—on the fifth day from this—God willing—
we shall march. I engaged two more pagazis,
besides two guides, named Asmani and Mabruki.
If vastness of the human form could terrify any
one, certainly Asman's appearance is well calculated to produce that effect. He stands considerably over six feet without shoes, and has shoulders broad enough for two ordinary men.

To-morrow I mean to give the people a farewell
feast, to celebrate our departure from this forbidding and unhappy country.

September 17th.—The banquet is ended. I
slaughtered two bullocks, and had a barbecue;
three sheep, two goats, and fifteen chickens, one
hundred and twenty pounds of rice, twenty large
loaves of bread, made of Indian corn flour, one
hundred eggs, ten pounds of butter, and five

gallons of sweet milk, were the contents of which the banquet was formed. The men invited their friends and neighbors, and about one hundred women and children partook of it.

After the banquet was ended, the pombe, or native beer, was brought in in five gallon pots, and the people commenced their dance, which continues even now as I write.

September 19*th.*—I had a slight attack of fever to day, which has postponed our departure. Selim and Shaw are both recovered. Selim tells me that Shaw has said that I would die like a donkey ; and that he said he would take charge of my journals and trunks, and proceed to the coast immediately, if I die. This afternoon, he is stated to have said that he does not intend to go to Ujiji, but that when I am gone he will stock the yard full of chickens, in order to be able to get fresh eggs every day, and that he will buy a cow, from which he will be able to procure fresh milk daily.

At night Shaw came to me while the fever was

at its height, to ask me to whom I would like to
have him write in case I should die, because,
said he, even the strongest of us may die. I told
him to go and mind his own business and not be
croaking near me.

About 8 P. M. Sheikh bin Nasib came to me
imploring me not to go away to-morrow, because
I was so sick. Thani Sakhburi suggested to me
that I might stay another month ; in answer, I
told them that white men are not accustomed to
break their words. I had said I would go, and I
intended to go.

Sheikh bin Nasib gave up all hope of inducing
me to remain another day, and he has gone away
with a promise to write to Syed Burghash to tell
him how obstinate I am, and that I am determined to be killed. This was a parting shot.

About 10 P. M. the fever had gone. All were
asleep in the tembe but myself, and an unutter
able loneliness came on me as I reflected on my
position and my intentions, and felt the utter
lack of sympathy with me in all around. Even

my own white assistant, with whom I had striven
hard, was less sympathizing than my little black
boy Kalulu. It requires more nerve than I possess to dispel all the dark presentiments that
come upon the mind. But probably what I call
presentiments are simply the impress on the mind
of the warnings which these false-hearted Arabs
have repeated so often. This melancholy and
loneliness, I feel, may probably have their origin
from the same cause. The single candle, which
hardly lights up the dark shade that fills the cor-
ners of my room, is but a poor incentive to cheerfulness. I feel as though I were imprisoned
between stone walls. But why should I feel as if
baited by these stupid, slow-witted Arabs and
their warnings and croakings? I fancy a suspicion haunts my mind, as I write, that there lies
some motive behind all this. I wonder if these
Arabs tell me all these things to keep me here, in
the hope that I might be induced another time to
assist them in their war with Mirambo! If they
think so, they are much mistaken, for I have

taken a solemn, enduring oath,—an oath to be
kept while the least hope of life remains in me,—
not to be tempted to break the resolution I have
formed, never to give up the search until I find
Livingstone alive, or find his dead body; and
never to return home without the strongest possible proofs that he is alive, or that he is dead.
No living man, or living men, shall stop me; only
death can prevent me.   But death—not even
this; I shall not die, I will not die, I cannot die!
And something tells me, I do not know what it is
—perhaps it is the ever-living hopefulness of my
own nature, perhaps it is the natural presump-
tion born out of an abundant and glowing vital-
ity, or the outcome of an overweening confidence
in one's self—anyhow and everyhow, something
tells me to-night I shall find him, and—write it
larger—FIND HIM!   FIND HIM!   Have I
uttered a prayer?   I shall sleep calmly to-night.

All this time there was no trustworthy news of
Livingstone.   At last, on the 20th of September,

1871, Stanley determined to set out for Ujiji by the southerly route. Fourteen days' travel in a south-westerly direction, with a gain of one degree of latitude, nearly every mile of the route presenting some new peril, found the expedition brought to a sudden halt by the report of another war between native tribes right in the line of march. So the course was changed to due west, through the forest, so as to strike Lake Tangan-ika further north than was at first intended. But from this time on we simply paraphrase Stanley's own story.

"On the 29th," says the journal, "we left camp, and after a few minutes we were in view of the sublimest, but ruggedest scenes we had yet beheld in Africa. The country was cut up in all directions by deep, wild, and narrow ravines trending in all directions, but generally toward the north-west, while on either side rose enormous square masses of the naked rock (sandstone), sometimes towering and rounded, sometimes pyramidal, sometimes in truncated cones, some-

times in circular ridges, with sharp, rugged,
naked backs, with but little vegetation anywhere
visible, except it obtained a precarious tenure in
the fissured crown of some gigantic hill-top,
whither some soil had fallen, or at the base of the
reddish ochre scarps which everywhere lifted
their fronts to our view.

"A long series of descents down rocky gullies,
wherein we were environed by threatening
masses of disintegrated rock, brought us to a dry,
stony ravine, with mountain heights looming
above us some thousand feet high. This ravine
we followed, winding around in all directions, but
which gradually widened, however, into a broad
plain, with a western trend. The road, leaving
this, struck across a low ridge to the north; and
we were in view of deserted settlements where
the villages were built on frowning castellated
masses of rock. Near an upright mass of rock
over seventy feet high, and about fifty yards in
diameter, which dwarfed the gigantic sycamore
close to it, we made our camp, after five hours

and thirty minutes' continuous and rapid marching.

"The people were very hungry; they had eaten every scrap of meat, and every grain they possessed, twenty hours before, and there was no immediate prospect of food. I had but a pound and a half of flour left, and this would not have sufficed to begin to feed a force of over forty-five people; but I had something like thirty pounds of tea and twenty pounds of sugar left, and I at once, as soon as we arrived at camp, ordered every kettle to be filled and placed on the fire, and then made tea for all, giving each man a quart of a hot, grateful beverage, well sweetened. Parties stole out also into the depths of the jungle to search for wild fruit, and soon returned laden with baskets of the wood-peach and tamarind fruit, which, though it did not satisfy, relieved them. That night, before going to sleep, the Wangwana set up a loud prayer to 'Allah' to give them food.

"We rose betimes in the morning, determined

to travel on until food could be procured or we dropped down from sheer fatigue and weakness. Rhinoceros' tracks abounded, and buffalo seemed to be plentiful, but we never beheld a living thing. We crossed scores of short steeps, and descended as often into the depths of dry, stony gullies, and then finally entered a valley, bounded on one side by a triangular mountain with perpendicular sides, and on the other by a bold group, a triplet of hills. While marching down the valley —which soon changed its dry, bleached aspect to a vivid green—we saw a forest in the distance, and shortly found ourselves in corn-fields. Looking keenly around for a village, we descried it on the summit of the lofty triangular hill on our right. A loud exultant shout was raised at the discovery. The men threw down their packs and began to clamor for food. Volunteers were asked to come forward to take cloth and scale the heights to obtain it from the village at any price. While three or four sallied off we rested on the ground, quite worn out.

"In about an hour the foraging party returned with the glorious tidings that food was plentiful ; that the village we saw was called " Welled Nzogera's'—the son of Nzogera—by which, of course, we knew that we were in Uvinza, Nzogera being the principal chief of Uvinza. We were further informed that Nzogera, the father, was at war with Lokanda-Mira, about some salt-pans in the valley of the Malagarazi, and that it would be difficult to go to Ujiji by the usual road, owing to this war ; but, for a consideration, the son of Nzogera was willing to supply us with guides who would take us safely by a northern road to Ujiji.

" *October* 31*st*. *Tuesday.*—Camp in jungle. Direction of road, north-by-east. Time occupied by march, four hours fifteen minutes. Our road led E. N. E. Soon we turned our faces north-west and prepared to cross the marsh ; and the guides informed us, as we halted on its eastern bank, of a terrible catastrophe which occurred a few yards above where we were preparing to cross. They

told of an Arab and his caravan, consisting of
thirty-five slaves, who had suddenly sunk out of
sight, and who were never more heard of. This
marsh, as it appeared to us, presented a breadth
of some hundreds of yards, on which grew a close
network of grass, with much decayed matter
mixed up with it. In the centre of this, and
underneath it, ran a broad, deep and rapid stream.
As the guides proceeded across, the men stole
after them with cautious footsteps. As they
arrived near the centre we began to see this
unstable grassy bridge, so curiously provided by
nature for us, move up and down in heavy languid
undulations, like the swell of the sea after a
storm   Where the two asses of the expedition
moved, the grassy waves rose a food high ; but
suddenly, one unfortunate animal plunged his feet
through, and as he was unable to rise, he soon
made a deep hollow, which was rapidly filling
with water.   With the aid of ten men, however,
we were enabled to lift him bodily up and land
him on a firmer part, and guiding them both

across rapidly, the entire caravan crossed without accident.

" On arriving at the other side, we struck off to the north, and found ourselves in a delightful country, in every way suitable for agriculturists. Great rocks rose here and there, but in their fissures rose stately trees, under whose umbrage nestled the villages of the people.

"*November* 1*st.*—Striking north-west, after leaving our camp and descending the slope of a mountain, we soon beheld the anxiously looked-for Malagarazi, a narrow but deep stream, flowing through a valley pent in by lofty mountains. Fish eating birds lined the trees on its banks ; villages were thickly scattered about. Food was abundant and cheap.

" About 10 A. M. appeared from the direction of Ujiji a caravan of eighty Waguhha, a tribe which occupies a tract of country on the south-western side of the Lake Tanganika. We asked the news, and were told a white man had just arrived at Ujiji from Manyuema. This news startled us all.

" ' A white man ?' we asked.

" ' Yes, a white man,' they replied.

" ' How is he dressed ?'   .

" ' Like the master,' they answered, referring to me.

" ' Is he young, or old ?'

" ' He is old. He has white hair on his face, and is sick.'

" ' Where has he come from ?'

" ' From a very far country away beyond Uguhha, called Manyuema.'

" ' Indeed ! and is he stopping at Ujiji now ?'

" ' Yes, we saw him about eight days ago.'

" ' Do you think he will stop there until we see him ?'

" ' Sigue' (don't know).

" ' Was he ever at Ujiji before ?'

" ' Yes, he went away a long time ago.'

"Hurrah ! This is Livingstone ! He must be Livingstone ! He can be no other ; but still—he may be some one else—some one from the West Coast—or perhaps he is Baker! No; Baker has no white hair on his face. But we must now march quick, lest he hears we are coming and runs away.

" I addressed my men, and asked them if they were willing to march to Ujiji without a single halt, and then promised them, if they acceded to my wishes, two doti each man. All answered in the affirmative, almost as much rejoiced as I was myself. But I was madly rejoiced ; intensely eager to resolve the burning question, ' Is it Dr. David Livingstone ?' God grant me patience, but I do wish there was a railroad, or at least horses in this country. With a horse I could reach Ujiji in about twelve hours.

" But we had no time to loiter by the way to indulge our joy. I was impelled onward by my almost uncontrollable feelings. I wished to resolve my doubts and fears. Was HE still there ? Had HE heard of any coming ? Would HE fly ?

" *November* 10*th*. *Friday*.—The two hundred

and thirty-sixth day from Bagamoyo, and the fifty-first day from Unyanyembe. General direction to Ujiji, west-by-south. Time of march, six hours.

"It is a happy, glorious morning. The air is fresh and cool. The sky lovingly smiles on the earth and her children. The deep woods are crowned in bright green leafage ; the water of the Mkuti, rushing under the emerald shade afforded by the bearded banks, seems to challenge us for the race to Ujiji, with its continuous brawl.

"We are all outside the village cane fence, every man of us looking as spruce, as neat, and happy as when he embarked on the dhows at Zanzibar, which seems to us to have been ages ago—we have witnessed and experienced so much.

"'Forward !'

"'Ay, Wallah, ay Wallah, bana yango !' and the light-hearted braves stride away at a rate which must soon bring us within view of Ujiji.

We ascend a hill overgrown with bamboo, descend into a ravine, through which dashes an impetuous little torrent, ascend another short hill, then, along a smooth footpath running across the slope of a long ridge, we push on as only eager, light-hearted men can do.

"In two hours I am warned to prepare for a view of the Tanganika, for, from the top of a steep mountain the kirangozi says I can see it. I almost vent the feelings of my heart in cries. But wait, we must behold it first. And we press forward and up the hill breathlessly, lest the grand scene hasten away. We are at last on the summit. Ah! not yet can it be seen. A little further on—just yonder, oh! there it is—a silvery gleam. I merely catch sight of it between the trees, and—but here it is at last! True—THE TANGANIKA! and there are the blue-black mountains of Ugoma and Ukaramba. An immense broad sheet, a burnished bed of silver—lucid canopy of blue above—lofty mountains are its valances, palm forests form its fringes! The

Tanganika!--Hurrah! and the men respond to
the exultant cry of the Anglo-Saxon with the
lungs of Stentors, and the great forests and the
hills seem to share in our triumph.

" We are descending the western slope of the
mountain, with the valley of the Liuche before
us.   Something like an hour before noon we have
gained the thick matete brake, which grows on
both banks of the river ; we wade through the
clear stream, arrive on the other side, emerge out
of the brake, and the gardens of the Wajiji are
around us—a perfect marvel of vegetable wealth.
Details escape my hasty and partial observation.
I am almost overpowered with my own emotions.
I notice the graceful palms, neat plots green with
vegetable plants, and small villages surrounded
with frail fences of the matete-cane.

" We push on rapidly, lest the news of our
coming might reach the people of Ujiji before we
come in sight and are ready for them.   We halt
at a little brook, then ascend the long slope of a
naked ridge, the very last of the myriads we have

crossed. This alone prevents us from seeing the lake in all its vastness. We arrive at the summit, travel across and arrive at its western rim, and— pause, reader—the port of Ujiji is below us, embowered in the palms, only five hundred yards from us.

" ' Unfurl the flags, and load your guns !'

" 'Ay, Wallah, ay Wallah, bana !' respond the men, eagerly.

" 'One, two, three—fire !'

" A volley from nearly fifty guns roars like a salute from a battery of artillery ; we shall note its effect presently on the peaceful-looking village below.

"Before we had gone a hundred yards our repeated volleys had the effect desired. We had awakened Ujiji to the knowledge that a caravan was coming, and the people were witnessed rushing up in hundreds to meet us. The mere sight of the flags informed every one immediately that we were a caravan, but the American flag borne aloft by gigantic Asamani, whose face was one vast smile on this day, rather staggered them at first. However, many of the people who now approached us remembered the flag. They had seen it float above the American Consulate, and from the mast head of many a ship in the harbor of Zanzibar, and they were soon heard welcoming the beautiful flag with cries of ' Bindera Kisungu !'—a white man's flag ! ' Bindera Merikani !' —the American flag ! .

"We were now about three hundred yards from the village of Ujiji, and the crowds are dense about me. Suddenly, I hear a voice on my right say :

"' Good-morning, sir !'

"Startled at hearing this greeting in the midst of such a crowd of black people, I turn sharply around in search of the man, and see him at my side, with the blackest of faces, but animated and joyous—a man dressed in a long white shirt, with a turban of American sheeting around his woolly head, and I ask :

"' Who the mischief are you ?'

" 'I am Susi, the servant of Dr. Livingstone,' said he, smiling, and showing a gleaming row of teeth.

" 'What ! Is Dr. Livingstone here ?'

" 'Yes, sir.'

" 'In this village ?'

" 'Yes, sir.'

" 'Are you sure ?'

" 'Sure, sure, sir. Why, I leave him just now.'

" 'Good-morning, sir,' said another voice.

" 'Hallo,' said I, ' is this another one ?'

" 'Yes, sir.'

" 'Well, what is your name ?'

" 'My name is Chumah, sir.'

" 'What ! are you Chumah, the friend of Wekotani ?'

" 'Yes, sir.'

" 'And is the Doctor well ?'

" 'Not very well, sir.'

" 'Where has he been so long ?'

" 'In Manyuema.'

"'Now, you Susi, run, and tell the Doctor I am coming.'

" 'Yes, sir,' and off he darted like a madman.

" But, by this time we were within two hundred yards of the village, and the multitude was getting denser, and almost preventing our march. Flags and streamers were out ; Arabs and Wangwana were pushing their way through the natives in order to greet us, for, according to their account, we belonged to them. But the great wonder of all was, ' How did you come from Unyanyembe ?'

" Soon Susi came running back, and asked me my name ; he had told the Doctor that I was coming, but the Doctor was too surprised to believe him, and, when the Doctor asked him my name, Susi was rather staggered.

" But, during Susi's absence, the news had been conveyed to the Doctor that it was surely a white man that was coming, whose guns were firing and whose flag could be seen ; and the great Arab magnates of Ujiji—Mohammed bin

Sali, Sayd bin Majid, Abid bin Suliman, Mohammed bin Gharib, and others—had gathered together before the Doctor's house, and the Doctor had come out from his veranda to discuss the matter and await my arrival.

"In the meantime the head of the expedition had halted, and the kirangozi was out of the ranks, holding his flag afloat, and Selim said to me, 'I see the Doctor, sir. Oh, what an old man ! He has got a white beard.' And I—what would I not have given for a bit of friendly wilderness, where, unseen, I might vent my joy in some mad freak, such as idiotically biting my hand, turning a somersault, or slashing at trees, in order to allay those exciting feelings that were wellnigh uncontrollable. My heart beats fast, but I must not let my face betray my emotions, lest it shall detract from the dignity of a white man appearing under such extraordinary circumstances.

"So I did that which I thought was most dignified. I pushed back the crowds, and, passing from the rear, walked down a living avenue of people, until I came in front of the semicircle of Arabs, in the front of which stood the white man with the gray beard. As I advanced slowly towards him I noticed he was pale, looked wearied, had a gray beard, wore a bluish cap with a faded gold band around it, had on a red-sleeved waistcoat, and a pair of gray tweed trousers. I would have run to him, only I was a coward in the presence of such a mob—would have embraced him, only, he being an Englishman, I did not know how he would receive me; so I did what cowardice and false pride suggested was the best thing—walked deliberately to him, took off my hat, and said :

" 'Dr. Livingstone, I presume?'

" 'YES,' said he, with a kind smile, lifting his cap slightly.

" I replace my hat on my head, and he puts on his cap, and we both grasp hands, and I then say aloud :

" ' I thank God, Doctor, I have been permitted to see you.'

" He answered, ' I feel thankful that I am here to welcome you.'

" I turn to the Arabs, take off my hat to them in response to the saluting chorus "Yambos" I receive, and the Doctor introduced them to me by name. Then, oblivious of the crowds, oblivious of the men who shared with me my dangers, we —Livingstone and I—turn our faces towards his tembe. He points to the veranda, or, rather, mud platform, under the broad overhanging eaves; he points to his own particular seat, which I see his age and experience in Africa has suggested, namely, a straw mat, with a goat-skin over it, and another skin nailed against the wall to protect his back from contact with the cold mud. I protest against taking this seat, which so much more befits him than me, but the Doctor will not yield : I must take it.

" We are seated—the Doctor and I—with our backs to the wall. The Arabs take seats on our left. More than a thousand natives are in our front, filling the whole square densely, indulging their curiosity, and discussing the fact of two white men meeting at Ujiji—one just come from Manyuema, in the west, the other from Unyanyembe, in the east.

"Conversation began. What about? I declare I have forgotten. Oh! we mutually asked questions of one another, such as :

" 'How did you come here?' and 'Where have you been all this long time ?—the world has believed you to be dead.' Yes, that was the way it began ; but whatever the Doctor informed me, and that which I communicated to him, I cannot correctly report, for I found myself gazing at him, conning the wonderful man at whose side I now sat in Central Africa. Every hair of his head and beard, every wrinkle of his face, the wanness of his features, and the slightly wearied look he wore, were all imparting intelligence to me—the knowledge I craved for so much ever since I heard the words, 'Take what you want, but find Livingstone.'

"The Doctor kept his letter-bag on his knee, then, presently, opened it, looked at the letters contained there, and read one or two of his children's letters, his face in the meantime lighting up.

"He asked me to tell him the news. 'No, doctor,' said I, 'read your letters first, which I am sure you must be impatient to read.'

"'Ah,' said he, 'I have waited years for a letter, and I have been taught patience. I can surely afford to wait a few hours longer. No, tell me the general news; how is the world getting along?'

"Shortly I found myself enacting the part of an annual periodical to him. There was no need of exaggeration—of any penny-a-line news, or of any sensationalism. The world had witnessed and experienced much the last few years.

"What a budget of news it was to one who

had emerged from the depths of the primeval forests of Manyuema.

"Not long after presents of food came in succession, and as fast as they were brought we set
to.   I had a healthy, stubborn digestion—the
exercise I had taken had put it in prime order ;
but Livingstone—he had been complaining that
he had no appetite, that his stomach refused
everything but a cup of tea now and then—he ate
also—ate like a vigorous, hungry man ; and, as
he vied with me in demolishing the pancakes,
he kept repeating, 'You have brought me new
life.   You have brought me new life.'

"'Oh, by George!' I said,. 'I have forgotten
something. Hasten, Selim, and bring that bottle ;
you know which ; and bring me the silver gob-
lets.   I brought this bottle on purpose for this
event, which I hoped would come to pass, though
often it seemed useless to expect it.'

"Selim knew where the bottle was, and he soon
returned with it—a bottle of Sillery champagne ;
and, handing the doctor a silver goblet brimful of

the exhilarating wine, and pouring a small quantity into my own, I said :

" ' Dr. Livingstone, to your very good health, sir.'

" ' And to yours,' he responded.

" And the champagne I had treasured for this happy meeting was drunk with hearty good wishes to each other.

" The Doctor and I conversed upon many things, especially upon his own immediate troubles, and his disappointment upon his arrival in Ujiji, when told that all his goods had been sold, and he was reduced to poverty. He had but twenty cloths or so left of the stock he had deposited with the man called Sheriff, the half-caste drunken tailor, who was sent .by the British Consul in charge of the goods. Besides which he had been suffering from an attack of dysentery, and his condition was most deplorable. He was but little improved on this day, though he had eaten well, and already began to feel stronger and better.

" This day, like all others, though big with happiness to me, at last was fading away. We, sitting with our faces looking to the east, as Livingstone had been sitting for days preceding my arrival, noted the dark shadows which crept up above the grove of palms beyond the village, and above the rampart of mountains which we had crossed that day, now looming through the fast approaching darkness ; and we listened, with our hearts full of gratitude to the great Giver of Good, and Dispenser of all Happiness, to the sonorous thunder of the surf of the Tanganika, and to the chorus which the night insects sang. Hours passed, and we were still sitting there with our minds busy upon the day's remarkable events, when I remembered that the traveler had not yet read his letters.

" 'Doctor,' I said, 'you had better read your letters. I will not keep you up any longer.'

" 'Yes,' he answered, 'It is getting late ; and I will go and read my friends' letters. Good-night, and God bless you.'

" ' Good-night, my dear Doctor ; and let me hope that your news will be such as you desire.' "

And now, dear reader, says Stanley in conclusion, having related succinctly " How I found Livingstone," I bid you also " Good-night."

CHAPTER III.

THROUGH THE DARK CONTINENT AND DOWN THE CONGO.

On a memorable Saturday in the spring of 1874, an imposing funeral cortege wound its way through the streets of London to the old abbey of Westminster, there to lay at rest the ashes of one more heroic soul to join the silent ranks of the illustrious dead already reposing in its cool recesses. The casket bore the simple inscription:

" DAVID LIVINGSTONE,
BORN AT BANTYRE, LANARKSHIRE, SCOTLAND,
MARCH 19, 1813,
DIED AT ILLALA, CENTRAL AFRICA,
MAY 1, 1873."

Truly, the workers die but the work goes on ! After the great exertions which Stanley had made to find Livingstone, it was only natural that he should watch with much interest the explorations of the latter in the wilds of that country where his own fame had been won. When the news came that Livingstone had closed his labors in death, he saw the great work of the Christian explorer unfinished, and the question came home with startling emphasis, "Why can I not complete the work?" Again and again the question arose, until he was seized with an anxious longing to plunge again into the wilds of Africa and make known to the world the secrets hidden there.

After having considered the matter for some time, the proprietors of the *New York Herald* and the *London Telegraph* resolved to send him out. The great lake region, which included about six degrees of longitude, reaching from the equator to fifteen degrees south latitude, had become one of the points on the African continent which possessed great interest to explorers and geographers. In this vast region lived a great many tribes as yet unknown, while it appeared as if the rivers which flowed into the lakes must furnish a medium of communication between the African interior and the outside world.

The records of the trials and triumphs of this second great expedition into the heart of Africa are told by the explorer in his *Through the Dark Continent.* Prof. Packard, in his *Stanley in Africa,* has given us a very remarkable summary of the record contained in the former book, and to these two works the present chapter is somewhat indebted.

Lakes Nyassa and Tanganika had been largely explored, but still there was much to learn respecting them ; while Victoria N'yanza, which was generally considered as being the source of the Nile, was almost entirely unknown. Notwithstanding the many and great efforts to find the source of the Nile, the question had not as yet been settled, and the mystery which hung about it only served to intensify the interest.

" The Victoria N'yanza, therefore, was to be

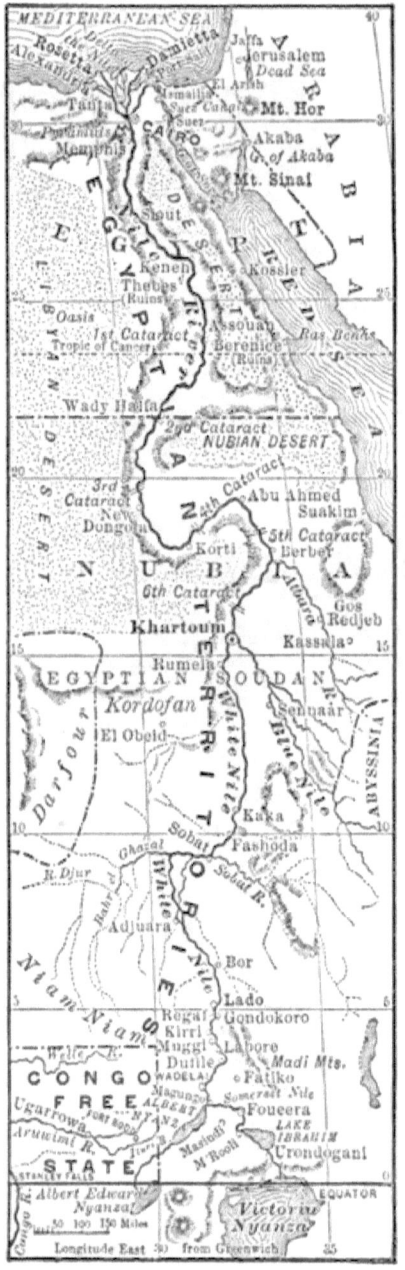

[The map shows the Valley of the Nile, from source to mouth, according to the latest discoveries, and depicts its true sources in the Victoria Nyanza and the Albert Edward Nyanza. The near approach of the Congo and the Nile watersheds is also apparent through the eastward trend of the Aruwimi-Ituri to almost within sight of the Albert Nyanza.]

THE NILE FROM SOURCE TO MOUTH.

Stanley's first objective point. He proposed to take a boat with him, and with this he intended to explore the lake which had been seen by Burton, Speke, and Livingstone. This boat he caused to be made in sections, so that he could the more easily carry it to its destination through the nearly one thousand miles which lay through African jungles.

" Having completed all necessary preparations, he left England, and toward the close of 1874, landed once again at Zanzibar. While here, he discovered that the person who had built his boat had made it very much heavier than he had ordered ; so heavy that even could it be carried into the interior, it must greatly retard his progress. Happily he found a man at Zanzibar who could reduce its weight so that it could be carried along by his attendants as he had intended. Thus completed, he named it *Lady Alice*. Having collected a force of a little more than three hundred men, and obtained several powerful dogs, he commenced his march into the interior."

After reaching Unyambe, instead of going directly west, they turned toward the north, and on the last day of the year 1874 reached the western frontier of Ugogo.

At the end of two days they came to Usandawa, a district abounding in elephants. Turning to the north-west, they entered the eastern border of Ukimbu, sometimes called Uyonzi. Stanley had hired guides in Ugogo, who had agreed to conduct him to Iramba ; but at this point they left him, leaving him to pursue the rest of the journey without a guide. "To add to his perplexity, they stood upon the edge of a vast wilderness, concerning which none of them knew anything. What should he do? Should he attempt to proceed, or should he go back and obtain fresh guides? These were questions of no little importance to the daring adventurer. On the previous day, before the guides had left him, one of them had informed him that three days' march would bring him to Urimi.

"But on the following morning, the path

which they were following became so greatly
mixed up with those pursued by the elephants
and rhinoceros, that Stanley was at a loss as to
which one he should take. Ordering the caravan
to halt, he sent back some of the men to look for
the lost path, but they soon returned having been
unable to find it. A sad fact now presented itself
to our hero—they were lost in the wilderness !
But still something must be done ; it would not
do to remain there, and it was contrary to Stanley's nature to lie down and die without making
a single effort to extricate himself from the trouble
which beset him. He resolved to push on, following the direction pointed out by his compass. He
therefore gave orders for the caravan to proceed,
while he went before it with the compass.

"But instead of getting out of the difficulty,
they soon found that they were in it deeper than
before. The path which they had adopted led,
after a few hours' march, into a dense jungle of
acacias and euphorbias, which seemed to forbid
further progress. The only way by which they

could proceed was by cutting the network of vines which blocked their path and crawling through the entrance thus made. This was slow work, but still the little party worked on, hoping in a short time to reach again the open country, where they could see just before them the village of Urimi."

For three days they thus toiled, and at nightfall again encamped in the wilderness. The lack of food began to tell fearfully upon Stanley's men, so that notwithstanding all their efforts they were able to proceed but fourteen miles that day. Around them was a continuous jungle, in which not a drop of water was obtainable. The men could not long hold out against such fearful odds. By-and-by they began to sink under their loads, their pace slackened, and many of the carriers fell some distance behind the main body. Those were indeed terrible days, notwithstanding the exertions of Stanley to make them as pleasant as possible. In spite of all his efforts many of the men straggled far behind, and as the path made by those in advance was very indistinct, they wandered from it and were lost. What their fate was we do not know, but most probably their bones lie to-day bleaching in the depths of that wilderness in which they fell exhausted.

On the fifth day they reached a little village which had been recently established. As its low huts greeted their vision, they rejoiced at the prospect of speedily obtaining food and drink; but when they reached the village they were doomed to disappointment. The inhabitants had scarcely enough for their own immediate wants, and therefore could spare nothing to the starving men of Stanley's caravan.

"Stanley's previous experience had taught him just how far he could urge an African carrier, and in those before him he saw plainly written a determination not to proceed until they had by some means, either fair or foul, obtained some food. He therefore ordered them to pitch their tents, resolving in some way, he scarcely knew what, to obtain some food for them.

When the camp was formed he selected twenty of his most able-bodied men, and sent them in search of provisions, with directions to proceed to the village of Suna, which lay, according to the report of the villagers, thirty miles distant, and which they said contained a large abundance of eatables.   After the men had departed, Stanley took his gun and went in search of game himself. The country had appeared before to abound in game, but now he could find nothing to shoot. He was about to return, when one of the men who had accompanied him discovered a lion's den in which they found two cubs.   These Stanley at once took, and having skinned them brought them to camp.   When he reached the camp and beheld his followers who had so faithfully followed him, and seeing their faces so pinched and wan, he was deeply moved, and but for adding to their depressed feelings, he would have wept.   It was true that he had two small cubs, but what were those among so large a number? If cooked in the ordinary way there would be scarcely a mouthful for each man. What should he do? At last he decided that if he could only make a soup of them, there would be at least a bowl full for each man. But even if he could thus provide for them, where could he obtain a kettle large enough to make a soup for so large a number of men? As he pondered the matter he chanced to think of a large sheet-iron trunk which was among his baggage, and which he knew was water-tight. Quickly turning out its contents he filled it with water—for that article was easily obtained—and placed it over the fire which one of the soldiers had made. He then proceeded to his medical stores, and having taken out five pounds of Scotch oatmeal and three packages of Revalenta Arabica, each containing one pound, he placed the whole in the trunk with the lions, and made that vessel full of broth, of which there was enough for each man to have a good bowl full. Stanley says that it was a rare scene to behold those half-starved men gather around that trunk, and place upon the fire fresh

fuel, endeavoring in every possible way to hasten
the soup to boil, while they stood around with
gourds in their hands, filled with water, which
they stood ready to empty into the trunk, should
its contents attempt to boil over, in which case they
would lose a little of the food which now possessed great value to them. Rare as the sight
was, he adds, ' It was a rarer sight still to watch
the famished wretches, as, with these same
gourds full of precious broth, they drank it down
as only starving men could. The weak and sick
got a larger portion, and another tin of oatmeal
being opened for their supper and breakfast, they
waited patiently the return of those who had
gone in quest of food.' "

But would those messengers who were sent for
food return ? Would they ever reach the place
where it was reported that provisions were to be
obtained in abundance ?

At last the messengers came in sight, and the
nearly starved men saw that they were laden

with large quantities of food. Then from that camp arose a joyful shout.

"Like ravening wolves the men fell upon the provisions, and sought to satisfy the cravings of their appetites. When they learned that there was indeed an abundance in the village from which the men had come, they forgot their weakness and begged Stanley to break camp and hasten thither that very day. This he was quite willing to do, for he longed to get out of the jungle which possessed such painful associations. He therefore cheerfully complied with the wishes of his men, and ordered everything to be got in readiness to move forward. On the following day they resumed their march, and having made a steady march for twenty miles, reached the district of Suna, in Urimi.

"Stanley was not a little surprised at beholding the phase of African life which presented itself to his gaze. Both men and women possessed great beauty and rare physical proportions, while all stood before him in a state of perfect nudity. There appeared to be no chief, but were controlled in their movements by the old men, whose longevity seemed to them to denote wisdom. With these wiseacres Stanley was forced to treat for permission to pass through the territory. This was no easy matter, since many men are more difficult to arrange terms with than one, whose word was supreme authority, would be. But after much talk the permission was granted, and food was also supplied to the hungry men."

A few marches farther on young Edward Pococke died, and was buried in the wilderness. This cast a gloom over the camp, concerning which Stanley says : "We had just finished the four hundredth mile of our march from the sea, and had reached the base of the water-shed where the trickling streams and infant waters begin to flow Nileward, when this noble young man died." They buried him at night at the foot of an acacia, Stanley reading the burial service of the Church of England over the body. At a later period,

when they had reached the head-waters of the
Nile, Stanley addressed the following tender letter
to the bereaved father :

"KAGEHYI, ON THE VICTORIA N'YANZA.
"*March 4th*, 1875.
" DEAR SIR :

"A most unpleasant, because sad, task de-
volves upon me, for I have the misfortune to
have to report to you the death of your son
Edward, of typhoid fever. His service with me
was brief, but it was long enough for me to know
the greatness of your loss, for I doubt that few
fathers can boast of such sons as yours. Both
Frank and Ted proved themselves sterling men,
noble and brave hearts, and faithful servants.
Ted had endeared himself to the members of the
expedition by his amiable nature, his cheerfulness,
and by various qualifications which brought him
into high favor with the native soldiers of this
force. Before daybreak we were accustomed to
hear the cheery notes of his bugle, which woke

us to a fresh day's labor; at night, around the camp-fires, we were charmed with his sweet, simple songs, of which he had an inexhaustible *repertoire*. When tired also with marching, it was his task to announce to the tired people the arrival of the vanguard at camp, so that he had become quite a treasure to us all; and, I must say, I have never known men who could bear what your sons have borne on this expedition so patiently and uncomplainingly. I never heard one grumble either from Frank or Ted; have never heard them utter an illiberal remark, or express any wish that the expedition had never set foot in Africa, as many men would have done in their situation, so that you may well imagine, that if the loss of one of your sons causes grief to your paternal heart, it has been no less a grief to us, as we were all, as it were, one family, surrounded as we are by so much that is dark and forbidding.

"On arriving at Suna, in Urimi, Ted came to me, after a very long march, complaining of pain in his limbs and loins. I did not think it was serious at all, nor anything uncommon after walking twenty miles, but told him to go and lie down, that he would be better on the morrow, as it was very likely fatigue. The next morning I visited him, and he again complained of pains in the knees and back, at which I ascribed it to rheumatism, and treated him accordingly. The third day he complained of pain in the chest, difficulty of breathing and sleeplessness, from which I perceived he was suffering from some other malady than rheumatism, but what it could be I could not divine. He was a little feverish, so I gave him a mustard plaster and some aperient medicine. Toward night he began to wander in his head, and on examining his tongue I found it was almost black and coated with dark-gray fur. At these symptoms I thought he had a severe attack of remittent fever, from which I suffered at Ujiji, in 1871, and therefore I watched for an opportunity to administer quinine—that is, when the fever should abate a little. But on the fourth

day, the patient still wandering in his mind, I
suggested to Frank that he should sponge him with
cold water and change his clothing, during which
operation I noticed that the chest of the patient
was covered with spots like pimples or small-pox
pustules, which perplexed me greatly. He could
not have caught the small-pox, and what the disease was I could not imagine ; but, turning to my
medical books, I saw that your son was suffering
from typhoid, the description of which was too
clear to be longer mistaken, and both Frank and
I devoted our attention to him. He was nourished with arrow-root and brandy, and everything
that was in our power to do was done ; but it was
very evident that the case was serious, though I
hoped that his constitution would brave it out.

   " On the fifth day we were compelled to resume
our journey, after a rest of four days. Ted was
put in a hammock and carried on the shoulders of
four men. At ten o'clock on the 17th of January,
we halted at Chiwyn, and the minute that he was

laid down in the camp he breathed his last. Our companion was dead.

"We buried him that night under a tree, on which his brother Frank had cut a deep cross, and read the beautiful service of the Church of England over him as we laid the poor, worn-out body in its final resting-place.

"Peace to his ashes. Poor Ted deserved a better fate than dying in Africa, but it was impossible that he could have died easier. I wish that my end may be as peaceful and painless as his. He was spared the stormy scenes we went through afterwards in our war with the Waturn; and who knows how much he has been saved from? But I know that he would have rejoiced to be with us at this hour of our triumph, gazing on the laughing waters of the vast fountain of old Nile. None of us would have been more elated at the prospect before us than he, for he was a true sailor, and loved the sight of water. Yet again I say peace be to his ashes; be consoled, for Frank still lives, and, from present appear-

ances, is likely to come home to you with honor
and glory, such as he and you may well be
proud of.

" Believe me, dear sir, with true sincerity, your
well-wisher,

"HENRY M. STANLEY."

As he continued in a north-westerly direction,
Stanley became more and more convinced that
the little stream which he saw, flowed into the
Nile, and he pushed on, confident that ere long
he would stand upon the shores of the Victoria
N'yanza, which was reached at last. Stanley and
his followers had endured much in order to reach
it, but that was now a thing of the past, and the
painful recollections of the march were forgotten
in the joy which they felt as they stood upon the
margin of the lake and viewed the broad expanse
of water before them. As for Stanley, he felt as
though he had won a great victory.

Never had the boat of a white man floated upon
the calm and placid water of the lake. All that

had been said concerning it was mere conjecture. Even Baker, whose description of the Albert Lake furnished a valuable addition to our geographical knowledge, could only say it is reported by the natives thus and so, while by actual observation he knew nothing.

Stanley longed to launch the *Lady Alice*, that he might solve the problem which had so long defied solution.

It was on the 28th of February, 1875, that they had reached the borders of the lake, and at the end of eight days they were ready to explore the lake and the adjoining region. Having launched the *Lady Alice*, he selected ten of the best oarsmen belonging to his party, and these, with himself and steersman, constituted the boat's crew, and with these he set out, determined to overcome whatever obstacles might lie in his path.

Sailing along the irregular coast on the eastern side of the gulf, they passed a section of the country possessing a greatly diversified appearance. Along their route they saw many villages, whose inhabitants fled at his approach, startled at the sight of a white man.

Pursuing their journey they at length came in sight of the high promontory of Majita, which rises nearly three thousand feet above the level of the lake, and around which is a low, brown plain, which, viewed from a distance, has the appearance of a broad sheet of water. It was doubtless this that Speke saw, which led him to suppose that the promontory was an island.

The next point of importance reached by the travelers was the coast of the Uriri district, whose fertile lands were dotted by fine herds of cattle. Continuing their journey in a northerly direction, he says: " We passed between the island Ugingo and the gigantic mountains of Ugegeya, at whose base the *Lady Alice* seems to crawl like a mite in a huge cheese, while we on board admire the stupendous height and wonder at the deathly silence which prevails in this solitude, where the boisterous winds are hushed and the turbulent waves are as tranquil as a summer

dream. The natives as they pass regard this
spot with superstition, as well they might, for
the silent majesty of these dumb, tall mounts
awe the very storms to peace. Let the tempests
bluster as they may on the spacious main beyond
the cape, in this nook, sheltered by tall Ugingo
isle and lofty Goshi in the mainland, they inspire
no fear. It is this refuge which Goshi promises
the distressed canoemen that causes them to sing
praises to Goshi, and to cheer one another, when
wearied and benighted, that Goshi is near to protect them."

Still sailing among the clustered islands, they
came at length to two islets which stood apart
from the rest, where they formed their camp for
the night. "There," says Stanley, "under the
overspreading branches of a mangrove tree, we
dream of unquiet waters, and angry surfs, and
threatening rocks, to find ourselves next morning
tied to an island, which from its peculiarity, I
called Bridge Island. While seeking a road to
ascend the island to take bearings, I discovered a

natural bridge of basalt, about twenty feet in
length and twelve in breadth, under which one
might repose comfortably, and from one side see
the waves lashed to fury and spend their strength
on the stubborn rocks which form the foundation
of the arch, while from the other we could see the
boat, secure under the lee of the island, resting
on a serene and placid surface and shaded by
mangrove branches from the hot sun of the equator. Its neighborhood is remarkable only for a
small cave, the haunt of fishermen.

After having carefully surveyed the mainland
near the islands, Stanley again set sail, and at
noon found, by observation, that he was directly
under the equator. Seeing before him an opening in the lake, which appeared at a distance like
the mouth of a river, he sailed into it, and found
that it was a bay. Upon the margin of this bay
was situated a village, which he approached and
endeavored to make peace with the inhabitants.
But the latter only " stared at them from under
pent-houses of hair, and hastily stole away to tell

their families of the strange apparition they had seen."

Leaving the bay, they continued their voyage of exploration, examining the streams which led to the Victoria Lake. But on the following day, having at last fairly entered the lake, Stanley began his explorations of it, and "surveyed its southern, eastern and northeastern shores. He made thorough work of it, entering every little indenture ; and examined every nook which he saw. The knowledge which he thus obtained was very valuable, for all the knowledge which men possessed concerning the lake was based upon a map made by Speke, and he had depended upon such information as the natives had imparted for his knowledge. Stanley corrected the map of Speke, and established the situation of the lake in a position different from that claimed by his illustrious predecessor. While upon the spot he took such notes as would enable him to make out a correct map of the lake and its surroundings, so that it could be easily found.

During his examination of the Victoria, he took thirty-seven observation, and found the extreme end of the lake to be 34° 35' east longitude, and 33' 43" north latitude.

"The travelers soon came to the point where the waters of the lake pass over the Ripon Falls and enter the Nile, which many miles farther on fertilizes the land of Egypt. Beyond this they came to the island of Krina. Here Stanley suc- ceeded in obtaining guides, who agreed to con- duct him to King Mtesa, who ruled over the whole adjoining region. Having sent messengers in advance to inform the king of their coming, Stanley continued to coast along the shore, past the land of the Uganda. The natives treated them with kindness, so far as words were con- cerned, but did not furnish them with provisions. While thus pursuing his journey, Stanley noticed a curious fact. He discovered an inlet where there appeared to be a tide which rose and fell at stated intervals. He inquired of the natives if this was an ordinary event, and they replied that it was, and afterwards told him that the same was true of all the inlets which indented the coast. When they arrived at Beya, they were met by a large number of canoes which had been sent out by the king to conduct them to him.

"Escorted by the envoys of the king, Stanley landed upon the 4th of April, while the natives waved their flags, discharged their muskets, and shouted and yelled in the ecstasy of delight at his arrival. He was promptly conducted to quarters which had been prepared for him, where he had hardly established himself, than there appeared several of the natives bearing large quantities of bananas, sweet potatoes, plantains, chickens, milk, rice, butter, together with sixteen goats, ten oxen, etc., etc.

"In the afternoon following his arrival, the king sent word to him that he was ready to receive the stranger. Leaving the quarters to which he had been assigned, Stanley entered a street eighty feet wide and half-a-mile in length. Upon either side of this street stood large num-

bers of the inhabitants, many of whom were the
personal guard, officers, attendants, and retinue
of the king. Glancing to the opposite end of the
avenue upon which he had entered, he could see
the residence of Mtesa, while in the doorway
sat the king himself. As our hero advanced the
natives kept up a horrible noise, discharging muskets and beating sixteen drums. When the
house was reached, the king arose and stretched
out· his hand without uttering a word. For
several minutes they regarded each other in
silence, and then the king resumed his seat and
bade Stanley be seated also. He did so ; and one
hundred of the king's chief captains did the same.
The silence which followed gave Stanley a chance
to glance at the king's person and to see what
manner of man he was. He describes him as
being tall and slim, yet possessing broad and
powerful shoulders. His eyes were large, and his
nose and mouth were far different from those of
the African race in general, while his face possessed an appearance both intelligent and amiable.

He was dressed after the manner of the Arabs. In his conversation he was courteous and affable, greatly superior, says Stanley, to the sultan of Zanzibar, and left an impression on your mind that he was a colored gentleman, whose manners had been refined and polished by his association with civilized, cultivated men, so that you would forget, for the time being, that he was what he was—a native of Central Africa, and had seen but three white men in the course of his whole life."

Stanley had already been away from his camp some time, and he began to deem it important to return. During the time he had remained in the village of Mtesa, he was kindly entertained, and the best of everything that the kingdom contained was at his disposal. But he had other work to perform, and he felt as though he must be "up and doing."

Under the escort of two canoes, belonging to Mtesa, he left the shore and sailed out again into the lake. After innumerable perils from savages, tempest, and threatened starvation, at about

three o'clock one morning "they entered Speke's
Gulf, from which they had sailed nearly two
months previous. The wind soon died away and
they were becalmed in the middle of the lake.
The experience of the past had taught them but
too well the meaning of this sudden calm. It
was the precursor of a coming storm. Soon the
fearful scenes, through which they had passed
twice before, were re-enacted, and amid the fury
of the storm and waves, the boat became unmanageable, and was hurried along at the mercy of
the wind and water. But they passed through
the storm in safety, which in the morning again
died away. Notwithstanding they were almost
under the equator, the morning dawned gray,
cheerless and raw. In order to learn his exact
situation, Stanley took an observation, and found
that they were only about twenty miles from his
camp, which lay in a south-easterly direction.
This information seemed to impart new life to
his comrades, and they at once made every effort
to reach that point. They ran the sails up, and

as if good fortune had indeed come to them at last, the wind, which had been unfavorable, shifted, and filled the sail, and they went bounding over the water, straight for the camp, where many hearts were anxious concerning them.

"Those in camp saw the boat when it seemed to be only a speck on the horizon, but as it drew nearer and they saw that it was indeed the *Lady Alice*, they hurried to the water's edge, where they shouted and danced with joy. Nearer and nearer came the boat, and then the shouts gave place to volleys of musketry and the waving of flags, while it might truly be said that 'the land seemed alive with leaping forms of glad-hearted men.'

"At last the boat touched the pebbly shore, and then fifty men rushed into the water and lifting Stanley from the boat, bore him on their shoulders to the camp, where in their joy they danced around him like persons bereft of their senses. They had been told by some of the natives that their leader was dead, and his long absence seemed to confirm the report. In view of these facts they saw no course left them to pursue but to turn back. But while they were considering how they might best do this, Stanley returned."

The next few days were devoted to the rest and repose which the weary explorers so much needed. How sweet and delightful this was to them can be best learned from his own words :

"Sweet is the Sabbath-day to the toil-worn laborer, happy is the long sea-tossed mariner on his arrival in port, and sweet were the days of calm rest we enjoyed after our troubleous exploration of the N'yanza. The brusque storms, the continued rains, the cheerless gray clouds, the wild waves, the loneliness of the islands, the inhospitality of the natives that were like mere phases of a dream, were now but the reminiscences of the memory, so little did we heed what was past while enjoying the luxury of a rest from our toils. Still it added to our pleasure to be able to conjure up in the mind the varied incidents of the long lake journey ; they served to enliven and employ the mind while the body enjoyed repose, like condiments quickening digestion. It was a pleasure to be able to map at will, in the mind, so many countries newly-discovered, such a noble extent of fresh water explored for the first time. As the memory flew over the lengthy track of exploration, how fondly it dwelt on the many picturesque bays, margined by water-lilies and lotus plants, or by the green walls of the slender, reed-like papyrus, inclosing an area of water, whose face was as calm as a mirror, because lofty mountain ridges almost surround it. With what kindly recognition it roved over the little green island in whose snug haven our boat had lain securely at anchor, when the rude tempest without churned the face of the N'yanza into a foaming sheet."

In reviewing the result of the journey, Stanley found that during his journey of two hundred and twenty miles, he had lost six men by drowning, five guns, and one case of ammunition. In addition to these, ten canoes had been wrecked,

and three out of four of his donkeys had died.
Having passed over a large portion of the distance
two and in some cases three times, he had really
traveled over seven hundred miles during the
fifty-two days which had passed since they had
left the margin of Speke's Gulf.

Having fairly rested themselves, Stanley
resolved to visit Mtesa and solicit aid in reaching
the Albert lake. Baker had previously visited the
lake, but his explorations had been very imperfect, for reasons which have been previously
stated. Concerning the region which lay between
the Victoria and Albert lakes very little was
known, and concerning which many strange tales
were told. The distance across this territory in a
straight line was about two hundred miles; but
of its exact size nothing was definitely known.
During the previous year Colonel Mason had
attempted to explore it, and had made a map of
the whole region, but the latter proved to be very
incorrect, so that Stanley had to lay it aside as
useless.

Stanley's computation of the size of Victoria
N'yanza (the native name is Lake Ukerewé)
showed it to contain twenty-one thousand five
hundred square miles, and that it lay at a point
nine thousand one hundred and sixty-eight feet
above the level of the sea. Directly west of this
lake is a second, whose name Stanley was told was
Mwutan Nzigi, concerning which his informants
could tell him but little save that its shores
abounded in cannibals. This lake he afterwards
proved to be none other than the Albert N'yanza.

When Stanley approached the capital of
Mtesa, he was disappointed to learn that that person was at war with the Wavuma, who had refused to pay their accustomed annual tribute. In
this war Mtesa had an army which numbered
about a quarter of a million soldiers. During the
many weeks of his absence Stanley assisted a
young educated Arab to translate a part of the
Bible, so that the king could have a portion of the
Scriptures to read when he returned. Stanley
states that he saw several naval engagements

between the two warlike forces. In one of these
he describes "the Wavuma dashing upon the
Waganda fleet (nearly eight hundred canoes engaged in action) with a hate approaching the sublime. The island is situated midway in the channel separating Uvuma from Uganda. Of course
a great many unfortunates were lost in this war,
as in other wars. I finally stopped it, that I
might prosecute my researches on Lake Albert,
by a stratagem which brought peace to Uvuma,
honor and glory to the Waganda, and aid to
myself."

The war over, Stanley had an opportunity to
consult with Mtesa. He expresses himself as
being greatly pleased with the king and his
household, which pleasure was strengthened each
day of his visit. The fact which pleased him the
most was the gentleness and the politeness which
he saw displayed. He thus describes the household of the king :

"If beautiful women of sable complexion are
to be found in Africa, it must, I thought, be in

the household of such a powerful despot as Mtesa, who has the pick of the flower of so many lands. Accordingly, I looked sharply amongst the concubines that I might become acquainted with the style of pure African beauty. Nor was I quite disappointed, though I had imagined that his wives would have all been of superior personal charms. But Mtesa apparently differs widely from Europeans in his tastes. There were not more than twenty out of all the five hundred that were worthy of a glance of admiration from a white man with any eye for style and beauty, and certainly not more than three deserving of many glances. These three, the most comely among the twenty beauties of Mtesa's court, were of the Wahuma race, no doubt from Ankori. They had the complexion of quadroons, were straight-nosed and thin-lipped, with large, lustrous eyes. In the other graces of a beautiful form they excelled, and Hafiz might have said with poetic rapture that they were 'straight as palm trees and beautiful as moons.' The only drawback was their hair—the short, crisp hair of the negro race—but in all other points they might be exhibited as the perfection of beauty which Central Africa can produce. Mtesa, however, does not believe them to be superior or even equal to his well fleshed, unctuous-bodied, flat-nosed wives ; indeed, when I pointed them out to him one day at a private audience, he even regarded them with a sneer."

It was now October, and Stanley began to turn his attention to the work before him. With a large force at his command, Stanley bade farewell to Mtesa, and amid the sound of drums and horns, and the waving of both English and American flags, the expedition started for the shores of the Albert N'yanza.

Taking a north-westerly direction they soon passed through Uganda, and reached the borders of Unyoro, where they halted and made prepara· tions for the fighting which was certain to follow an attempt to proceed. Stanley describes the country of Unyoro as extending along the whole shore of the Albert Lake. That which lies upon the southern shore is called Ruanda; its western *shore bears the name of Ukonju, and is inhabited by cannibals; and its extreme north-western shore was called Ulegga.

Entering the kagera, the "main feeder" of the Victoria lake, Stanley discovered the lake to which Speke had given the name of Windermere. This he explored, and passing still farther up the stream, he came to a second lake, which was some nine miles in length and six in width. Beyond this he found a third, smaller than either of the others, being only a mile long. Having ascended an eminence near by, he found that the lakes and the river formed parts of one great lake, a portion of whose surface was covered with a mass of vegetation similar to that which obstructed Baker's path when he endeavored to ascend the Nile. This partially concealed lake he estimated to be about eighty miles long and fourteen wide. An examination of the region revealed

the fact that there were seventeen small lakes,
which were "parts of one stupendous whole."

As a result of this journey of exploration, •
Stanley declares that he was thus able to discover
the true source of the Nile. Continuing his
journey southward, he reached Ujiji. While
upon the borders of the Victoria Lake, Stanley
wrote the following letter to a friend, which
furnishes a clear view of camp-life in the African interior :

" Kagehyi is a straggling village of cane huts,
twenty or thirty in number, which are built
somewhat in the form of a circle, hedged around
by a fence of thorns twisted between upright
stakes. Sketch such a village in your imagination, and let the center of it be dotted here and
there with the forms of kidlings who prank it
with the vivacity of kidlings under a hot, glowing
sun. Let a couple of warriors and a few round-
bellied children be seen among them, and near a
tall hut, which is a chief's, plant a taller tree.
under whose shade sit a few elders in council

with their chief; so much for the village. Now outside the village, yet touching the fence, begin to draw the form of a square camp, about fifty yards square, each side flanked with low, square huts, under the eaves of which plant as many figures of men as you please, for we have many, and you have the camp of the exploring expedition, commanded by your friend and humble servant. From the center of the camp you may see Lake Victoria, or that portion of it I have called Speke Gulf, and twenty five miles distant you may see table topped Magita, the large island of Ukerewé, and. toward the north-west a clear horizon, with nothing between water and sky to mar its level. The surface of the lake, which approaches to within a few yards of the camp, is much ruffled just at present with a north-west breeze, and though the sun is glowing hot, under the shade it is agreeable enough, so that nobody perspires or is troubled with the heat. You must understand there is a vast difference between New York and Central Africa heat. Yours is a

sweltering heat, begetting langour and thirst—
ours is a dry heat, permitting activity and action
without thirst or perspiration. If we exposed
ourselves to the sun, we should feel quite as
though we were being baked. Come with me to
my lodgings, now. I lodge in a hut little inferior
in size to the chief's. In it is stored the luggage
of the expedition, which fills one half. It is
about six tons in weight, and consists of cloth,
beads, wire, shells, ammunition, powder, barrels,
portmanteaus, iron trunks, photographic appara-
tus, scientific instruments, pontoons, sections of
boat, etc., etc. The other half of the hut is my
sleeping, dining and hall-room. It is dark as
pitch within, for light cannot penetrate the mud
with which the wood-work is liberally daubed.
The floor is of dried mud, thickly covered with
dust, which breeds fleas and other vermin to be
a plague to me and my poor dogs.

"I have four youthful Mercuries, of ebon color,
attending me, who, on the march, carry my personal weapons of defense. I do not need so many

persons to wait on me, but such is their pleasure. They find their reward in the liberal leavings of the table. If I have a goat killed for European men, half of it suffices for two days for us. When it becomes slightly tainted, my Mercuries will beg for it, and devour it at a single sitting. Just outside of the door of my hut are about two dozen of my men sitting squatted in a circle and stringing beads. A necklace of beads is each man's daily sum wherewith to buy food. I have now a little over one hundred and sixty men. Imagine one hundred and sixty necklaces given each day for the last three months—in the aggregate the sum amounts to fourteen thousand necklaces ; in a year to fifty-eight thousand four hundred. A necklace of ordinary beads is cheap enough in the States, but the expense of carriage makes a necklace here equal to about twenty-five cents in value. For a necklace I can buy a chicken, or a peck of sweet potatoes, or half-a-peck of grain.

"I left the coast with about forty thousand

yards of cloth, which, in the United States, would
be worth about twelve and a-half cents a yard,
or altogether about five thousand dollars; the
expense of portage as far as this lake, makes
each yard worth about fifty cents. Two yards of
cloth will purchase a goat or sheep; thirty will
purchase an ox; fifteen are enough to purchase
rations for the entire caravan. These are a few
of the particulars of our domestic affairs. The
expedition is divided into eight squads of twenty
men each, with an experienced man over each
squad. They are all armed with Snider percus
sion lock muskets. A dozen or so of the most
faithful have a brace of revolvers in addition to
their other arms."

As Stanley descended the slopes leading to
Ujiji, and saw the huts of the village rising just
before him, he remembered with pleasure the first
time he had visited the place. "He seemed to live
over again those hours and days during the few
minutes which elapsed from his first seeing it and
reaching the village. He remembered how glad

the sight of Ujiji had been to him when searching for Livingstone. It was then the end of his
journey. Livingstone was there, and *he* had
found him. But now Livingstone 'was not, for
God took him,' and Stanley had left the comforts
of home to complete the work which the explorer
had been unable to do, and it must be many
weary months before it would be completed."

Glancing to the right, he saw the beautiful
Tanganika as it lay half-hidden among the hills,
and could see the cattle as they came down to the
water's edge to drink. At last the village was
reached, and Stanley and his weary companions
gave themselves up to the enjoyment of that rest
which they needed. Making his home in the
village, he proposed, if possible, to lift the curtain
of mystery which hung around Tanganika.

There was certainly a deal of mystery connected
with the lake, and Stanley resolved to unravel it,
and set out on the 11th of June upon his tour of
exploration. As he proceeded, Stanley found
additional proofs of the steady rise of the lake,

and the question very naturally arose in his mind, "If Tanganika has an outlet, why does it continue to rise? why do not its waters pass off by means of this outlet?" And this continual rise seemed to shake his idea of there being an outlet to the lake. After a time, they came to the Lukuga river, where the natives gave conflicting accounts concerning the river, as to whether it sustained the position of an outlet or that of an inlet to the lake. One of the natives most earnestly declared that its waters flowed both ways. The spot where two years before Cameron had pitched his tent, was now covered with water. As Cameron reached what he believed to be the outlet of Tanganika, he says that the entrance of the stream was something more than a mile wide, but was closed up by a grass sandbank, with the exception of a channel three or four hundred yards wide. Across this there is a rill where the surf breaks heavily, although there is more than a fathom of water at its most shallow part.

"Carefully examining the river, Stanley found

that it was an affluent instead of an outlet of the lake. If such was indeed the case, why had Cameron declared that it flowed from, instead of into the lake? Upon what had he based his conclusions? And then one of the inhabitants had stated that at different times the stream flowed in different directions—why was this? There seemed to be strange contradiction here, and well might the reader inquire : 'Who was right?' We reply, 'Stanley.' He declares that no such outlet exists, and that the Tanganika is a great inland sea with waters flowing into it, but none flowing out. He did find, however, a small stream flowing westward from the lake, but it was nothing but a mere brook and could not be termed an outlet of a lake whose length was nearly twice that of Lake Ontario. Stanley gives it as his opinion, that at some time in the past the bed of the river had been raised to a higher level, and that the land was subsequently sunk by some convulsive throe of nature, in which the Lukuga had been taken with it, and forming a dam at its

mouth, which explains the cause of the steady
rise of the river.

"When Stanley returned to Ujiji, he found
that the small-pox had broken out in his camp,
and that the Arabs were filled with dismay on
account of it. This was an unlooked-for event,
as he thought that he had taken all necessary precautions before starting to guard against this terrible disease, since he had vaccinated, as he supposed, every member of his party. He had been
able to pass from the sea to the Victoria Lake
without losing a single man by it, but now,
having reached Ujiji, it entered his camp, and in
a few days bore away eight victims. The appearance of this fearful disease created a panic among
the men, who began to desert in such large numbers that Stanley saw that he soon would be left
alone.

"Among the very last persons that Stanley
expected would desert him, was Kalulu, the negro
boy whom he had purchased at Unyanyembe
when searching for Livingstone. He had become

strongly attached to him, and when he returned, after accomplishing the object of his mission, he took Kalulu home with him, and afterwards had placed him at school in England for eighteen months. And now he had forsaken him. Certainly Stanley might think that if he could not be trusted, there was none among his men who could be. Meanwhile desertions continued, and he sent Pococke (brother of the one who died), and a faithful chief, together with a squad of men, to hunt up the deserters and bring them back to camp. Returning to Ujiji, the scouts found six of the men, whom they secured after a short fight, and returned to Stanley. Soon after, Kalulu was found on a neighboring island and brought in.

"Stanley now determined to push on to the Lualaba, and after exploring the country through which he must pass in order to reach it, to follow its course to the sea. Livingstone desired to do this, but had been denied the privilege ; Cameron also had wished to explore it, but had been refused

permission to proceed, and now Stanley, the last
of all, resolved to undertake the task, with the
determination to succeed.   Turning his back upon
the main portion of the equatorial lake region, he
set out for the Lualabe."

During Stanley's march to Manyuema, there
occurred very little of importance. Passing over
nearly the same ground which had been trodden
by Livingstone, he entered the borders of this
strange country on the 5th of October.   "Know-
ing that the missionary had once spent several
months in this district, Stanley resolved to halt
here for a few days. The natives are represented
as being a very peculiar people, and their weapons
are described as being excellent. Among other
things, Stanley's attention was directed to one
peculiar custom ; the men wore lumps of mud,
variously shaped, upon their bodies, and also daubs
of it upon their hair and beard. The women
wove their front-hair into head-dresses, which
somewhat resemble bonnets, while their back-
hair fell in beautiful ringlets over their shoulders.

Their villages had one or more wide streets running through the centre of them, which were
from one hundred to one hundred and fifty feet
wide, upon either side of which square huts were
ranged, each furnished with well-beaten, cleanly-
kept clay floors, and to which they cordially invited the travelers.

"Stanley reached a village situated on the
banks of the Luma, on the 12th of October. It
was at this point that both Livingstone and Cameron had left the river, and going directly west,
had proceeded to Nyangwé. Our hero proposed
to pursue a different route. He intended to follow
this stream until it joined the Lualaba, and then
proceed by the latter stream to the same place.
On his way down the river, he found the inhabitants very kind, and possessing many curious
traditions and customs. Reaching the Lualaba,
they passed down that river, and soon reached
Tubunda, and a few days later arrived at a point
near Nyangwé.

"This point lies about three hundred and fifty

miles from Ujiji, and it required forty days of
marching to reach it. Livingstone was the first
white man who ever succeeded in reaching the
place, and he was still remembered by many of
the inhabitants. When Stanley appeared among
them, they at once supposed that he must know
the white man who had been there previous to
the visit of Cameron, and dwelt among them,
breaking to them the Bread of Life.

" ' Did you know him ?' eagerly inquired an old
chief of Stanley.

" ' Yes, I knew him,' was the reply.

" Turning to his companions, the chief said :

" 'He knew the good white man. Ah ! we
shall hear all about him.'

" Then turning to Stanley, he asked :

" ' Was he not a very good man ?'

" ' Yes,' was Stanley's reply, ' he was good, my
friend ; far better than any white man or Arab
you will ever see again.'

" ' Ah,' said the aged chief, ' you speak true ;
he was so gentle and patient, and told us such

pleasant stories of the wonderful land of the white people. The aged white man was a good man, indeed.' "

As he stood upon the last point which Livingstone had reached, Stanley recalled to mind the earnest words which that hero had uttered when pressed to return home :

"No, no, no ; to be knighted, as you say, by the queen, welcomed by thousands of admirers, yes—but impossible ; it must not, can not, will not be !"

"This," says Stanley, "is a most remarkable region,—more remarkable than anything I have seen in Africa. Its woods, or forest, or jungles, or brush,—I do not know by what particular term to designate the crowded, tall, straight trees, rising from an impenetrable mass of brush, creepers, thorns, gums, palm, ferns of all sorts, canes and grass—are sublime, even terrible. Indeed, nature here is remarkably or savagely beautiful. From every point the view is enchanting, the outlines eternally varying, yet always beautiful, till the whole panorama seems like a changing vision. Over all, nature," he says, "has flung a robe of varying green ; the hills and ridges are blooming, the valleys and basins exhale perfume, the rocks wear garlands of creepers, the stems of the trees are clothed with moss, a thousand streamlets of cold, pure water stray, now languid, now quick, toward the north and south and west. The whole makes a pleasing, charming illustration of the bounteousness and wild beauty of tropical nature. But, alas ! all this is seen at a distance. When you come to travel through this world of beauty, the illusion vanishes. The green grass becomes as difficult to penetrate as an undergrowth, and that lovely sweep of shrubbery a mass of thorns, the gently rolling ridge an inaccessible crag, and the green mosses and vegetation in the low grounds that look so enchanting, impenetrable forest belts."

While in the vicinity of Nyangwé, Stanley chanced to meet Tippoo Tib, who had befriended Cameron while on his journey. We shall meet with this old gentleman again ere our tale is done. From him he learned that Cameron had been unable to explore the Lualaba, and thus the work which Livingstone had not been able to complete was as yet unfinished.

" Not believing, as Livingstone did, that the Lualaba was the remote southern branch of the Nile, but having the same conviction as Cameron, that it was connected with the Congo, and was the eastern part of that river, and having, what Livingstone and Cameron had not, an ample force and sufficient supplies, he determined to follow the Lualaba, and ascertain whither it led. He met with the same difficulty that Livingstone and Cameron had encountered in the unwilling-ness of the people to supply canoes. They informed him, as they had the two previous explorers, that the tribes dwelling to the north on the Lualaba were fierce and warlike cannibals, who would suffer no one to enter their territories, as the Arab traders had frequently found to their cost. That between Nyangwé and the cannibal

region the natives were treacherous, and that the
river ran through dreadful forests, through
which he would have to make his way—information which afterward proved to be true. He
nevertheless resolved to go ; but it was not easily
accomplished, as the people of Nyangwé filled his
followers with terror by the accounts they gave
of the ferocious cannibals, the dwarfs with
poisoned arrows who dwelt near the river, and
the terrible character of the country through
which they would have to pass ; which had such
a disheartening effect upon them that difficulties
arose which would have been insurmountable to
any one but a man of Stanley's indomitable per-
severence, sagacity and tact. He overcame all
obstacles ; succeeded in getting canoes, and in
engaging an Arab chief and his followers to
accompany him a certain distance ; an increase of
his force which gave confidence to his own people.

  "Those who are acquainted with the dangers
and difficulties of African exploration, and who
know how frequently the most sagacious conclu-

sions, founded upon what seemed to be reliable information, have not only been attended by failure, but with the most disastrous results, can alone fully appreciate what Stanley undertook, and the hazard which he ran in determining to follow the river in its northerly course. The river ran to the north, apparently in the direction of the sources of the Nile. He had Livingstone's conviction that it was the remote source of that river. He knew nothing of the fact that the southern part of the Mwutan Nzige (Albert N'yanza) had been explored by Gessi, and that no large river flowed into it. The theory, moreover, that he had formed of the course of the Lualaba was different from that of Cameron's conclusion, that a little above Nyangwé it turned to the west and flowed to the Atlantic coast ; whereas Stanley's conviction was, as subsequently proved to be the fact, that it flowed on to the north, beyond the equator, and then turned to the west as part of the Congo. To follow the river, however, in its northerly course, might lead him, if his theory should not be verified, into the interior of northern Africa, where he would be, with a large body of followers, without supplies, and in a state of utter destitution.

"He fully appreciated the great risk he ran. It was to him a matter of painful and anxious thought, but, after fully considering it in all its bearings, he came to the bold and fixed determination to follow up his theory; and in this he exhibited the same geographical instinct which he has referred to as such a remarkable faculty in Captain Speke, the discoverer of Lake Ukerewe."

Writing from Nyangwé, Stanley says: "I am determined to stick to the Lualaba, come fair or foul, fortune or misfortune. I have supplies for six months; beyond that Heaven knows what will become of us if we should find the Lualaba running into some unknown river, with not a single bead or cowrie with which to buy food."

"It required no little heroism on the part of Stanley to face the dangers which he knew must lay between him and that point, one thousand eight hundred miles distant, where the Congo, ten miles wide, rolls into the broad bosom of the Atlantic. Notwithstanding all the dangers which lay before them, Tippoo Tib agreed to accompany Stanley with his soldiers the distance of sixty marches, for $5,000."

Stanley rested until the 5th of November, when, having been joined by Tippoo Tib with seven hundred men, he set out upon his journey.

As the expedition left Nyangwé, it numbered eight hundred and seventy-six men. Of these, one hundred and seventy-six were regularly attached to the expedition, while the remainder belonged to Tippoo Tib. Of Stanley's men, sixty-three were armed with muskets, and the remainder with rifles, double-barreled guns, and pistols; while Tippoo Tib's men had one hundred flint-lock muskets, and the remainder were armed with spears and shields. Besides these, there were some sixty-eight axes belonging to the party, which Stanley had purchased at Nyangwé.

Besides their weapons the men carried upon
their shoulders all the provisions, large quantities
of cloth, beads, wire and ammunition, in addition
to the *Lady Alice*, which was carried in sections.

Traveling through the virgin jungle was terribly trying to all ; from three to six miles a day
was all that could be accomplished. At last, on
the 19th of March, they reached the Lualaba,
which swept grandly on to swell some stream
beyond. The point where they reached the river
was at 3° 33′ 17″ south latitude, being forty-one
geographical miles north of Nyangwé. Our hero
at once determined to proceed by the river, the
men having desired that he should do so. The
Lady Alice was then put together, and he
says : "I formed the resolution never to abandon
the Lualaba until I learned its destination."

He made an encouraging speech to his men,
telling them that they had promised at Zanzibar
to follow him for three years, wherever he wanted
to go, and that there was one year left. " I will

not," he said, "leave this river until I reach the sea, and I promise you that we shall reach it before the year is out. All I ask of you is to follow me in the name of God." Upon which fifty of the youngest stepped forward and shouted, "In the name of God, then, master, we will follow you."

The river at this point was nearly three-quarters of a mile wide, and its opposite shore appeared like a dark and gloomy forest. They had scarcely launched the boat, than the farther shore seemed to swarm with human beings, and as Stanley approached it he saw several canoes tied to the trees. He endeavored to hire the natives to take the expedition across the stream, but they stubbornly refused. He then resolved to carry his men across the stream by detachments in the *Lady Alice*. The first load contained thirty men, and having reached the shore, Stanley told the natives that if they would assist him in carrying the rest of the men across, they should be well paid for it. After a great deal of talk they agreed to do so, and soon the entire party were carried safely over the stream.

Stanley now decided to change the name of the Lualaba to that of Livingstone, and pushed on down the river. Himself and thirty-three men proceeded by water in the *Lady Alice*, while the remainder of the party, under the direction of Frank Pococke, went by land, "communication between the two parties being kept up by occasional taps given upon drums, by which either party was able to know the situation of the other. As before, the villages which they passed were deserted at their approach, the inhabitants leaving everything behind them as in terror they fled. At one point they found six canoes, which had been abandoned, some of which were injured very badly, while others with a little labor could be used by the travelers. These they repaired, and having lashed them together, they became a sort of floating hospital, in which the sick of the land party were placed. The exposure which they had undergone had greatly increased the number of the sick, so that the finding of the canoes was indeed fortunate. In the afternoon of the same day, they reached the first rapids which they had seen upon the river. In endeavoring to pass them several of the boats were upset, and four Snider rifles lost. The natives accepted this as a good opportunity to attack the party, and accordingly sent a shower of arrows and spears among the men ; they were, however, soon beaten off."

Their progress down the Livingstone was very slow, and consequently very monotonous. The natives continued hostile, and ever and anon they would dart out from some hiding-place and make an attack upon Stanley's company, while they kept up a continual tooting of horns and pounding their war-drums. At last the natives beat a hasty retreat. The force which Stanley had with him in this running fight numbered forty men ; of these, four were killed and thirteen wounded.

"The night after the retreat of the savages was

dark and stormy. One could see but a short distance before him. Upon the opposite side of the
river, farther up the stream, Stanley saw the
enemy's camp fires shine brightly, and he determined to play a trick upon them. Leaping into
the *Lady Alice*, he pushed on towards the distant
camp-fire, while Frank Pococke was stationed a
short distance below him to assist in his venture.
Carefully approaching the camp, he saw some
forty canoes moored to the shore. He soon cut
their moorings, when they were secured by
Pococke and conveyed to camp. This done, Stanley knew that the natives could not cross the river
to attack him, and he retired to rest, conscious of
having a little undisturbed sleep. On the following day he repaired to the camp of the natives,
and offered to make peace with them. This offer
was gladly accepted, they desiring only that their
canoes might be returned. After an exchange of
blood, Stanley returned fifteen canoes, retaining
twenty-three."

Tippoo Tib now informed Stanley that he should

go no farther with him, as his men were rapidly dying from exposure ; and, instead of reaching the end of their difficulties, they had but just begun them. " Really, he and his men were more of a hindrance than a help, a large number of them being sick, and Stanley saw that, rid of them, he could proceed with boats, they having enough to carry the remainder of the party. There was but one thing that was to be feared ; the effect which the withdrawal of so large a force would have upon the men. But he determined to brave it. He called the company together, and announced the chief's intention, after which he talked kindly with them, and asked if there had ever been a time when he had not been kind to them, looked after their interests, and performed all his agreements with them ; and then told them if they would only trust him, he would bring them at last to the ocean, and see that they were carried back to Zanzibar. He closed by saying : ' As a father looks after his children, so will I look after you.' The men replied with a loud shout and decided to remain with him."

Preparations were at once made for continuing the journey. The canoes were repaired, provisions gathered, and everything done to assist them to proceed speedily when once they had set out. On the 28th Stanley mustered his force, now numbering only one hundred and forty-six men, and made ready to continue his route down the river.

The record of the next few weeks was a succession of perils from cannibals and cataracts. At length they came to the sixth cataract, over which they could not pass in safety, and therefore were forced to haul their canoes around it. Says Stanley :

"It will give an idea of a short hour we lived through while hauling our canoes past one of the cataracts under the equator. By night a road had been cut, about five hundred yards in length, through a thick forest and thicker undergrowth, and what we have clipped out of the woods we have arranged on the ground, over which, at sunrise, a working party has been detailed to haul the canoes. The women, children and goods, before dawn, under an escort, have been taken to the new camp, with its impenetrable stockade. At the old camp are a dozen sharpshooters lying in wait outside in the jungle. Along the flank on the forest side are the sharpshooters which have been detailed for the defense of the working-party in the new camp. Frank and a dozen good men are sent to defend it. It is an hour that no one must be idle in, for it is absolutely necessary that the early daylight should be spent in moving from one camp to the other, before the cannibals have gathered in the woods in force, as they have been accustomed to. For we have found that the night hours are the best to work in, the cannibals having a horror of the dark, dread wood, with its weird noises and startling interruptions."

The river reached at last, they push onward, notwithstanding the savages are near and showers of arrows fall among them. At last they

come to the seventh and last of the series of cataracts, when, as usual, they are obliged to fight
in order to pass round it.   This series of cataracts
extended the distance of forty-two geographical
miles, and to pass them they were forced to drag
their boats more than thirty miles by land, and
cut a track of thirteen miles through a dense
forest.   At this point, which was beyond the
equator, in 0° 14′ 52″ north latitude, the river
gradually widened until it became a noble
stream.

"When they had reached between the 24th
and 25th degrees of north longitude, they came to
a magnificent tributary flowing into the river,
with a width of two thousand feet, which Stanley
supposed might be the Welle of Schweinfurth, or
else the Aruwima.

"As they approached the mouth of the large
affluent, which flowed into the river, they were
suddenly attacked by a force of fifty-four armed
canoes, that rushed down upon them with such
fury that four of their canoes became panic-

stricken. One of these hostile canoes was of great size, being propelled by about eighty paddles, and was guided by eight steersmen, with a planking in front holding about ten men, armed with spears, and a planking along its sides traversed by armed men.

"In a second, almost, we were surrounded, and clouds of arrows were darted upon us for ten minutes ; but after a very serious contest, which at times was somewhat doubtful, these formidable assailants were repulsed, and the explorers proceeded in safety down the river."

Stanley was now in doubt what to do— whether to go up a great tributary which they had found—the Aruwimi, which at one time Stanley thought might be the Congo. But they kept on down the main stream.

"On reaching very near the second parallel of north latitude, the river made a great curve to the west, and then flowed south-westerly with a width varying from two to ten miles, and was filled with islands, between which he was enabled to

pass with less danger. Here a new trial awaited
him. All attempts to communicate with the
natives proved fruitless, and they had now
before them the peril of starvation, having passed
three days without food.

"On the 14th of February, Stanley arrived
among the tribes of Bangala, or Mangala, negroes
who live on the right bank of the Livingstone
river, in latitude 1° 16′ 50″. Sixty-three canoes
met the hardy explorers in the stream and, without warning, attacked them with muskets and
missiles. Stanley immediately returned the fire,
allowing his boat to float with the current. The
battle lasted from noon to sunset, when, after a
floating fight of ten miles, the fierce assailants
drew off. This was the thirty-first fight of the
expedition and the last but one."

On approaching the next village they found the
natives friendly and willing to furnish them with
provisions. Stanley asked an aged chief the
name of the river. The old man replied, "Aku-
ta-ya Kongo." The great problem was, then,

solved. The Lualaba of Livingstone and the
Congo of the Portuguese proved to be the same
river. This was indeed joyful news for Stanley,
who believed that now there would be but little
difficulty in reaching the ocean, which lay eight
hundred and fifty miles distant, they now being
twelve hundred miles from Nyangwé.

Stanley was now out of the region where the
cannibals lived, and had, therefore, nothing to
fear from them. But the dangers of the journey
were not yet over. Before him the river rushed
maldly on, now rolling along in boiling rapids,
and then plunging over rocks in frightful cataracts. The whole aspect of the country had
changed, and now bore a wild and cheerless look.

"After going a few miles the river assumed
the form of two stretches of rapids and a cataract. The first of these was passed in safety ; but
the passage of the second was more difficult.
Having no fear of being attacked by the natives,
Stanley went into camp ; and while the men
rested themselves, he and Pococke explored the

shore in order to ascertain the best method of
passing the lower rapids. They decided that it
was not safe to attempt to go down in the boats,
but that the best way was for the whole party to
proceed by land, carrying their baggage with
them, while the boats were to be hauled along
the stream by ropes. When at last they reached
the calm and level water below the rapids, the
men were almost fainting for want of food.

"The large size of the canoes—one being
eightly-five and another seventy feet long, hewn
out of a solid tree—and the exhausted condition
of the men was such, that it required nearly
three days to pass this point. When navigable
water was again reached, Stanley found the men
so exhausted as to be unable to proceed, and
therefore ordered a halt, and the whole party
went into camp. After resting a few days they
pushed on down the stream, and on the 25th of
March were confronted by impassable rapids.
An attempt was again made to haul the boats
through them by ropes, but so strong was the

current that it wrenched one of the canoes from the grasp of the men leading it and dashed it against the rocks, which raised their ugly forms above the seething tide. While endeavoring to get the boats in safety past these rocks several of the men were injured, one having his shoulder dislocated, while Stanley was thrown into a chasm thirty feet deep, but succeeded in escaping with some slight bruises, having been fortunate enough to strike upon his feet as he fell. Two days were occupied in getting past this 'cauldron,' as Stanley terms it, during which they came very near losing their largest canoe. On the 28th they were again afloat in smooth water, but it was only for a short distance, for they soon came to the 'Rocky Falls.' Having passed these in safety, two men were sent ahead to examine the river and country. They soon returned, and reported that at a point about a mile beyond, there was a great cataract, and at the head of it was a sandy bay, which would afford then a good camping-place. It was at

once determined to push on and, if possible, reach
this camping place before dark.   In order to pass
along in safety, it was necessary for them to hug
the shore very closely, so as not to be drawn into
the current and carried over the falls.   Stanley
led the way, keeping close to the right bank, and
carefully feeling his way along."   He says :

"I led the way down the river, and in five
minutes was in a new camp in a charming cove,
with the cataract roaring loudly about five hundred yards below us.   A canoe came in soon after
with a gleeful crew, and a second one also arrived
safe, and I was about congratulating myself for
having done a good day's work, when the long
canoe, which Kalulu had ventured in, was seen in
mid-river, rushing with the speed of a flying
spear towards destruction.   A groan of horror
burst from us as we rushed to the rocky point
which shut the cove from view of the river.
When we had reached the point, the canoe was
half-way over the first break of the cataract, and
was then just beginning that fatal circling in the

whirlpool below. We saw them signaling to us for help ; but alas ! what could we do there, with a cataract between us? We never saw them more. A paddle was picked up about forty miles below, which we identified as belonging to the unfortunate coxswain, and that was all."

Leaving this point, and passing on down the river, they soon came to a series of rapids. These they passed in safety, Stanley conducting the boats, while Pococke led the main party, who carried the goods, overland. Thus one day after another was passed in fighting the rough and turbulent river along which they were passing. At some points the water was so rough that it was impossible to shoot the boats through them, when they had to be hauled to the land and pulled around the dangerous point. It was slow and worrying work, and the progress which they made seemed very little. But still they worked on and on, strengthened by the thought that sooner or later they would reach the ocean.

" While they were passing through scenes like

these, although the natives were very kind and furnished them with large supplies of provisions, yet all these things had to be paid for, and it was a question of no little moment which presented itself as to how long their currency would last. Although they had already gone many hundred miles, still they had several more to go, and they could not tell how long they would be in doing it. The time occupied in reaching the point now attained had been far beyond what Stanley expected it would require to reach the open sea ; and therefore he was still unable to tell how long it would be before they would reach the coast. The next rapids which they came to well-nigh capsized the *Lady Alice,* and nearly drowned Stanley. Both, however, escaped.

As he advanced he saw many signs which told him that he was approaching the shore. Many of the articles used by the natives were of English make, and such as he knew could not be obtained without communication with the coast. While this was encouraging he could not tell how many weeks must pass before the goal of his ambition would be reached, if reached at all; and hence it became necessary that he should be economical in the use of his goods and provisions, particularly meal. For lack of the latter, he prepared some very palatable dishes from vegetables, fruit and oil.

For ninety-three miles it had been almost a continual struggle with cataracts and rapids, there being only an occasional stretch of smooth water in all that distance. To pass this ninety-three miles it had required one hundred and seventeen days. The season had now advanced into July, and although some were confident that ere long they would reach the coast, several who were sick seemed to have some doubts of it. As they continued down the river they occasionally came to dangerous rapids, but they succeeded in passing them in safety. Presently, Stanley found himself very near the sea. Great was the joy of his followers when he announced the glad news to them.

" On the 30th of July they reached a point near
the Falls of Isangila. While here Stanley learned
that they were only five day's march from Embomma, and that the distance was generally
passed by the natives overland, on account of the
large number of obstructions in the river between
them and that village. Besides this, the real
object of the expedition had been accomplished,
since from that point to the sea the river was
well known, having been previously explored. In
view of these facts, Stanley resolved to leave the
river and made the rest of his journey by land.
Just as the sun sank behind the distant hills, they
drew the *Lady Alice* out of the river, and placed
it upon some rocks near the bank, where they
proposed to leave it. Having been his companion
during all that long and toilsome journey, it
seemed to Stanley like parting with a friend. But
it must be done, and after bidding it farewell they
passed on.

" It was with the greatest difficulty that they
could obtain food. Such things as they had been

accustomed to exchange for provisions now possessed but little value. As a general thing, rum was demanded in exchange for such things as were needed by the travelers. On the 3d of August they reached Nsanda. The king of this district told Stanley that he had only three days more of marching to make before reaching the ocean. Stanley then asked him to carry a letter for him to Embomma. This the king refused to do, but after being urged for nearly four hours, he at last consented to furnish guides, who would conduct three of Stanley's men to the village. Having secured this promise from him, Stanley repaired to his tent to write the letter," which was as follows :

"NSANDA, *August 4th*, 1877.

"To any gentleman who speaks English at Embomma.

" DEAR SIR : I have arrived at this place from Zanzibar with one hundred and fifteen souls, men, women and children. We are now in a state of imminent starvation. We can buy nothing from the natives, for they laugh at our kinds of cloth, beads and wire. There are no provisions in the country that may be purchased except on market-days, and starving people cannot afford to wait for these markets. I therefore have made bold to despatch three of my young men, natives of Zanzibar, with a boy named Robert Ferugi, of the English mission at Zanzibar, with this letter, craving relief from you. I do not know you, but I am told there is an Englishman at Embomma, and as you are a Christian and a gentleman, I beg of you not to disregard my request. The boy Robert will be better able to describe our condition than I can tell you in a letter. We are in a state of the greatest distress, but, if your supplies arrive in time, I may be able to reach Embomma in four days. I want three hundred cloths, each four yards long, of such quality as you trade with, which is very different from that we have; but better than all would be ten or fifteen man-loads of rice or grain, to fill their pinched bellies immediately, as, even with the cloths, it would require time to purchase food, and starving men cannot wait. The supplies must arrive within two days, or I may have a fearful time of it among the dying. Of course I hold myself responsible for any expense you may incur in this business. What is wanted is immediate relief, and I pray you to use your utmost energies to forward it at once. For myself, if you have such little luxuries as tea, coffee, sugar and biscuits by you, such as one man can easily carry, I beg you on my own behalf, that you will send a small supply, and add to the great debt of gratitute due to you upon the timely arrival of supplies for my people. Until that time, I beg you to believe me,

"Yours sincerely,

"H. M. Stanley,

"Commanding Anglo-American Expedition for Exploration of Africa.

"P. S.—You may not know my name ; I therefore add, I am the person that discovered Livingstone. "H. M. S."

When the letter was finished, Stanley gathered his men around him, and told them that he intended to send to Embomma for food, and desired to know who among them would go with the guides and carry the letter. No sooner had he asked the question, than Uledi sprang forward exclaiming, "O, master, I am ready!" Other men also volunteered, and on the next day they set out with the guides.

Passing along the banks of the Congo, they reached the village soon after sunset, and delivered the letter into the hands of a kindly disposed person. For thirty hours the messengers had not tasted food, but they were now abundantly supplied. On the following morning—it was the 6th of August—they started to return, accompanied by carriers who bore provisions for the half-starving men, women and children with Stanley.

Meanwhile, he and his weary party were pushing on as fast as their tired and wasted forms would let them. At nine o'clock in the morning they stopped to rest. While in this situation, an

Arab boy suddenly sprang from his seat upon the grass, and shouted :

"I see Uledi coming down the hill !"

Such was indeed the fact. Uledi was the first to reach the camp, and at once delivered a letter to his master. By the time Stanley had finished reading it, the carriers arrived with the provisions, and need we say that those half-starved people did them justice? After he had given to each one as much food as he desired, Stanley turned to his own tent to open the packages which had been sent expressly for him. Deeply grateful for the substantial answer to his letter, he immediately penned another, acknowledging their safe arrival. The letter ran as follows :

"DEAR SIRS : Though strangers I feel we shall be great friends, and it will be the study of my lifetime to remember my feelings of gratefulness when I first caught sight of your supplies, and my poor faithful and brave people cried out, 'Master, we are saved—food is coming !' The old and the young men, the women and the children lifted their wearied and worn-out frames and began lustily to shout an extemporaneous song in honor of the white people by the great salt sea (the Atlantic), who had listened to their prayers. I had to rush to my tent to hide the tears that would come, despite all my attempts at composure.

"Gentlemen, that the blessing of God may attend your footsteps, whithersoever you go, is the very earnest prayer of,

"Yours faithfully,

"HENRY M. STANLEY."

The remainder of the day was spent in feasting, and in a good time generally, and on the next morning they started forward in high spirits. On the third day, as they were passing down a slope, they saw men approaching bearing hammocks, and soon Stanley stood face to face with four white men. After a short conversation they declared that he must get into one of the hammocks ; and borne on the shoulders of eight men be carried into the village of Embomma—or Boma, as it is now called. He reluctantly consented, and was thus borne in triumph into the village, where he was received with great rejoicing. Remaining here one day, they took a steamer for the mouth of the river, and shortly reached Kabinda. So great was the re-action from almost starvation to plenty, that several of the caravan died. One of them was buried at this point ; four died at St. Paul, and three more while on the passage to Cape Town. It was with the greatest exertion that Stanley saved himself from falling victim to a similar fate. After remaining eight days at Kabinda, they embarked on board a Portuguese vessel for St. Paul de Loanda. It will be remembered that it is from this point that most of the caravans bound for the interior start.

"Arriving here, the governor-general kindly offered to give him passage in a gunboat to Lisbon. It was a tempting offer, but Stanley polite-

ly declined it. He had promised to see his followers landed at Zanzibar, and he meant to keep that
promise. Soon after, a passage to Cape Town
being offered him on board the British ship
Industry, he embarked with his expedition. He
was gladly welcomed at Cape Town, and at the
request of some of the leading men of the place,
he delivered a lecture there, in which he briefly
narrated the journey which he had made, particularly that part of it relating to the Congo. Passage was offered him in a British vessel bound
for Zanzibar, which he accepted, and on the 6th of
November, almost six months after they had
reached the coast, they sailed for that place. In
due time they reached their destination, where
they were received with great rejoicing."

The great journey was now over, and after
paying the men the sum agreed upon, and the
relatives of those lost what they would have
received, Stanley bade his men adieu. The mystery of the Congo, and of the source of the Nile,
had at last been revealed. It had been a great

undertaking, but it had been accomplished. Stanley's own words will best describe the condition of those daring travelers while passing down the Congo: "On all sides," he says, "death stared us in the face; cruel eyes watched us by day and by night, and a thousand bloody hands were ready to take advantage of the least opportunity. We defended ourselves like men who knew that pusillanimity would be our ruin among savages to whom money is a thing unknown. I wished, naturally, that it might have been otherwise, and looked anxiously and keenly for any sign of forbearance or peace. My anxiety throughout was so constant, and the effects of it, physically and otherwise, have been such, that I now find myself an old man at thirty-five."

CHAPTER IV.

THE FOUNDING OF THE CONGO FREE STATE.

No classic legends or mythic stories are clustered around the banks of the mighty Congo,
whose tawny torrent far exceeds in volume the
floods rolled to the sea by either the Old or the
New World "Father of Waters." Peopled by
savage tribes, the banks of this mid-American
water-way are equally barren in records of
human weal or woe, and only within the last
decade has the keel of the adventurous Anglo-
Saxon cleft its waves from source to sea, or the
strokes of his hammer and ax awakened unac-
customed echoes in the gloomy forests that clothe
its precipitious banks.

During the long centuries when the adventurous blades of northern Europe were carving out
new empires "across the Western Ocean," the

EMIN PASHA (DR. SCHNITZLER.)

great southern continent near at hand remained
a *terra incognita,* save for a narrow belt of coast
country dominated by Portuguese traders ; while
the gaps of the interior were peopled by the
guessing geographers of the day with "savage
pictures" in lieu of inhabitants, and with "elephants for want of towns." Even in our own
day so little were the possibilities of the Congo
country suspected, that Livingstone is reported to
have said that "he would not be made into black
man's pot" for the sake of it. The slave-catcher
and the ivory-trader were the virtual monarchs
of this vast domain.

True, the intensest rivalry prevailed among the
factors of the English, Dutch, and Portuguese
coast settlements for a lion's share of the profitable commerce in such native commodities as
palm-oil, rubber, copal, ivory, and palm nuts.
But these confined themselves to their factories,
seldom ascending higher than Yellala Falls, the
lowest of the Livingstone series of cataracts.
Communication was had with the tribes of the

interior (and is still) by means of the middleman,
or "lingster," a half-Europeanized native or
Arab, for whom the climate had no terrors. And
although the Portuguese have been on the ground
for nearly four centuries, they have added but
little to our stock of knowledge concerning the
great river whose yellow flood ceaselessly laves
the jetties of their trading-posts. The armed
ships of various other nations, too, occasionally
anchored inside Banana Point, but usually
departed as unenlightened as they came.

Captain Tuckey, in 1816, was dispatched by the
British Government on an exploring expedition
to the Congo region. The prospects for a rich
harvest of geographical and ethnological data
were never more promising; yet never was the
ending, even of an Arctic errand, more disastrous
or discouraging. Within less than three months
of reaching the scene of their labors eighteen of
the officers and scientists died of African fever,
including Captain Tuckey. The results of this
attempt were *nil*, with the additional unfortunate

effect of deterring all further scientific missions for a full half century. Until Stanley's heroic feats Europeans had never ascended the Congo further than the Livingstone Falls.

In 1866 Dr. David Livingstone began the journey, destined to be his last, whose object was the survey of the water-shed between Lake Nyassa and Lake Tanganika. The following year he discovered a large river flowing westward, and, in common with many other savants of his day, believed he had at last hit upon the most southerly head of the Nile. He followed the course of the new river, which was named Chambezi, until it entered Lake Bangweolo, under the native name Luapula, and flowed almost due north. After expanding into another lake, named Mweru, he last saw it as the Lualaba, now of mighty proportions, in the Manyema country, about fifteen hundred miles from its source. Livingstone died at Illala in 1873, ignorant of the fact that unwittingly he had come very near to making the greatest discovery of his life.   But his mantle fell on worthy shoulders.

In the year 1876 an expedition was sent to Africa under the combined patronage of *The New York Herald* and the London *Daily Telegraph*, commanded by Henry M. Stanley, to gather up the dropped threads of Livingstone's unfinished explorations.   Arriving at the native town of Nyangwé, in Manyema, Stanley resolved to solve all doubts by following the mysterious stream to its mouth.   Two hundred and eighty-one days later the battered canoes of these African Argonauts reached the Atlantic Ocean, having navigated the river for one thousand six hundred and sixty miles, and made portages around Stanley and Livingstone Falls of one hundred and forty miles, and proving conclusively that the Chambezi, the Luapula, or the Lualaba, was none other than the Congo.   The story of the descent of this unknown river, through frequently hostile tribes, is told in the preceding chapter.

The Congo is the Livingstone of modern explorers and the Zaire of the Portuguese, to which latter name they most devotedly cling, though the word "Zaire" means simply, in the native tongue, "the great river." In the *Lusiad*, Camoens speaks of

"That lucid river, the long-winding Zaire."

The mouth of this noble stream was discovered by Diego Cam, a courtier and naval commander of Joao Second, of Portugal, in 1484–85, when coasting along Africa for the purpose of discovering a water-way to the East Indies. In accordance with the custom of the time the discoverer erected a pillar on the southerly side of its entrance, now called Shark's Point, and for some years thereafter the stream was known as "the Pillar River, flowing through the kingdom of Congo." But about the beginning of the seventeenth century, English map-makers began to call the stream the Congo, though the Portuguese to this day write and speak of it as the Zaire.

Banana Point and Shark's Point are respectively

the northern and southern boundaries of the
mouth of the Congo, which has no delta, entering
the sea by a single channel. These "points" are
both arc-shaped sandy spits, similar to our Sandy
Hook or Cape Cod, within which is anchorage
ground for the largest ocean greyhound of our
day, and which are backed north and south by
lofty, dark green verdure-clad hills, through a
cleft in which the Congo issues like "a broad
stream of daylight, parting the mass of woods
into two sections," and bearing down upon the
spectator "a majestic stretch of river, twenty
miles long, of immense volume and force." The
distance from Shark's Point to Banana Point is
seven and a-half miles, while across what may be
called the real embouchure of the river, bounded
by Boulambemba Point and Viva Creek, is three
and a-half miles.

The Congo factories, flying the flags of various Powers, occupy nearly the whole of the sandy
peninsula known as Banana Point, and on the
harbor side are constructed the jetties. So low is

this sand-spit that "the dark hulls of the shipping in the bay (viewed from the ocean,) seem to be riding on a higher plane than the ground covered by the buildings." Behind each of the Points are shallow creeks bearing the same names.

It may be mentioned here that the Congo is, except at its mouth, virtually tide-less. At Banana there is a rise of six feet ; this is diminished at Ponta da Lenha, twenty-eight miles up stream, to twenty-one inches ; and at Boma, twenty miles further, to two or three inches. The ebb runs with great velocity near the mouth and continues twice as long as the flood. But the sea is not admitted into the estuary of the Congo. The phenomena of the flood tide is "simply the effect of the pressure of the sea upon the current of the river, which, checked in its velocity, rises to the heights above mentioned." Furthermore, as with the Amazon, its great American prototype, the ocean is stained a muddy green or a pale brown by the fierce discharge of its impetuous

torrent to the distance of a full day's steaming
from its mouth.

But the height of the river varies constantly
during the year on account of rains in the interior. The first or lesser rise happens in the latter
part of March, and increases until the end of
May ; then there is a decline until August. The
greater rise occurs between September 1st and
December 25th and from January 15th to March
10th there is again a falling river, to be succeeded
in turn by the lesser rise. These fluctuations are
as steady and never-failing as the annual overflow
of old Father Nile from a similar cause—an equatorial rainfall.

The entire length of the Congo is over three
thousand miles, broken up as follows : from
Banana to Vivi a navigable stretch of one hundred and ten miles ; thence to Isangila, innaviga-
ble, fifty-two miles ; from Isangila to Manyanga,
a fairly navigable reach of eighty-eight miles ;
thence to Leopoldville, along the upper series of
the Livingstone Falls, partly navigable, eighty-

five miles ; then comes the Upper Congo, from Leopoldville to Stanley Falls, an unobstructed stretch of 1068 miles ; from the lowest fall of this series to Nyangwé, three hundred and eighty-five miles; from Nyangwé to Mweru four hundred and forty miles, including the length of Lake Mweru, sixty-eight miles ; thence to Lake Bang-weolo two hundred and twenty miles ; and from thence to its sources the Chambezi has a length of three hundred and sixty miles ; the total length from sea to source being 3,035 miles.

"The Dark Continent had been traversed from east to west ; its great lakes, the Victoria Nyanza and the Tanganika, had been circumnavigated ; and the Congo River had been traced from Nyangwé to the Atlantic Ocean. The members of the late exploring expedition had been taken to their homes, the living had been worthily rewarded, and the widows and orphans had not been neglected."

Such are the modest yet memorable words in which Stanley summarizes what was perhaps one of the greatest achievements of our modern conquistadores. "Bula Matari," the natives named him—"Breaker of Rocks"—and in numberless ways he deserved his sobriquet.

On reaching Europe in January, 1878, with a frame shattered by famine and fatigue and the perils and privations of the Congo downward journey, the last anticipation that entered Stanley's mind was that in less than a year he would be again threading the mazes of an African wilderness, alternately scorched by its sunshine and chilled by the cool breezes that sweep up the funnel-shaped gorge of the Congo. But even while he was in the wilds of the Dark Continent, steps had been taken looking to the formation of an association of capitalists and philanthropists, having for its object the opening up of the Congo Basin to trade and civilization. At Marseilles railway station, then, the sick and weary explorer was met by two envoys from the King of the Belgians, who informed him that their royal master "intended to undertake to do something for Africa," and that Stanley was expected to assist him. In his then frame of mind and body, and with the memory of untold hardships still vividly present, what wonder that such munificent plans awoke no responsive thrill ! Stanley commended the project as a wise one, but for himself he said : " I am so sick and weary that I cannot think with patience of any suggestion that I should conduct it."

But Stanley the invalid, and Stanley re-invigorated by six months' rest and a brief pedestrian tour in Switzerland, were different beings. " With restored health," he naively says, " liberty became insipid and joyless ; that luxury of lounging which had appeared desirable to an ill-regulated and unhealthy fancy became unbearable ; with such views a letter from one of the commissioners requesting an interview, and appointing a meeting in Paris, was very acceptable."

From this meeting, which occurred in August, 1878, Stanley dates the formation of the project of the first enterprise to open up the rich region of the Congo. "For as yet it was only generally understood that, as the Congo was explored, and the core of the Dark Continent accessible by it, *something* ought to be done to render it serviceable to the humanities that were encompassed around by roadless regions fatal to all good doing. All readily concurred in the proposition that my descent of the Congo had opened a highway into Africa, were it possible to utilize it." But how make use of this highway? What enterprise should be undertaken? In what character should a new expedition be despatched to the Congo? Should it be purely geographical, philanthropic, or ·commercial? Or should the construction of a railway to join the Upper and Lower Congo be at once adventured on? The discussion and decision of these and various other equally weighty questions consumed the next three months. In November, 1878, Stanley was summoned to the Palace at Brussels, and there found "various persons of more or less note in the commercial and monetary world, from England, Germany, France, Belgium, and

Holland." He was subjected anew to a fusillade of queries as to the commercial outlook and the geographical and political features of Congo land. The upshot of the conference was that then and there a fund was subscribed to equip an expedition. The new body assumed the title *Comité d' Etudes .du Haut Congo*—"Committee for Study of the Upper Congo." One hundred thousand dollars were paid in for immediate use, and every member pledged himself to respond to each call for further funds, and a president, secretary, and treasurer were chosen. In the words of Stanley : " The expedition was to be immediately organized and equipped, and I was honored with the charge of its *personnel* and *materiel* to effect the object for which the committee was constituted. I was to erect stations, according to the means furnished, along the overland route—after due consideration of their eligibility and future utility— for the convenience of the transport and the European staff in charge ; to establish steam communication wherever available and safe. The stations

were to be commodious and sufficient for all
demands that were likely to be made on them.
By lease or purchase ground enough was to be
secured adjoining the stations so as to enable
them in time to become self-supporting if the
dispositions of the natives should favor such a
project. If it were expedient, also, land on each
side of the route adapted to traffic was to be
purchased or leased, to prevent persons ill-dis-
posed toward us from frustrating the intentions
of the committee through their love of mischief
or jealousy. Such acquired land, however, might
be sub let to any European, at a nominal rent,
who would agree to abstain from intrigue, from
inciting the natives to hostility, and from disturb-
ing the peace of the country." This was the her-
culean task, albeit narrated in such matter-of-fact
fashion, set before our "Breaker of Rocks." It
could not have been committed to worthier hands,
as the sequel shows.

We cannot follow Stanley through the mazes
of preparation. Steamers were to be chartered

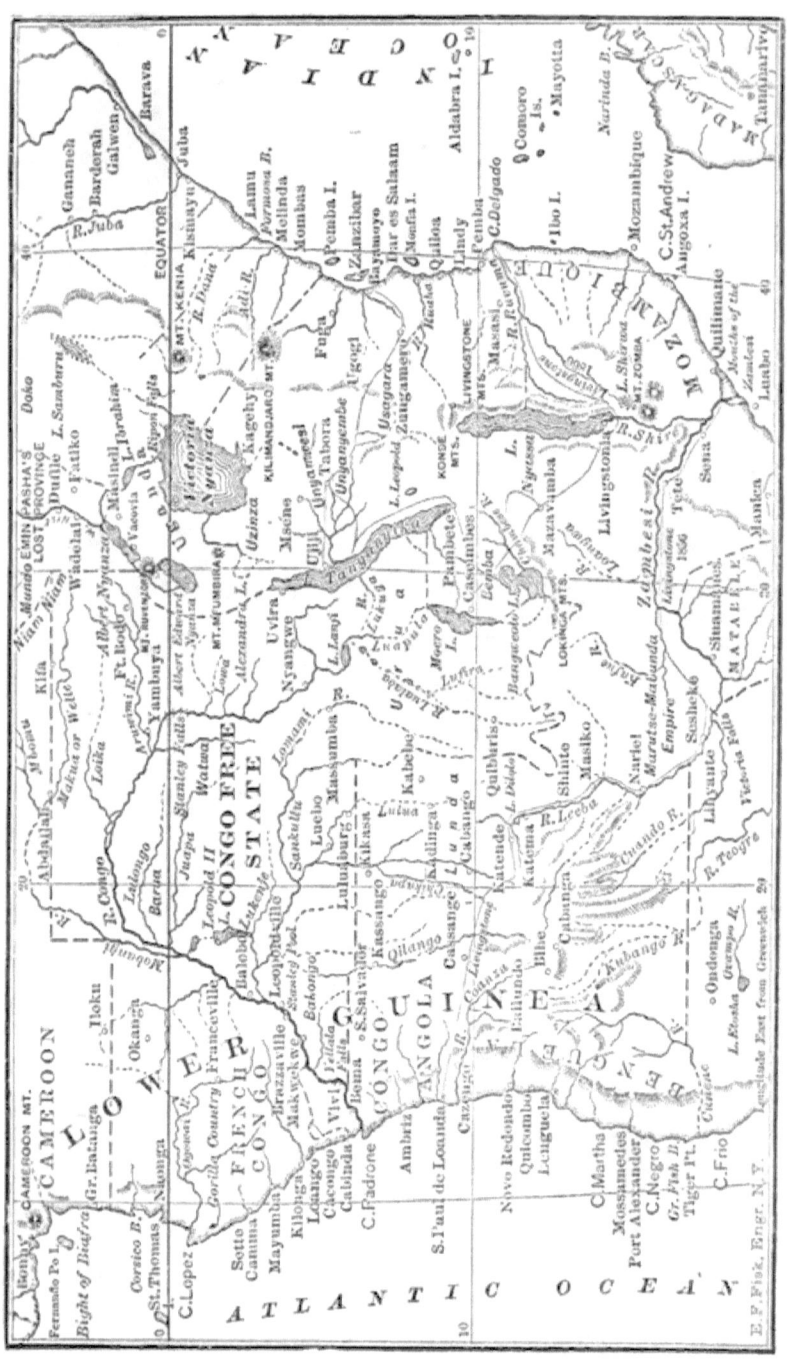

or built; lighters, steel whaleboats, portable houses, and wagons constructed for use in hauling the launches around rapids and waterfalls; tools and weapons purchased; provisions and clothing packed; and the thousand and one articles of merchandise necessary to the traveler in Africa, from a bundle of brass rods to a musket, from a gaudy pocket handkerchief to an embroidered robe, from a string of colored beads to a roll of scarlet cloth, from a toy looking-glass to a japanned trunk, were to be selected and shipped. Meanwhile, Stanley was to proceed to Zanzibar, on the east coast of Africa, in the steamer *Leith*—specially chartered—there to re-engage as many of his former comrades, Zanzibaris, as would volunteer for another journey up the great river. In the interim it was hoped that all the boats and *materiel* would have arrived off the mouth of the Congo, ready for the coming of the chief. By the latter part of May, 1879, the steamer *Albion*, with a body of sixty-eight Zanzibaris on board, departed on her long voyage to

the Congo *via* the Red Sea and the Mediterranean.
On August 14, 1879, just two years from the time
when, footsore and famished, he had last set eyes
on Banana Point, the intrepid explorer once more
arrived off the mouth of the river, this time at
the head of a well-equipped expedition charged
with "the novel mission of sowing along its
banks civilized settlements, to peacefully conquer
and subdue it, to re-mold it in harmony with
modern ideas into national states, within whose
limits the European merchant shall go hand in
hand with the dark African trader, and justice
and law and order shall prevail, and murder and
lawlessness and the cruel barter of slaves forever
cease."

But little time was lost in preliminaries.
Onward and upward was literally the watchword
of the expedition, and seven days after the arrival
of the *Albion* in Banana Creek the flotilla was
ready for ascending the Congo. Early on the
morning of August 21, a chorus of steam whistles
aroused the echoes of the African hills, and pro-

claimed the dawn of a new era for Congo land,
" just as a grander array of mighty ships in the
year 1869 inaugurated the union of the Red Sea
with the Mediterranean." With their sterns to the
sea and their stems pointing toward the interior
the little fleet, consisting of the *Albion*, the *Bel-
gique*, sixteen horse-power and thirty tons
measurement, the *Royal*, the *Esperance*, the *En
Avant*, two steel lighters of twelve and six tons
capacity, the *Jeune Africaine* steam launch, and a
wooden whale-boat, proceeded up a channel from
sixty to nine hundred feet deep, stemming slowly
a nine-knot current. A full head of steam is kept
up, and in exactly four hours Ponta da Leuha
(" Wood Point,") is reached, twenty-eight miles
from Banana, the shores of which are cloistered
by dark green groves, embowered in which are
the whitewashed, low-roofed, broad-verandahed
Dutch factories. As far as this trading-station
the *Great Eastern* might have ascended with perfect safety and be moored to the wharf close in
shore. But a few miles above a treacherous

shifting sand bar forbids the passage of any but
craft of moderate draught—say sixteen feet.

The scenery of this stretch of the lower Congo
deserves a word of description. " On either hand
the dark green walls of mangrove, intermixed
with palm fronds, are apparently impenetrable,
though the charts tells us that many a lazy creek
traces its winding course amid the cool and silent
shades of embracing leafage. A break here and
there shows the entrance of one of these, within
the mazes of which a flotilla of piratical canoes
might hide. The scene is devoid of all animate
nature. Not a bird is seen, not a movement
breaks the melancholy interest with which we
regard it ; neither on the north bank, nor on the
south bank, nor yet on the river, is there aught to
disturb this lifelessness of sleeping nature. The
river-flood glides serene in one unbroken, unruffled
mass, but yet with an unmistakable resistless,
though silent, energy. On the wooded shores
there is a solemn loneliness as of death ; in the
tranquil mass of ceaseless moving water we only

see the peace of an undisturbed **slumber.**" From bank **to bank,** just above **Ponta da Lenha,** the river measures **four and a-half miles.**

Four hours' further steaming brought the fleet to Boma, forty-eight miles from **Banana Creek.** This is the chief trade depot **on the Congo, and consists** of a motley, but picturesque collection of factories and residences of the English, Dutch, French, and **Portuguese merchants, the** whole curving along **the wooded shore,** and in front of **the wharves of** which **was** a goodly array of foreign and native shipping.

Altogether **there are seven or eight steamers** plying constantly **beween Boma and Banana,** conveying native **produce** and European goods for barter, not to mention scores **of** native canoes **from up-river.** So that this stretch of water-way, dotted with trading-stations, "cannot be said to be quite devoid of evidences of trade movement" and of **the all**-powerful influences of European thrift and industry. Nevertheless, **says** Stanley, "**the** general **prospect,** whether over river or

land, is not prepossessing ; the eye is dissatisfied ;
it hungers after more evidences of man and commerce.   Probably the human gregarious instincts
are shocked or chilled by the unaccountable feeling
of loneliness.   Look resolutely away, or over the
factories at your feet, from the crest of yonder
hill, and you will understand why.   There is a
grand sweep of massive hills lifting and falling
to the north ; a long undulating line of hilly land
is visible across the river, stretching away into the
dim distance ; there is a mighty breadth of living
water slowly moving toward the sea, but I can
detect no boat, large or small, just at this present
moment, on any part of its hundred square miles
of surface.   Over all the vast area of land visible,
upland and plain, I see no aspiring tower or dome
or chimney, nor even the likeness of human
structure.   Unfortunately, not a column of smoke
threads the silent air to suggest the thought that
I am not alone.   All is nature—large, ample,
untouched, and apparently unvisited by man.
From all I can see, I may have been the first man

black or white, who has ever stood on the un-
grateful soil under my feet."

The peculiar quality of the African sunshine
has been spoken of by nearly every traveler of
note, and plays an important part in producing a
feeling of inhospitality in all who visit equatorial
Africa. It must be remembered, says Stanley, that
there are different qualities of sunshine. "For
instance, there is the hard, white, naked, undis-
guised sunshine of north-eastern America; there
is the warm, drowsy, hazy sunshine of the English summer; there is the bright, cheery, purified
sunshine of the Mediterranean. African sunshine, however, always appears to me, with its
great heat, to be a kind of superior moonlight,
judging from its effects on scenery. Once or
twice I speak of 'solemn-looking' hills. I can
only attribute this apparent solemnity to the
peculiar sunshine. It deepens the shadows and
darkens the dark green of the foliage of the
forest, while it imparts a wan appearance or a
cold reflection of light to naked slopes or treeless

hill-tops. Its effect is a chill austerity, an inde-
scribable solemnity, a repelling unsociability.
Your sympathies are not warmed by it ; silence
has set its seal upon it ; before it you become
speechless. Gaze your utmost on the scene,
admire it as you may, worship it if you will, but
your love is not needed. Speak not of grace nor
of loveliness in connection with it. Serene it
may be, but it is a passionless serenity. It is to
be contemplated, but not to be spoken to, for
your regard is fixed upon a voiceless, sphinx-like
immobility, belonging more to an unsubstantial
dreamland than to a real earth.

Boma has a hideous history. For two centuries
it was the port of shipment for the cargoes of
black humanity whose destination was the United
States, the Brazils, and the West Indies. The
emissaries of the slave-catcher and the slave-
trader harried all this wide land, from the sea to
Stanley Pool, until there was scarcely a native
village that had not been forced to contribute its
quota of defenseless men, women, and babes, who

never returned to the palm thatched huts whence they were torn. This wholesale depopulation of one of earth's fairest regions explains why to day so many miles of these rich plateaus remain grass-grown and untilled, roamed by the elephant and the antelope. The memory of the Congo slave-traffic has justly become a by-word in the annals of even that "sum of all villainies."

One of the chief objects of the expedition was, as we have seen, the founding of permanent stations for present observation and future trade. All available spots below and around Boma were already pre-empted, and, as was only natural, the trading firms already in possession viewed with none too friendly eyes the new venture. Stanley hoped to find some site above them all well adapted for the purpose in view. So, while the other steamers were unloading their freight at Boma and preparing to return to Banana for the remainder, the launch *Esperance*, the most powerful and speedy of the fleet, was prepared and provisioned for a dash up-stream "which

should fix forever the ultimate point of navigability and the site for the principal station of the
Comité d' Etudes du Haut Congo." At a distance
of thirteen hours from Banana by a nine-knot
steamer, the plateau of Vivi appears on the north
bank at the head of a stretch of very swift water,
but at the foot of a wide and comparatively tranquil reach. Castle Hill, as it has since been
named, towers almost perpendicularly three
hundred feet from the river, but slopes gently on
the landward side. From the base of this cliff-
faced rock there projects a "level-topped isolated
spur," sloping on the western side to a sandy
river beach. Here the native guide, De-De-De,
proposed that the new-comers should build.

Stanley was not at first prepossessed in favor
of the site. Rank grass covered it, waving high
above their heads, so that it was well-nigh
impossible to discern the conformation of the
little plateau. However, the grass was fired, and
in an hour the flames had licked the ground clear
and revealed "a sand plot one hundred yards

long and fifty yards deep, which to our strange eyes led nowhere except to a grassy forest some fifteen feet high or back again to the deep forceful river, or up that tall, upright, grim rock !"

A more minute inspection, however, revealed to Stanley the fact that though this site at Vivi possessed some disadvantages, not the least among which would be the difficulty of making a wagon-road to what must be the landing place, still, on rehearsing to himself what it was he desired and wished to discover, the value of this Vivi platform became more and more evident. As his thoughts shaped themselves the indispen- sable requisites were seen to be : A place easy of access from the sea, a neighboring population of conciliating tendency, salubrity of position, and a spot whence a feasible route to the interior might be made.

Soundings made up and down the river, a palaver with the aborigines from the neighboring village of Chinsalla, and a rapid survey of the country inland, proved that Vivi possessed most of these advantages, and, ever quick to decide, the native lords of Vivi were summoned to a second consultation, in which Stanley's plans and proposals to purchase from them enough land to found a station were set forth by means of interpreters. Finally, for goods of the value of £32 and a rental of £2 per month, the site of Vivi was secured, with the additional right to make roads into the interior, the natives pledging themselves neither to make war on those using the roads nor to allow any other white man to settle in the region round about without Stanley's permission. In his diary Stanley records that he is not entirely pleased with his purchase; but necessity compelled him, for it is the highest point of navigation on the lower Congo opposite which a landing could be effected by steamers.

The story of the founding of Vivi reads like an heroic epic. It tells of difficulties overcome and of well-night insurmountable obstacles subdued. "A more cruel or less promising task than to conquer the sternness of that austere and

somber region could scarcely be imagined," writes
Stanley. "Its large, bold features of solidity,
ruggedness, impassiveness, the chaos of stones,
worthless scrub, and tangle of grass in hollow, or
slope, or summit, breathed a grim defiance that
was undeniable. Yet our task was to temper
this obstinacy, to make the position scalable,
even accessible ; to quicken that cold lifelessness ;
to reduce that grim defiance to perfect submis-
sion ; in a word, to infuse vigorous animation
into a scene which no one but the most devoted
standard-bearer of Philanthropy could ever have
looked at twice with a view to its value. Our
only predecessors in this region had been men
despatched on an errand of geographical exploration, or tourists who had hastily passed through
to visit the Falls of Yellala. Trade had shunned
it ; religious zeal saw no fit field here for its
labors; perhaps its grimness of feature had
daunted the zealot. But let us see what wakeful
diligence, patient industry, and a trustful faith
can make of it. The power of man is great,

though he is a feeble, perishable creature ; with
little strokes but many he has before this performed marvels ; his working life counts but a
handful of hours, but with every hour—industry
inspiring him—he makes his mark, and many
marks make a rood." The heroic spirit breathing
throughout this last sentence strikes the keynote
of Stanley's career in Congo land. It earned
him his title of "the Rock-breaker," and it
brought him, not unscathed, but undaunted, to
the goal of his labors at the foot of Stanley
Falls.

Work began at once in earnest. Boats were
despatched down stream for provisions, tents,
tools, and a hundred men. Then, on the morning
of October 1st, the task of leveling the plateau
and of building a road to the landing-place was
attacked with vigor. The sites of the corruga
ted-iron storehouses sent out from England, of the
native houses, and of Vivi headquarters were
staked out ; a garden was made by dint of carrying 2000 baskets of black loam from the valley on

the backs of the natives ; stables, poultry-houses, blacksmiths and carpenters' sheds were built, and by February 6th, 1880, Stanley was able to write to the committee that the lower station was complete in all its details ; time, three months twenty-four days. The termination of this stage of the labors of the expedition was celebrated by a day's holiday and a banquet. Then to work again.

Just above Vivi all navigation of the lower Congo is checked by the lower series of the Livingstone cataracts, which comprise Yellala, Iuga, and Isangila Falls, and several miles of intervening rapids. The distance from Vivi to Isangila is fifty-two miles, and a portage must be made for this distance around the obstruction. At this writing surveys have been made on the south bank for a railway to span this gap, but to Stanley it was virgin forest. The problem confronting him at the commencement of this second stage was to make a practical wagon road through an unknown country, over which could be drawn heavy steel wagons con-

taining the hull, boilers, and machinery of the
boats destined to be used on the higher reaches.
In addition was to be transported all the *materiel*
of the expedition in packs on the backs of the
trusty Zanzibaris, the goods necessary for barter
and for presents to the rude potentates, and the
food for the large force of men that would neces-
sarily be engaged.   Supplies of native produce
could doubtless be obtained, but must not be
entirely relied on.

A sentence from a letter to the committee at
home about this time furnishes some idea of the
labor thus involved : " It is going to be a tedious
task, I perceive very clearly, and a protracted
one, to make a road fifty-two miles long, then to
come back and transport a boat which may be
moved only a mile a day perhaps, then to come
back, hauling the heavy wagon with us, to transport another heavy launch, and move on a mile a
day again, then back for another heavy launch,
and repeat the same operation for three heavy
boilers three times, by which we see we have to

drag the heavy wagon nine times over a fifty-two
mile rough road, total nine hundred and thirty-
six miles, before we can embark for our second
station, without counting the delays caused by
constant parties conveying provisions."

A rapid reconnaissance to Isangila was first
undertaken, in course of which many savage
potentates were interviewed, and by a judicious
use of presents treaties were drawn up guarantee-
ing the integrity of the road from Vivi, and the
comforting assurance was afforded that no serious
obstacle of any kind would be offered by the
native tribes. This preliminary, though very
cursory survey of the country between Vivi and
Isangila revealed a few of the obstacles to be
overcome in road-building. There were ravines
to be filled up, morasses to be crossed, bridges to
be built, jungles to be penetrated, mountains to
be flanked, and rocks to be removed. The native
pathways running boldly "up and down inclines
and declines of formidable steepness, and sometimes along a six-inch wide ledge of rock around

the ends of water-courses," were simply out of the question ; and the task that weighed most heavily upon the chief of the expedition was the necessity of "finding available—in Nature if possible, by laborious industry if necessary—either continuous stretches or detached pieces of level land which might be deftly connected together by a passable and safe road." .The country between the two objective points is a cruel one, but by dint of rambling about the hills and along the river, tracing the courses of streams and plunging into the depths of a perfect wilderness, Stanley was at length able to map out a feasible route to Isangila from Vivi Station.

On the 18th of March, 1880, the initial blow was struck on the first road through the tropic land, with its enervating heats and treacherous changes of temperature. The narrative of this first day's labor is so vivid and lifelike that we shall allow the gallant commander to tell it in his own words : " On the 18th of March, 1880, we marched to the Loa River and valley, and formed a camp, all the Vivi laborers being employed in conveying seventy sacks of beans, peas, lentils, rice and salt, as a first instalment of provisions for the pioneer force. During the rest of the morning we traced the line of road by means of flagstaffs bearing white cloth streamers, and a tall step-ladder to guide through the high grass the bearers of the half-mile cord and reel. It must be remembered that the grass in many cases was ten feet high, and in loamy hollows about fifteen feet. In the months of July, August, and September fires consume the old grass ; but so quick is the growth from the moment that the rains begin in September that by the middle of March it is as tall as a young forest. At mid-day the pioneers were formed in line, hoes in hand, along the cord, and at a signal the work of uprooting the grass began. By night there was a clear roadway made fifteen feet wide and two thousand five hundred feet long." On April 22 there were twenty-two and a-third miles of road completed, from Vivi Station to Makeya Manguba, at the junction of the Bundi River with the Congo. For the present it was decided that the steamers, when hauled thus far, should transport the goods and equipage up the Bundi to the point found best adapted for further progress by means of the wagon road up the Bundi valley. By the 30th of July all the *materiel*, amounting to fifty-four tons, destined for the Congo, had been transported to Makeya Manguba, to do which it had been necessary to actually travel nine hundred and sixty-six miles, although the real distance from camp to camp was only twenty-two miles on the road to Stanley Pool, nearly fifteen hundred miles away! By this time the road from Vivi had become so hard and well-trodden that it presented the appearance of an old-country turnpike.

Then the work of road-making up the Bundi valley was undertaken—a repetition of the toils, tribulations, and triumphs of the first stretch from Vivi to Makeya Manguba. In one year—or, to be absolutely correct, three hundred and sixty-six days, from February 21, 1880, to February 21,

1881, the overland route was completed to Isangila camp, above the cataract, and three days later the boats, all scraped, cleaned, and painted, were launched, ready for a second stage of river transit. During the year the various marchings, haulings, and countermarchings reached a total of 2,352 miles—an average of six and a-half miles a day—to gain an advance into the interior of only fifty-two miles! "This was no holiday affair," writes the chief, "with its diet of beans and goat-meat and sodden bananas in the muggy atmosphere of the Congo cañon, with the fierce heat from the rocks and the chill, bleak winds blowing up the gorge and down from seared grassy plateaus. Let the deaths of six Europeans and twenty-two natives and the retirement of thirteen invalid whites, only one of whom saw the interior, speak for us." And with naive modesty, at the conclusion of the record of this stupendous feat of engineering, without a word of self-glorification, Stanley adds : "And now we were all prepared to commence another section of our work of a somewhat different character to that which was now happily terminated."

By the committee Mr. Stanley had been instructed to build three stations—one at Vivi, one at Manyanga, and one on the shores of Stanley Pool; also to convey a steamer and a boat to the former place, and another steamer and boat to the latter. From Isangila to Manyanga— between the cataract of Isangila and the cataract of Ntombo Mataka—was eighty-eight miles, Manyanga being distant from Vivi Station one hundred and forty miles. In fourteen round trips up and down the various reaches of this eighty-eight miles of open river the boats and steamers transported by May 1, 1881, the houses, equipage, and baggage to the site of the second permanent station.

But now the uniform good health enjoyed by the chief of the expedition failed, and a severe attack of African fever brought him to the gates of death. Again, however, his magnificent physique brought him through, and during his

convalescence the news of the arrival of re-enforcements from Zanzibar acted like a bracing tonic.
Though still weak and feeble, he was able to
direct the building of the Manyanga Station, and
to superintend the commencement of another
wagon road toward Stanley Pool.

What of the climate on the lower and upper
Congo? We have seen that even Stanley's seasoned frame succumbed, while the large roll of
invalided Europeans during the first three years
would seem to augur a malign influence, if not
actual insalubrity, for Europeans. The popular
belief in a pestilential belt of coast country at the
mouth of the Congo is a mere bugbear. From the
sea to Vivi, one hundred and ten miles up the river,
Africa has no terrors to those who will accommo-
date themselves to the changed atmospheric conditions. The scourge that decimates the ranks of
explorers and residents on the Congo is not the climate, but their own crass stupidity and obstinacy
in refusing to abandon the habits of diet, drinking,
and dressing suitable to temperate latitudes. Un-

limited whiskey and gin, wine and bottled ale, may
do for the parallels of London or New York, but
are suicidal within a few degrees of the equator.
" From the moment of arrival," says Stanley,
" the body undergoes a new experience, and a
wise man will begin to govern his appetite and
his conduct accordingly. The head that was
covered with a proud luxuriance of flowing locks,
or bristled bushy and thick, must be shorn close ;
the body must be divested of that wind and rain-
proof armor of linen and wool in which it was
accustomed to be encased in high latitudes, and
must assume, if ease and pleasure are preferable
to discomfort, garments of soft, loose, light flannels. The head-covering which London and Paris
patronize must give place to the helmet and
puggaree or to a well-ventilated light cap with
curtain. And as those decorous externals of
Europe, with their somber coloring and cumbrous
thickness, must yield to the more graceful and airy
flannels of the tropics, so the appetite, the extravagant power of digestion, the seemingly uncon-

trollable and ever-famished lust for animal food,
and the distempered greed for ardent drinks, must
be governed by an absolutely new *régime.* Any
liquid that is exciting, or, as others may choose
to term it, exhilarating or inspiring, the unsea-
soned European must avoid during daylight,
whether it be in the guise of the commonly
believed innocuous lager, mild Pilsen, watery
claret, *vin ordinaire*, or any other 'innocent'
wine or beer. Otherwise the slightest indiscretion,
the least unusual effort or spasmodic industry
may in one short hour prove fatal. It is my duty
not to pander to a depraved taste, not to be too
nice in offending it. I am compelled to speak
strongly by our losses, by my own grief in
remembering the young, the strong, and the
brave, who have slain themselves through their
own ignorance.

"'*Un petit verre de Cognac*—a glass of small
beer—what can they matter?' asks the inexperi-
enced, pleadingly.

"To me, personally, nothing ! To you, a sudden

death, perhaps a *coup de soleil!* A frantic and insensate rush to the hot sun out of the cool shade, an imprudent exposure, may be followed by a bilious fever of who knows what severity, or a rheumatic fever that will lay you prostrate for weeks, perhaps utterly unfitting you for your work and future usefulness. You were inspired by that *petit verre* of Cognac—which, had you not taken, you might have been more deliberate in your movements, and more prudent than to needlessly exert yourself in the presence of an enemy so formidable as is the tropic sun to a white man's head when sensitized by the fumes of Cognac.

"Should you recover, you will blame Africa. 'Africa is cruel! Africa is murderous! Africa means death to the European!' And your stupid unreflecting friends, with their cowardly jargon, in Europe will echo the cry—simply because a weakling like you could not resist your *petit verre* at mid-day. Must all this continent be subjected to the scourge of your vituperative powers?

"'A man cannot exist on tea and coffee, or be

continually drinking soup and water " whines one whose propensities are alarmed.

"I do not demand that you should confine yourself to tea, or coffee, or soup— or water, or lemonade, or seltzer, or Apollinaris, or whatever other agreeable liquid you may wish to quench your thirst. I only suggest that if you wish to enjoy Africa, and do your pledged duty, avoid stimulants, under whatever name, during the day; in the evening, moderate indulgence with your dinner in clarets, madeira, or white wines or champagnes is not harmful, but beneficial. At the same time this advice is not especially intended for you, but for young men desirous of distinguishing themselves for their ability to live and work in Africa. The brave man is he who dare live, and will not yield to death without a contest."

The mean highest temperature is 90° Fah., the lowest 67°, while the heat of the sun on a clear day is from 110° to 115°. Clad in suitable garments—light flannels—a European can perform as

much work on the Congo as he can in England,
provided a roof or awning is above his head. For
three months of the year it is decidedly chilly in
the interior, owing to the high altitude ; while
during the rest of the year cloudy or partially
cloudy days are frequent, and there is always a
cooling breeze blowing. The nights are invariably
cool, and a blanket is, after a very short sojourn,
found requisite for comfort. The sun is the only
real enemy of the European, and a few judicious
and timely precautions rob him of half his terrors.

On July 15, 1881, Stanley started with a small
company to reconnoitre the ground between
Manyanga and Stanley Pool, and to obtain an
eligible site for a station contiguous to the point
where the navigability of the upper Congo com-
mences. Owing to the indifference or hostility of
the natives on the north bank, inspired by Mala-
meen, the former sergeant of M. de Brazza, no
ground could be secured there, and Stanley was
forced to cross over to the south shore. The politics of these primitive communities are as compli-

cated as those of the petty German States in the last century, and an explorer finds it extremely difficult to be on friendly terms with one tribe or village and escape the enmity of every other in all that section of country. After a tedious palaver and an extravagant outlay of finery for presents, amounting to hundreds of pounds, an admirable site for a station was secured, about a mile below the village of Kintamo. This, the principal station on the upper Congo, was named Leopoldville, "in honor of the munificent and royal founder of the Association Internationale du Congo," to which the old name of ˙ Comité d'Etudes du Haut Congo had given place since the departure of the expedition from Europe. Below the station foam the rapids of Kintamo ; above it opens out the lake-like, island-dotted expanse of Stanley Pool, from which there is an unbroken stretch of one thousand and sixty-eight miles of clear and unobstructed river to Stanley Falls.

The native concession once obtained, the founding and building of Leopoldville went on apace, though the nominal chief of Kintamo, the crafty and fawning Ngalyema, gave no end of trouble. This episode deserves a book to itself, says Stanley. Ngalyema's peculiar temper requires more than a few phrases before an exact representation of the man can be given. He is a grasping, greedy savage, whose bland roguery and smirking simplicity remind us irresistibly of Pecksniff. "It cost more money to overcome this man peacefully than the aggregate expenditure on all the chiefs of the country who possessed something substantial to give us in exchange. Through long patience, liberality, and a timely hint now and then that he might be sorry for going beyond certain bounds, he was at last fairly won to good behavior and a stout and friendly alliance," which last happy result gave Stanley leisure to prepare for his long-deferred journey up river on an errand of exploration.

Leopoldville stands just within the Garden of the Congo. The belt of rough and sterile country through which we have accompanied our brave

explorers may be compared to the rough and
rugged shell surrounding a sweet and meaty ker-
nel. The beauty and fertility of the country on
whose threshold they now stood baffle calculation.
Millions of acres of unsurpassed fertility greet the
eye from the summit of any eminence. "Even
now it is almost idyllic in appearance, yet there
are only the grass huts of Kintamo conspicuously
in view ; the rest is literally only a wilderness of
grass, shrubs, and tree-foliage. But my mind,
when I survey this view, always reverts to the
possibilities of the future. It is like looking at
the fair, intelligent face of a promising child ; we
find naught in it but innocence, and we fondly
imagine that we see the germs of a future great
genius—perhaps a legislator, a savant, a warrior,
or a poet. Supposing the rich fertile soil of that
plain, well-watered as it is by many running
streams, were cultivated, how it would reward the
husbandman ! How it would be bursting with
fullness and plenty ! In all the Mississippi valley
there is no soil to equal it, yet here it lies a

neglected waste." And perhaps for generations
yet the prospect will possess the same idle slum-
berous appearance it presents to-day !

The situation of Leopoldville is most fortunate.
On a natural grassy plateau of easy ascent from
the river, in a crescent-shaped indentation of the
shore, the station commands a view of the wide
expanse of Stanley Pool and its islands. Water
was handy ; fuel was abundant ; a one-story
block-house, impregnable to attack and proof
against fire, offered safe refuge in case trouble
should arise with the surrounding natives. Such
a contingency, however, seemed very remote.
So that it was with feelings of perfect security
that Stanley left Leopoldville under the command
of a subordinate, while he made a dash up-
stream.

On this tour of observation another small
station—the sixth in all—was founded at Mswata,
fourteen hours' steaming from Leopoldville.
And then, while waiting for the arrival of the
Europeans and stores left at Vivi and destined

for the upper Congo, Stanley utilized the time by exploring the Kiva River, a south bank tributary of the Congo, "in order to discover whether any special advantages would result from a more intimate acquaintance with that river and its tribes." Once more the little steamer *En Avant* turned her prow toward the center of the continent, her commander, undeterred by weird tales of perils in the way, such as volcanic waters, rocky impassable barriers, and savage natives whose spears were longer and sharper than any others. The steamer was equipped for a nine days' absence, and on the 19th of May, 1882, was commenced one of the most fateful journeys ever undertaken by "Bula Matari."

Three hours and forty minutes from Leopold-ville, or four hundred and forty miles from the sea, the deep and rapid embouchure of the Kiva, four hundred and fifty yards wide, was entered. The stream proved to be very tortuous, though the current perceptibly slackened as the ascent progressed. But wood for the engine was scarce,

and the natives on either shore suspicious and dis-
obliging.   Progress under these conditions was
much slower than Stanley had calculated, and
soon the provisions ran low.   A few fish were
obtained from the natives, so Stanley pressed on,
for rumors of a great lake ahead of a nature well
calculated to fire the soul of an ardent explorer
were rife among the tribes dwelling along the
Kiva.   This river, about eighty miles from its
mouth, splits into the Mfini and Mbihé.   Steering
boldly into the former branch, which varied from
two hundred and fifty to four hundred yards in
breadth, with a current of two and a-half knots an
hour, on the morning of the 26th a sudden widen-
ing of the horizon ahead, the receding of the
banks on either hand, and an almost total cessa-
tion of the current, told that some abrupt change
in the riverine scenery was at hand.   Neither of
the native guides had ever been so far, nor was
their dialect now intelligible to the denizens of
the banks of the Mfini.   Stanley soon suspected
that he had discovered another central African

lake hitherto unkown to Europeans. Conjecture soon became certainty. From the 26th to the 31st of May were spent in the circumnavigation of this newly revealed body of water, which Stanley named Lake Leopold II. At two o'clock on the afternoon of the 31st the *En Avant* arrived once more at the mouth of the Mfini, and the survey was completed. Lake Leopold II. covers a total area of eight hundred square miles—rather smaller then Lake Erie—lies in the midst of a delightful climate and country, though so near the equator, and is fed by innumerable small streams, discharging its waters by means of the Mfini into the Congo.

The natives on the shores of this inland lake were paralyzed with terror at the advent of these strange beings in their demoniac, hissing, and smoke-belching steamer. Here is a ludicrous account of the way a party of fishermen were surprised in mid-lake, when the *En Avant* approached them in the vain hope of acquiring some information.

" About ten o'clock, as we were issuing out of a long bay-like bight in the shore, we saw half-a-dozen small canoes well out in the lake, and one probably two miles further out, and after passing the rocky point we saw the village to which these canoes evidently belonged. I thought this an excellent opportunity to obtain some information respecting the country, and perhaps obtain fresh fish and food. We bore down upon the fisher-men, who, all engrossed in hauling their seines aboard, permitted us to approach within a mile of them before they were aware of our presence. And such a presence as we must have been to them! A large white boat with outspread and ample wing, emitting strange noises, which was unlike the sounds sent out by any animal they had ever heard! They lift their hands up in dismay. One, with more presence of mind than the others, claps his hands to his paddle, and instinctively skims away. "An admirable idea," the others seem to cry, and all strike their paddles deep in the black water, and urge their tiny dugouts until they appear to fly over the lake. But the other—the canoe all alone in the watery waste—in which the fisherman, profoundly abstracted in his task, sits heedlessly hauling his seines aboard! When, hark! what is that? What strange sighing sound, what harsh grating and plashing noise, is that? He turns toward our direction and beholds a strange structure, all white, with lofty awning, and a pair of revolving clappers striking the lake water into long, trailing waves behind. He falls sideways into his little canoe, completely paralyzed, as if striving to realize that the vision is not all a dream. No doubt the thought flashes into his mind, "But a moment since I swept my eyes around, and saw naught strange to inspire fear or anxiety in me. But this! Whence could this have issued? It must be a dream, surely.'

"But again the gentle wind bears to his ears the strong pulsating sounds, and the deep but sharp sighing ; he hears the desperate whirl of the paddle wheels ; he sees the trail of rolling wavelets astern. Leaping to his feet with frantic energy, he takes one short glance around and realizes that he, insensate fool, while indulging in Waltonian reveries in mid-day, has been abandoned by his friends! However, there is hope while there is life ; he bends his back, and draws, with long-reaching grasp, the water sideways, this way and that, and the tiny pirogue, sharp as a spear-point, leaps over the water, obeying his will dexterously.

"Nearer and nearer the steamer draws on the fugitive, but by a whirl of the paddle the dark man shoots at right angles triumphantly away, while the *En Avant*, confused by this sudden movement, careers madly along. In a short time, however, she is in full chase again, this time carefully watching every movement. The man has kept throwing wild glances over his shoulders ; he observes the monster rapidly gaining on him, and each time it seems to loom larger and larger upon his excited imagination ; he hears the tremendous whirr of the wheels and the throbbing of the engines, and the puffing of the steam. Another glance, and it seems to be overwhelming him, when, 'Ach, Gott!' he springs overboard, and we sweep past the empty canoe!"

But not to drown, for the crew of the *En Avant* carefully fish him out, limp with terror, and proceed to question him. Between his fright and his unfamiliarity with the language spoken by Stanley's guides they can make nothing of him, save that he takes them for slave-catchers. In compensation for his bath and the loss of his morning's catch of fish they fill his two hands with bright beads, place a dozen bright handkerchiefs in his canoe, and then invite him to step in. This he did, slowly and carefully, but "did not seem to realize that he was a free and a rich man until there was such a distance between us that he thought it impossible for us to catch him again, even if we tried. When he seemed a small speck in the lake we saw the figure rise to its

height, and then we knew that he was conscious
that his old life had begun again."

But this voyage of discovery up the Kiva was
fraught with dire results to Stanley. Ere the
prow of the *En Avant* was turned down stream
on the return its crew were suffering the pangs
of hunger. But worse than all were the symptoms of a severe sickness which oppressed the
chief. While Leopoldville was yet distant a day's
steaming Stanley became unconscious, and at
last was obliged to be carried ashore. A week
later he decided to return to Vivi, that being the
sanitarium at which enfeebled Europeans from
the upper Congo could recover health and
strength. But on the 28th of June, at Manyanga,
incipient gastritis made itself felt, with swelling
of the lower limbs, and to the recent sun-roasting
on Lake Leopold II. he attributed this illness.
But the bracing air of Vivi failed to afford the
desired relief. So, with intense reluctance, Stanley resolved to proceed to Europe, invalided. His
work on the Congo was left, as he thought, in

competent hands, and might be safely deprived
of its controlling mind for a few months. In
October, 1882, he arrived in Europe, greatly
bettered by the sea-voyage, and before many days
were over had laid before the Committee of the
Association Internationale du Congo a report of
the true condition of affairs at the front.

In brief, the problem now confronting the pro-
jectors was to secure what had been hitherto
gained by the toils of the years 1878–1882.
Frankly, Stanley declared that in its present state
the Congo Basin was not worth a two-shilling
piece, and to reduce it to proper order a railway
must be constructed between the lower and the
upper Congo. (In the summer of 1885 a survey-
ing party of Belgian engineers departed to survey
both banks of the Congo between Vivi and Stanley Pool, and this survey, as already stated,
has been completed.) The cost of such a road
would be between two and three million dollars.
To render it even prospectively valuable, he told
the king and the committee, " You must first

have a charter from Europe that you shall be permitted to build that railroad, that you shall
govern the land through which it passes, that, in
short, the guardianship of it shall not pass into
the hands of any power but your own." It was
seen that at first such a road would not only be
unremunerative, but would entail a large annual
outlay, and could never become a source of profit
either to the Association or Africa unless commercial men and emigrants could be attracted to
the upper Congo. The members of the Association were unanimously of the same opinion, and
declared themselves ready to face the further
enormous outlay, provided Stanley would continue
in charge of the work. Though shattered in
health, Stanley consented to return to the Congo
and complete the establishment of stations as far
as Stanley Falls, provided an efficient subordinate
or assistant chief could be found to relieve him of
all direct concern for the welfare of the stations
on the lower Congo. The committee engaged to
find and send such a person, and on these condi-

tions Stanley arranged to return to the scene of his labors at the end of six weeks.

In the preceding paragraph we have touched on a fruitful source of annoyance and hinderance to progress at the scene of action—the, with a few bright exceptions, general untrustworthiness of those filling subordinate positions in the employ of the association. Half-pathetic, half-humorous, are the records of incompetency, petty jealousy, and absurd bickering among the European staff. "The right man in the right place" was a scarce commodity on the Congo, and a greater number of round pegs in square holes was probably never before gathered around an enterprise of such pith and moment. Gentlemen accepted service under the flag of the Committee with the idea, in many cases, that hunting big game and flirting with dusky maidens were the chief ingredients of life in Africa under the equator. The hard work attending the ascent of the river and the founding of stations they had not bargained for, and after a taste of the discomforts and dangers such

frequently resigned in indignation and disgust.
But the malingerer was the worst foe to order and
discipline.   Some of these gentry, by unwise
excesses or by an assumption of wounded dignity
ill-suited to the mode of life in which they had
embarked, were often for months an incubus on
the hands of the chief. Time and again they
would resign and incontinently quit their posts,
while Stanley, five hundred miles up the river,
would receive the first intimation thereof by
letter when the writer was well on his way to
Europe. No wonder he thus gives vent to his
feelings and speaks in plain terms : "These people
had given me more trouble than all the tribes put
together. They had inspired such disgust in me
that I would rather be condemned to be a boot-
black all my life than to be a dry-nurse to beings
who had no other claim to manhood than that
externally they might be pretty pictures of men."
But much of the ineffectiveness of some Europeans on the Congo, Stanley thinks, is due simply
to nostalgia, intensified perhaps by the inhospit-

able and austere appearance of the scenery to which allusion has been made. Yet it is impossible to view such ill-timed petulance with much indulgence.

If the want of efficient and trustworthy assistants had been apparent before Stanley's illness and departure for home, their urgent necessity was reiterated with ten-fold force ere he set foot on shore at Vivi on his return to the Congo in December, 1882. Reports of resignations, desertions, and wholesale neglect of duty came pouring in from all the stations ; the steamers had been allowed to rust at their moorings ; at the upper stations the stocks of provisions had been allowed to diminish through petty squabbles among the various chiefs left in command ; at Leopoldville there existed an armed truce between the garrison and the natives, and the former were nearly reduced to want ; at all a general lack of personal responsibility and *esprit du corps.* And yet but six months had elapsed between his departure and his return ! However, the salutary influence of

his presence was soon felt ; the judicious exercise
of authority and a little needful tact, tempered
with a dash of severity, soon restored matters to
their former condition of decent prosperity.

These disagreeables settled, and matters placed
on their former footing, the chief was free to
enter on the final stage of his Congo labors—the
planting of a station at Stanley Falls and of
another one midway between that place and
Leopoldville. On the 9th day of May, 1883, a
little flotilla streamed out into Stanley Pool, consisting of the steam launches *Royal* and *A. I. A.*
and our old friend the *En Avant,* the first and last
named towing the large sixty-foot canoe and the
steel whale-boat respectively. A force of eighty
men, with six tons of *materiel,* consisting of
every necessary article for the equipment of two
small stations, and provisions for the garrisons
for at least six months, loaded all the boats to the
load-line. Amid the cheers of the garrison at
Leopoldville the tiny fleet pushes out into the
stream on its thousand-mile voyage into the

real heart of equatorial Africa, carrying the flag
of the Association to almost the limit of Congo
navigation.

On June 13, at a distance of four hundred and
twelve miles above Leopoldville, and seven hundred and fifty-seven miles from the sea, Equator
Station was founded, in the Wangate country, at
0° 1' 0" north latitude. Here a lieutenant and
twenty-six men were left as a permanent garrison,
with a further temporary contribution of twenty
men to assist in building, etc. This is Stanley's
ideal depot, and though usually anything but
enthusiastic or optimistic, his account of the
beauties of its surroundings is radiant. On
October 16 the flotilla steams out of Equator
Station for the last six hundred miles of river
travel separating them from Stanley Falls, making
verbal treaties with the tribal chiefs en route.

On November 23 the explorers reached a point
nine hundred and twenty-one miles above Leopoldville, where they encounter a stretch of country
on either bank recently devastated by a raid of

Arab slave-takers.   Smoking villages, decaying
corpses, and ruined gardens blot one of the fairest
landscapes.   The fiends had harried a country
exceeding Ireland in area and formerly peopled
by a happy primitive people numbering over one
million souls.   One hundred and eighteen villages
had been destroyed for the scant return of about
two thousand five hundred slaves and two thousand ivory tusks.   The stoppage of this iniquity
will be one of the beneficent results of the domi-
nation of all this zone by enlightened Europeans.

A week later the lower rapids of Stanley Falls
came into view.   They consist in all of seven distinct cataracts, spread out along a curvature of
the river fifty-six miles long, and separated by two
navigable stretches twenty-two and twenty-six
miles in length respectively.   From the highest
of the Stanley Falls to Nyangwé, where Stanley
commenced his descent of the Congo, is three
hundred and eighty-five miles of clear navigation.

The usual protracted palavers with the natives
were inevitable, but finally, at a cost of £160

worth of goods, the right to settle in the country of the Wane Rusari tribe was purchased. Stanley chose an island of the same for the site of the final station of the association, and because of the placid nature of the water between the island and the north bank, affording an admirable berth for the steamers, the depot was named Still Haven. About four acres of ground were cleared ; an abundance of tools, food, etc., carried ashore, and Still Haven was placed in command of one Binnie, "a little Scotchman, five feet three inches in height," the person whom Stanley had carried from the Atlantic to the interior to take charge of the station begging at the last moment to be returned to the coast ! This Ultima Thule of the Congo Expedition was reached only one day later—December 1, 1883— than that set down by Stanley to the Committee at Brussels. Nothing more could be done in the way of station building or trade development until the right of protectorate over the districts between station and station, from Vivi to Stanley

Falls, had been obtained by the concert of the great Powers.

The next milestone in the reclamation of the Congo Basin was the meeting of the Berlin Conference in 1884–85, and the constitution thereby of the Congo Free State, dominated chiefly by the African International Association, though France and Portugal possess a princely domain therein. We may not close this chapter without a brief survey of the area and products and trade prospects of this new equatorial empire. "To define the geographical basin of the Congo, whether explored or unexplored," said Mr. Stanley, in an address before the conference, "is a very easy matter, since every school-boy knows that a river basin—geographically speaking—includes all that territory drained by the river and its affluents, large and small. The Congo, unlike many other large rivers, has no fluvial delta ; it issues into the Atlantic Ocean in one united stream between Shark's Point on the south and Banana Point on the north, with a breadth of seven miles and an

unknown depth. But when you ask me as to what
I should consider the commercial basin of the
Congo, I am bound to answer you that the main
river and its most important affluents constitute
means by which trade can influence a much larger
amount of territory than is comprised within the
geographical basin. To define the commercial
basin of the Congo is very simple : Commencing
from the Atlantic Ocean I should follow the line
of 1° 25′ south latitude east as far as 13° 13′ long.
east of Greenwich, and along that meridian north
until the water-shed of the Niger-Binué is reached :
thence easterly along the water-shed separating
the waters flowing into the Congo from those
flowing into the Shari, and continuing east along
the water-parting between the waters of the
Congo and those of the Nile, and southerly and
easterly along the water-shed between the waters
flowing into the Tanganika and those flowing
into the affluents of Lake Victoria, and still cling-
ing to the water-shed to the east of the Tanganika
southerly until the water-parting between the

waters flowing into the Zambesi and those flowing into the Congo is reached ; thence along that
water-shed westerly until the head-waters of the
main tributary of the Kiva is reached, whence
the line runs along the left bank of the Kiva to
7° 50' south latitude ; thence straight to the Loge
River, and thence along the left bank of that
river westerly to the Atlantic Ocean.   By this
delineation you will have comprised the geographical or commerical basin and its present commercial delta."   These were substantially the
boundaries agreed on by the Berlin Conference as
the limits of the Congo Free State.

The principal commercial product of the Upper
Congo is ivory, and it will probably take several
generations to exhaust the supply.   Next in
importance are palm oil, rubber, orchilla, camwood,
nutmegs, gum-copal, and wild coffee—all in
practically unlimited quantities.   In the lake
region are gold, silver, copper, and iron deposits
—the two latter of surpassing richness.   Bananas,
oranges, and every kind of semi-tropical vegetable

product, as well as many of those of temperate zones, thrive amazingly. Spices and gums are indigenous, and the timber will repay the most expensive transportation. The rich river bottoms and the ancient lake basins yield marvelous crops of rice and grain ; while there is pasturage for many million head of cattle.

The area of the Congo Basin proper was thus divided by the Berlin Conference :

	Sq. M.	Pop.
French Territory	62,400	2,121,600
Portuguese "	30,700	276,300
Unclaimed " . . .	349,700	6,910,000
Free State of the Congo .	1,065,200	42,608,000
	1,508,000	51,886,000

The total area of the Congo Free State is 2,400,000 square miles, of which France possesses 257,000 square miles, Portugal 741,343 square miles,, and Great Britain 5,056,000,000 acres.

European trade with the Congo country has

increased very rapidly within the last half decade. Exports and imports now amount to many millions of dollars annually. In 1882 the annual exports from Liverpool were computed at $5,000,000 in value. At present nearly the whole of the rich Congo trade is controlled by two Liverpool companies, one Paris company, one Hamburg firm, and a Rotterdam house.

Finis coronat opus are the appropriate closing words of Stanley's thrilling narrative of work and exploration on the Congo. The superstructure of a new equatorial empire had been laid, and yet the only self-gratulation permitted the builder was the modest expression of the belief that his royal patron was satisfied (as well he might be) with the manner in which his intentions had been consummated ! Nevertheless, we must not allow ourselves to be borne away on a wave-crest of enthusiasm by the bright horoscope predicted for the empire carved out by these fortuitous endeavors. There yet remain many intricate problems to be solved and many weighty obstacles

to be surmounted ere the roseate dawn of civilization shall illumine the night of the Dark Continent. But scant assistance can be expected from
its aboriginal peoples, except as they are dominated and directed by European brain and brawn—
doubtless these children of the forest would
infinitely prefer to be left unmolested and enshrouded in their centuries-old Cimmerian gloom
and ignorance. But *Capital* is ever alert for a
new field for conquest, and the reclamation of
Africa to *Commerce* and *Christianity* is simply a
question of years. Be this result speedy or tardy,
humanity must unite in according a large meed
of praise to the men whose philanthropy and
fortitude rent the veil of mystery and doubt
which so long enshrouded Congo Land.

CHAPTER V.

EMIN BEY AND THE EQUATORIAL PROVINCES.

We must now suspend the regular course of our narrative to glance for a few pages at the history of the man who was the immediate cause of Stanley's last journey into the wilds of Africa, and incidentally to acquaint ourselves with the great empire known as the Equatorial Province.

In February, 1888, an important volume was published in Germany of the letters and journals of Emin Pasha during the whole period of his administration of the Equatorial Provinces. This volume was translated into English, and a perusal of its pages shows us how great a man Emin Pasha really is : his extraordinary gifts as a scholar and a scientific investigator, his powers of administration, his conscientiousness, his faithfulness, and his marvelous unselfishness. The mantle of Gordon had indeed fallen on an heroic lieutenant. We cannot follow him in the various journeys he made throughout the length and breadth of his province, nor note the scientific data he was able to collect and register ; whenever he was free from administrative cares—on the march, in camp, or at his headquarters—he devoted his time to scientific research. In whatever character we view him, we learn to admire his genius, earnestness and sincerity.

Emin Pasha was born in Oppeln, in the Prussian province of Silesia, on 28th March, 1840. His real name is Edward Schnitzer.

He is of Hebrew parentage. His father died when Edward was still in swaddling clothes, and his mother then removed to Neisse. At fifteen Edward entered college at Neisse, where he carried off nearly all the prizes during his term. His close application to study almost cost him his eyesight, however, and his physician ordered him to desist from reading and writing for at least a year. He obeyed, and his eyesight became some-

what restored. He then visited the universities
of Breslau, Berlin and Konigsberg, studying
medicine and paying particular attention to bot-
any. The latter became a hobby with him. From
its study came the desire to visit strange lands,
and especially tropical climates, where unknown
plants and trees were to be found. He made the
acquaintance of Ismail Pasha while the latter was
traveling in Germany.

After Ismail Pasha's death, Emin married his
widow, a Grecian woman of great beauty and
talents.

He entered the Egyptian service in 1876, and
was sent as chief medical officer to the Equatorial
Provinces. Gordon Pasha, who was then governor of the Equatorial Provinces, sent him on
tours of inspection through the districts that had
been annexed to Egypt, and employed him on
several diplomatic missions. Subsequently, in
1878, a few months after, Gordon was made Governor-General of the region.

Gordon, on his retirement, left the Equatorial

Provinces in a fairly satisfactory state. Colonels Prout and Mason, who at first succeeded him, remained only a short time ; and the native gov· ernors who were then appointed in a few months reversed all the beneficial effects of Gordon's rule ; so that when Emin took up the reins of govern- ment, the province was in a very bad state. But he threw himself into his work with a brave heart. In order to sink his Frankish origin and gain "an unhampered entrance into the Mohammedan world," he had previously assumed the Turkish name of Emin—" the faithful ; " he is, however, a Turk in name only—a fact that does not appear to be sufficiently well known in this country. "Don't be afraid ; " says Emin, in a letter to his sister ; " I have only adopted the name ; I have not become a Turk." He rapidly introduced law and order, extended his province by peaceful negotiations with native chiefs, established stations and a weekly post, made roads, cultivated the soil, and, in a word, built up an independent civilized state out of the ruins of a broken pro-

vince.   Instead of his finances showing a yearly
deficit, he was able, by the end of 1882, to return
a handsome surplus to Khartoum, after paying
his own way.   With what patient and honest
labor he accomplished this result will in time
become a matter of history.   He was met at every
turn by opposition from his corrupt Egyptian
colleagues and subordinates ; his applications to
the central government at Khartoum were either
unheeded or rejected—at the best, it was months,
sometimes years, before they were answered.
What wonder that he cried, "No progress is
possible until the Equatorial Provinces are separated from the central government at Khartoum !"
It was able to stand on its own legs, but its
demoralized guardians weighed it down.

Then came the insurrection in the Soudan.
Lupton Bey, the governor of the Bahr-el-Ghazel
province, was rapidly overwhelmed ; he himself
was taken prisoner to Khartoum, where he is still
supposed to be.   But Emin, although he was
obliged to withdraw his garrisons and intrench

himself in his more southerly stations, made a brave and successful stand against the Emir Keremallah and the Mahdi's followers. Emin's letters and journals at this dark period of events in the Soudan are most important ; they add to the consensus of opinion that is rapidly gaining ground that the insurrection of the Mahdists, and its rapid success, was the direct result of Egyptian misrule and corruption. Had Gordon or Emin been in Khartoum at the time of the outbreak, they could have crushed the insurrection with a handful of loyal troops.

Surrounded by enemies on all sides, his own people disaffected, and hard pushed to find the means of existence, Emin Pasha still held loyally to his post, and refused the escape offered to him.

The Colonel H. G. Prout, just referred to, is known in the Soudan by the Oriental title of Baroud Bey. He was with Gordon, and later with Emin, and from an article from his pen in a late number of *Scribner's Magazine*, the following facts are condensed :

From where the Nile leaves the Victoria Nyanza to the Damietta mouth in the Mediterranean is
a little over thirty degrees of latitude. The
distance, in a straight line, is 2,137 miles. As the
Nile runs it is about 3,300 miles.

In this 3,300 miles is found a great diversity of
climate, topography, and people. That region is
the most important part of what has been known
since 1869 as the Provinces of the Equator (El
Gahat El Khat El Istiwa). It is the region to
which the authority of the Khedive was first
carried in 1869 by Sir Samuel Baker; where
Gordon did the best of his African work from
1874 to 1876; and where Emin was governor-
general for twelve years.

For the first five or six hundred miles of its
course, from the Victoria Nyanza to a point somewhere north of Lado, the Nile is known to the
Arabs as the Bahr-el-Gebel, the River of the
Mountains. This is the most beautiful part of the
river. The country is diversified with mountains
and forests, green hillsides and bright brooks.

For stretches of many miles the river is broad and slow. In other parts are wooded islands and foaming rapids. About half-way between the Victoria Nyanza and Lado the Nile flows through the northern end of the Albert Nyanza. About twenty-five miles above the Albert Lake are the Murchison Falls. Below the lake, for more than one hundred miles, the stream is broad and placid, traversing a comparatively level country and always navigable for vessels drawing four or five feet. In this part of its course, about forty miles below the Albert Lake, it passes Wadelai, the headquarters of Emin's government.

All the country of the Bahr-el-Gebel is habitable, and much of it is quite thickly peopled. There are regions, particularly in the country of the Moogi, some seventy-five miles south of Lado where the straw huts of the negroes shine on the grassy slopes for miles like one continuous village. Then there are other regions where a village will not be seen in a two days' march.

From some indefinite line north of Lado, but

not far north of it, to Khartoum, what we know
as the Nile is called by the Arabs El Bahr-el-Abiat,
the White Nile. Going north from Lado, the
forests and hills gradually disappear, and finally
even the banks of the river are lost, and from
about the seventh degree of latitude until after the
mouth of the Sobat is passed—over three hundred
miles, as the river runs—its course lies through a
most heart-breaking land. The desert is cheerful
compared with the vast swamps of the White
Nile. The boundaries of the swamp region are
not accurately known, but Baroud Bey estimates
the area roughly at twenty-five thousand square
miles. An occasional hillock breaks the monotony
of level marsh, and here and there a solitary tree
is a landmark for many miles. As one sails
through the flat wilderness of papyrus and tall
grasses there is no other sign of life than an occasional aquatic bird, or, more rarely, a hippopota-
mus, and clouds of ravenous mosquitoes. Gordon,
whose experience had covered many lands, said

that the mosquitoes here were worse even than at the mouth of the Danube.

Throughout this three hundred miles the stream is extremely crooked. It is one of the discouraging features of the journey that after hours of sailing one appears to come round again to the same place from which he started. It is in this part of the White Nile that, from time to time, forms the " sudd," that vegetable barrier which completely closes the river to navigation.

The northern frontier of the Provinces of the Equator was, in Gordon's time, marked by the reach of the Nile running from the mouth of the Gazelle River (Bahr-el Ghazal) easterly to the Sobat, and the latter stream lay within his government. In about this latitude the character of the country changes. The swamps give place to rolling steppes, and in the Shillock country, from the bend of the Nile to Fashoda, the land adjacent to the river is very thickly peopled. Farther north the Bedouin tribes have encroached upon the country of the negroes, and the slave-traders

have scattered the blacks and driven them south
or to the interior, and villages are rarely seen.
The grassy steppes, with occasional forests, continue to about the latitude of Khartoum and then
gradually give place to the desert. Great areas of
absolute desert are not found, however, until we
come considerably farther north. From the
Sobat to the Blue Nile, some four hundred miles,
there are no affluents other than brooks, carrying
the drainage of small areas in the rainy season,
and dry most of the year. In truth it may be
said that the Nile receives no tributary from the
west in the last two thousand miles of its course.

The Nile is the one overwhelming physical fact
of the whole Egyptian empire. It is the highway
from province to province, from the capital to the
equator. It made and sustains the best part of
Egypt and the Equatorial Provinces.

The first people met south of the Sobat are the
Nouer. Then comes the great tribe of the Dinka
These two tribes cover a great territory, and
have furnished to the Arabs a vast number of

slaves. The regular regiments of the Khedive in the Soudan were largely made up of Dinka slaves. South of the Dinkas, beginning about latitude 6°, is the Shir tribe, said by Emin to be a division of the Baris. The Bari tribe, with many subdivisions, occupies about two degrees of latitude, and then come the Madi, the Shooli, the Lango, and finally the powerful Wanyoro and Waganda, who people the countries of Unyoro and Uganda, immediately south of the Provinces of the Equator. All of these people are heathens, with the most rudimentary notions of religion. They have their coojoors or magicians, who are their only priests, and to whom are attributed various superhuman powers. While the other men wear no covering, the coojoor usually has a skin of some kind hanging down his back. He wears curious charms and amulets, and frequently carries a gourd rattle, or a horn to blow upon. He often carries a horn filled with dust, or with various odds and ends, which is supposed to have magical virtues. By his native craft he keeps alive the faith of the people in his magic. He controls the weather, and sometimes the fate of war. He is, of course, the physician, and whether his patient be a cow or a man, the result is probably more favorable than it would be if his pharmacopœia were larger. The treatment, so far as the duties of the physician go, is ordinarily by dances and incantations on his part.

The rain-maker is often a chief and ruler as well, but even then his calling is not always a comfortable one. Sometimes, if the crops suffer too much for want of rain, he gets killed.

All of the tribes are village people, and not nomadic. They live in huts made with a frame of light sticks thatched with straw. These are usually cylindrical to a height of three or four feet, with a high conical roof. This is the universal type of the "tokel" throughout the Soudan, far north of the negro country. Of course it varies considerably among the negro tribes of the south, often being nothing but a low hemisphere, and sometimes having the roof projecting and supported by posts to form a low veranda around the whole structure. In and about the villages are usually numerous "googas" for storing grain. These are cylindrical struc-tures made of straw wattled in light frames, and daubed inside and out with clay. They stand a few feet from the ground, on three or four posts, and have a cover of thatch. Around the village is often, and among the more warlike tribes usually, a hedge of thorns, which is called by the Arabs a zereba. Against an enemy armed only with spears and bows and arrows, this is a very efficient fortification. A high hedge of the *Euphorbia candelabra* is often seen instead of the thorny zereba.

Most of the negroes of the upper Nile breed cattle, and some of them have great herds. These are ordinarily driven at night into zerebas near the villages and guarded. Where the mos-quitoes are very troublesome fires are lighted in the cattle-yards, and a dense smoke is kept up all night. The watchmen often sleep in the ashes, and turn out in the morning a fine iron gray. When one goes up the Bahr-el-Gebel, soon after he passes the swamp region, he will be startled, if it is his first journey, by the sudden appearance on the bank of the stream of a group of these gray negroes. Each one carries a spear, and probably he stands on his left foot with the hollow of the right foot against the inside of the left knee. His balance is kept by the spear, which is held upright in the right hand, the butt resting on the ground. Very likely each man has stuck in his hair two short feathers, one standing straight up on each side of his head. The traveler naturally expects to see black negroes, but gray ones he is not prepared for. These are hardly any more fantastic, however, than the bright red ones whom he will meet soon after. It is much the fashion with many of the tribes to color the whole body with red ochre, or any other convenient coloring-matter, mixed with grease. Among the Madi it is not uncommon to see a man with red legs and a black body, or the reverse ; or perhaps only his head and arms will be painted. Of course it is well known that the practice of greasing the body is ancient, and still very common in hot countries. In the Egyptian Soudan, far north of Khartoum, castor oil is made and largely used for this purpose.

With very few exceptions the men, boys, and girls from the Sobat, as far south as Unyoro, are seen in the natural state. The men wear rings around their arms, ankles, and necks, made of iron, copper, ivory, rhinoceros' hide, or serpent's skin. Tattooing and painting the face or body are little practiced, except the broad style of treatment of large surfaces in red before mentioned. In some of the tribes the men insert long pieces of quartz or of glass in the lower lip ; but such mutilations are by no means universal, and are more frequent among the women. Many of the Bari and Madi men carry about a small stool, which is hung to the left arm by a thong, and is almost an article of dress. This stool is perhaps four by eight inches on top, and four or

five inches high.   The top and the four legs are
all worked out of one piece of wood.   Beads are
worn by both sexes as necklaces, armlets, girdles,
or in other ways.

The costume and ornaments of the women do
not differ greatly from those of the men.   Invariably, however, or almost invariably, they
wear a small apron, or what is considered its
equivalent, in a bunch of green leaves.   This apron
may be made of a strip of cotton, or of strings
twisted from the bark of trees, or spun from
wool.   Sometimes iron beads made by native
smiths are woven in with the bast or woolen
strings.   Among various tribes it is the custom
for married women to wear a tail.   This is made
of loose strings, perhaps two feet long, thinner
and shorter than a horse's tail, but still quite a
substantial brush.   There is no other article of
dress or ornament so grotesque and perpetually
amusing as this appendage.   It seems to grow
naturally from the person, and when the wearer
is in lively motion her flaunting tail is most

expressive.   This custom explains at once the ancient legends of people with tails, which are still current all over Africa.

Throughout the great area included in the Equatorial Provinces the tribes are all finer people than the West Coast negro whom we see in America.   The head is higher, the face less prognathous, the features more agreeable, and the limbs more symmetrical, and muscled well down to the extremities.   The long heel and crooked shin which we consider characteristic of the true negro, do not belong to the negro of the upper Nile.

All of these people are armed with spears, and many of them carry bows and arrows as well. Shields are by no means universal.   Such of the tribes in the immediate vicinity of the Nile as carry no shields seem to dread the shields of the Makraka warriors from the west, the occasional allies of the troops of the Provinces, quite as much as they fear their fierce courage and reputed cannibalism.   The arrows particularly are

often fiendishly contrived to lacerate terribly, and
to be withdrawn only by free cutting. Poisoned
spears and arrows are also used.

Cattle are the most valuable property. They
are not killed for food, but the milk is used.
Stealing other people's herds and keeping one's own
from being stolen are constant cares. Cattle raids
are the most frequent causes of fights between
tribes. For many years the slave-traders have
allied themselves with one chief after another to
attack his neighbors. When the raiders are successful the women and children are carried off for
slaves, the cattle for barter and to feed the slave-
trader's stations, and the ivory to be sent to the
Khartoum market. This predatory warfare goes
on constantly in the regions much frequented by
the Arab slave-traders. In other regions it is less
general.

Beans of two or three kinds, tobacco, sesame,
and several other crops are grown to a greater or
less extent in all the country south of latitude 6°
N. Poultry, the common barnyard fowl, is found

very commonly in all the villages. A few sheep and goats are also kept. The grain crop furnishes much the most important part of the food of the people. Milk, poultry, the vegetables already mentioned, and such game as they manage to secure, supply the rest; although the white ant, which can hardly be called game or poultry, should not be forgotten. Throughout great regions these insects are eaten at certain seasons of the year. They are collected at night by people who light fires near the ant-hills, to attract the males, which swarm out and are gathered up and roasted and stored away for a time or are eaten raw.

The great quantity of game, small and large, in all the upper Nile country, is sufficient evidence that the natives are but moderately good hunters. Elephants are found everywhere in the country of which we write, but their numbers vary in different regions. There are not many of them left just about Lado and Gondokoro, although in Gordon's time a small herd swam the river one

night at that place, climbed the steep bank in front
of his house, and charged through the enclosure,
overturning banana trees and huts, and making
considerable excitement.   Wild boars are occasionally met with.   Gordon killed one with a
revolver as it was crossing the trail by which he
was traveling from station to station.   They are
not very common.   Lions, leopards, cheetah cats,
giraffes, and several other varieties of antelopes,
are all found in greater or less numbers in many
parts of the Provinces.   Hippopotamuses and
crocodiles abound everywhere in the White Nile
and Bahr-el-Gebel.   Crocodiles frequent the same
locality, having found it a good hunting-ground.

The country and the people here briefly
described were suddenly brought to the knowledge of the civilized world by Speke; Grant, and
Baker, from twenty to twenty-five years ago.
Before that time but little was known about them
except to the traders of Khartoum, and even they
had but very inaccurate notions of much of the
country.   Fortunes were made, however, in the

slave and ivory trade with those regions. Ismail
Pasha, the fifth viceroy of Egypt, and the first to
bear the title of Khedive, succeeded to the rule in
1863, at the age of thirty-three. He is the son of
Ibrahim, and the grandson of the great Mohammed Ali. He and his father and grandfather
were not only the ablest men of their dynasty,
but would have been men of great ability and
power in any time and place. There is no doubt
that Ismail's ambition was to establish a great
Nile empire, and to make it independent of
Turkey. There is little doubt that he would have
succeeded in getting his independence, as Mohammed Ali and Ibrahim would have done before
him, if the European Powers had not prevented it. In the development of his ambitious
projects Ismail undertook the subjugation of the
countries in the upper Nile basin, and in 1876 his
forces conquered Darfour. Some years before
this, Ismail had turned his attention to the White
Nile, and in 1869 he placed Sir Samuel White
Baker in command of a great expedition, "organ-

ized to subdue to our authority the countries
situated to the south of Gondokoro." Other
specified objects of this expedition were to sup-
press the slave trade, to introduce legitimate
commerce, and to open to navigation the great
lakes of the equator.

In February, 1874, Gordon arrived in Cairo to
take command of the Equatorial Provinces.
He was then forty-one years old, a colonel of
Royal Engineers in the English army, and had
made his name immortal as "Chinese Gordon."
Although he was already a man of high distinction, and had come to take a position of great
power and some honor, nothing could be simpler
or less ostentatious than his appearance and
manners. He was rather under than over
medium height, of well-proportioned figure, by no
means heavy, but muscular and vigorous in all
his movements. His hair was brown, and curled
rather closely. His complexion was ruddy. He
wore a short mustache and small whiskers, and
shaved as carefully when he was in the heart of

Africa as when he was in London. His mouth was resolute, but full of humor. His smile was quick, and his whole expression was kind, bright, and ready, but absolutely self-reliant. Only a dull person could fail to see that here was a man who had nothing to ask or to fear. His most striking feature was his eyes. These were bright blue, and the blue and white were of that pure unclouded quality that one sees only in the eyes of a baby. Only a baby's eyes could be so direct and sincere. You felt that they looked right into your soul and laid bare your motives.

He reached Khartoum March 14th, left there March 22nd, and April 16th was at Gondokoro. October 6, 1876, two years and a-half later, he left Lado finally and forever. The work done in those two and a half years has been briefly and adequately told by various writers. Much the best account of it is to be found in Gordon's letters, and on them no one who wishes to tell the story can improve.

When Gordon reached his Province he found

three stations occupied — Gondokoro ; Fatiko, some one hundred and sixty miles south ; and Foweira, about seventy miles farther south. When he gave up the government he had a chain of stations established from Lado to Mrooli in the south, three hundred and sixty miles, at easy stages. Communication between all of these stations was regular, and between those on the upper Nile it was safe and frequent. Generally one man could go from station to station with no risk. From one end to the other of the Provinces there was peace with the negroes. Ferries had been established at crossings of the larger streams, and at one or two points on the Nile. Regular communication was kept up with Khartoum, and wood stations for the steamers were established at convenient intervals. The journey could be made easily in sixteen days up and eight days down. A twin-screw steamer and two steel life-boats had been transported to Dufili, erected there, and were available for communication with the Albert Lake and the stations above. Another steamer had been hauled up to Moogi and taken to pieces, and the sections were lying there ready for transportation to Dufili or elsewhere. It was perfectly practicable to assemble several thousand porters, for this or other work, on short notice. The soldiers in the garrisons were paid, clothed, and fed with tolerable regularity, and were subordinate and generally contented. The debt of the Provinces was being paid off by the surplus revenue from the sale of ivory. Above all, the chiefs and natives throughout the whole land knew Gordon, and feared him and trusted him, so far as a savage can trust any one.

This is a very brief statement of what Gordon had done ; and he had done it alone.

Death, disease, and the process of eliminating the tricky and the worthless, shortly left the Provinces under Gordon with a *personnel* which remained practically unchanged under Emin.

The legacy which Gordon left for his successor was to keep the frontiers from the encroachment of the Soudan government ; to maintain the

discipline and order already established ; to improve the routes of communication ; to introduce
some other means of land transportation than
porters ; to solidify and extend the position of the
Provinces to the west, and to bring King Kaba
Rega, of Unyoro, and King Mtesa, of Uganda,
into such a position of acknowledged dependence,
that trade, instead of going to Zanzibar, would be
turned down the Nile. It was not proposed to
annex these countries, but to convince their
rulers that they would be annexed if they did not
behave themselves. The first step was to get a
steamer afloat on the Nile above Foweira.
From the Albert Nyanza to that point the river
is not navigable. At Moogi was lying a steamer
ninety feet long, of about twenty tons. The
engine and boiler were carried on the heads of
men. In this work over two thousand men were
employed. Many of them were from the surrounding country, and a valuable contingent
came from the Makraka country in the west.
The difficulty in this part of the work was simply

in getting and keeping the porters. The boiler was a harder problem. This must be transported entire, and one water-course of considerable size must be crossed. The others could be headed, or crossed where they were very small, by keeping well up on the slopes. The boiler was mounted on skids, or runners, made of tree trunks, and hauled by a couple of hundred men. These fellows learned to stop and start at the sound of a bugle, but a coojoor was a necessary assistant. He marched by the boiler, and when the starting signal sounded he threw dust in the air, blew a blast on a horn, and beat the boiler vigorously with a stick, and away went the procession on the wings of magic. This steamer was afterward erected at Dufili, and was for years regularly running there in Emin's service.

In 1878 Emin was made Governor-General of the Provinces of the Equator. Then came the Mahdi's rebellion, which so entirely shut Emin off from the Soudan that for months he knew less of what was going on there than was known

in the United States. His only communication
with the outside world was by infrequent letters
through Zanzibar. The Mahdi's men threatened
Emin in his own provinces. He withdrew to
Wadelai, Lado and the lower stations being open
to attack by parties coming up the river. His
Danagla in the outlying stations revolted and
gave in their allegiance to the Mahdi. The
negroes about Lado and farther north, the Bari
and Dinka, who had received from Gordon and
Emin only the kindest treatment, and had been
relieved by them from the scourge of the slavers,
repeatedly attacked his garrisons at Lado and
Rejaf. The minds of his officers and men were
filled with fear and confusion. For a long time
they refused to believe that Egypt had lost the
Soudan. Their isolation made it impossible to
replenish their stock of ammunition and cloth,
but they did not suffer for food, and accumulated
a vast store of ivory, which was perforce left
behind when Emin and Stanley took up the
march for the coast.

CHAPTER VI.

STANLEY TO THE RESCUE.

Up to within two years ago the name of Emin
Pasha was unfamiliar to the public. He, however, was not without friends in Europe, and his
scientific work had for many years enriched the
transactions of several societies ; but for a period
of about three years no communication had been
received from him : he was entirely cut off from
intercourse with the outer world. Dr. Robert W.
Felkin, of Edinburgh, was the first to hear of his
critical position. In the letters he received from
Emin an urgent appeal for help was made.
Emin, according to these letters, was almost
entirely without resources. The Royal Scottish
Geographical society at once took the matter up,
and petitioned the English Goverment either to
send out an expedition for his relief or to assist

the society in despatching one. The society, moreover, took every step to give publicity to the position of Emin Pasha ; and in a very short space of time the name and the deeds of Emin were world-known. In the meantime a private syndicate of gentlemen in London obtained the consent and assistance of the Goverment to organize an expedition for the relief of Emin Pasha, and the grant of the Egyptian Government was placed at its disposal. Stanley was chosen as the leader of the expedition, and its organization was rapidly completed.

The question of routes was for some time a matter of public debate. The Royal Scottish Geographical Society at once recommended an East Coast route as the best and surest, and their recommendation received the support of all experts. Stanley himself was inclined to prefer an East Coast route ; but his better judgment—or perhaps his peculiar position—was overruled by the King of the Belgians, who offered to place all the resources of the Congo Independent State at his disposal if the expedition went by way of the Congo. King Leopold's wish was, of course, equivalent to a command, and, at the last moment (in spite of the delay it occasioned), the Congo route was definitely selected.

The story of Stanley's last journey across the Dark Continent is one of the most thrilling ever penned, and Stanley alone has the right to tell it to the world in full. But we can give a résumé of his journeyings, mostly compiled from his own letters, and from the reports that have reached us from the Congo and the Aruwimi, that will show the magnificence of the work accomplished and the dangers which the gallant explorer passed through.

The journey just brought successfully to a conclusion, after nearly three years' absence from civilization, will rank in many ways as the greatest ever made by any African explorer. Time and time again Stanley was reported dead. Deserters from his little army brought to the posts on the Congo, and slave-dealers carried to

Zanzibar, the rumors that he had been betrayed by his men and slain. But, as usual with him, he turned up again all right.

For months the world was left in doubt as to where he was, and for months he was supposed to be that mysterious personage known to modern African history as "the White Pasha," who, with a few hundred followers, was forcing his way northward though the Bahr-el-Ghazel country and fighting off the advance forces of the Mahdi's hordes. The mystery of "the White Pasha" is still unsolved, and doubtless Stanley brings with him the solution, since it appears to be certain that after joining forces with Emin he fought several hard battles with the Mahdi and captured one of the Prophet's most treasured standards. One of the most persistent rumors was to the effect that both he and Emin had been taken prisoners at Wadelai. For two years, in fact, Stanley's probable fate was a subject that interested the entire civilized world.

It was while just beginning a lecture tour in

this country in the winter of 1886 that Stanley received the imperative summons to seek out Emin Bey, supply him with ammunition and necessaries, and, if required, to bring him back. At the time we write of, it was known that the Mahdists were pressing Emin hard ; that he was struggling heroically against odds, refusing to abandon his post, as he might easily have done, and that to hold his own he must have aid. Stanley at once accepted the task assigned him, proceeded to Cairo, where he was told by the Khedive that Emin could expect no aid from the Egyptain Government, and hurried on to Zanzibar, on the East Coast, where he organized his expedition and chose his course. Rejecting three possible routes from the East Coast into the interior (one being that by which he returned), he sailed around the Cape of Good Hope to the West Coast, to ascend the Congo River, passing through the great country which his former journeys had opened up to civilization, pushing eastward from Stanley Falls. This course carried

him into the Aruwimi River country, through
dense forests and hitherto unexplored country.
It is thought by many that it was this very fact,
and the desire of adding new territory to the map
of known Africa, which induced the adoption of
this route. The reason given, however, was that
the Aruwimi River would afford water convey-
ance for his heavy baggage for a great distance.

Before proceeding to the west coast Stanley
engaged a body of trained natives as porters at
Zanzibar ; and there, too, he made an agreement
with the great slave-trading chief, Tippoo Tib, on
whom he conferred the dignity of Governor of
Stanley Falls, securing a promise of his assistance
to the expedition. The Congo route would have
been quite impractical, however, with such a mass
of stores as Stanley had to convey, but for the help
of the King of the Belgians, who, as sovereign of
the Free State, placed the whole resources of
that body at the disposal of the expedition, and
gave them use of the steam vessels which kept up
communication on the river. This example was

followed by the various missionary societies, and by the American Trading Company under Mr. Sandford, who also lent their vessel, the *Florida*, although at the time without engines, to be used as a cargo boat. The expedition left Zanzibar in the end 'of February, 1887, landing at the mouth of the Congo on the 18th of March. Stanley had about seven hundred men with him, and was some one thousand two hundred and fifty miles from the mouth of the Aruwimi, where his overland march was to begin.

The expedition disembarked from the steamship *Madeira*, at Banana Point, March 18, and left the following day in river boats, reaching Matada on the 21st. It was not until April 26th that it was enabled to leave Leopoldville, on Stanley Pool, and it was not until the second week in June that it reached the Aruwimi, much delay having been caused by defective means of transportation and a scarcity of provisions. The flotilla consisted of the steamer *Stanley*, towing the *Florida*; the *Henry Reid*, towing the *En Avant*; and the

Advance (Stanley's steel boat) and the *Peace*, towing two whale boats. The *Stanley* was then sent
back to Kouamenda to bring up Major Barttelot
and Dr. Parke's party to Bolobo. Mr. Stanley
and the main body proceeded to the Aruwimi
River, and disembarked at Yambuga village on
the 19th of June. The *Henry Reid*, with Major
Barttelot and Mr. Walker, proceeded in charge of
Tippoo Tib's party to Stanley Falls, five days'
steaming from the Aruwimi River. At Yambuga,
Stanley proposed to wait for re-enforcements,
which he had arranged that Tippoo Tib should
send him from Stanley Falls. He delayed there
several days, but Tippoo Tib failed to come up to
his contract. It is possible that he was unable to
do so, as the natives all around the Falls were in
revolt against the Arab slave-traders, of whom he
was the chief. Stanley himself passed up the
Aruwimi as far as Yambuga without meeting
hostilities on the part of the natives, though they
fled on his approach, thinking that he was the
leader of a new slave-raiding horde. Tippoo's

supposed treachery caused some alarm for Stanley's safety at the time. It was known that he should have been able to command the principal routes from the Congo to Wadelai. He had agreed to furnish six hundred carriers at $30 a man, and he was to be paid for them out of Emin's stock of ivory, of which Dr. Junker had reported there was about seventy-five tons at Wadelai, and this Tippoo's men were to transport to the coast.

The " Tippoo Tib " above alluded to is rather a remarkable old gentleman. His real name is Hamid Ben Mohammed, his *nom de guerre* being a phonetic effort on the part of the natives. Tippoo has a pleasing way of going round in the early morning surprising peaceful villages where ivory is reported to be stored and pegging away with his rifles. The natives used to say that the sound of his gun was like " Tip, Tip, Tip," hence they called him " Tip, Tip," which Europeans rendered into the now famous Tippoo Tib. Tippoo is as wealthy as he is rapacious.

Stanley's acquaintance with these Arab slave-traders began early.   They are the curse of Equatorial Africa.

"A few years ago," says Henry Drummond, "the well-known German explorer, Captain Wissmann found himself within a few degrees of the equator, in the heart of Africa.   It was a region of great beauty and fertility, with forests and rivers, and great and many-peopled towns. The inhabitants were quiet and peaceable, and lived a life of artless simplicity and happiness. For generations they had been established there ; they grew many fruits in their gardens, and excelled in the manufacture of cloth, pottery, ironware, and wood-carving.   No Arab slaver had ever visited this country.   Within its borders the very report of a gun had never once been heard.   But as the explorer walked among the palm trees and met the kindly eyes of the country people who came to gaze upon the white man, his heart sank.   This Arcadia could not last.   He knew, from what had happened in adjacent dis-

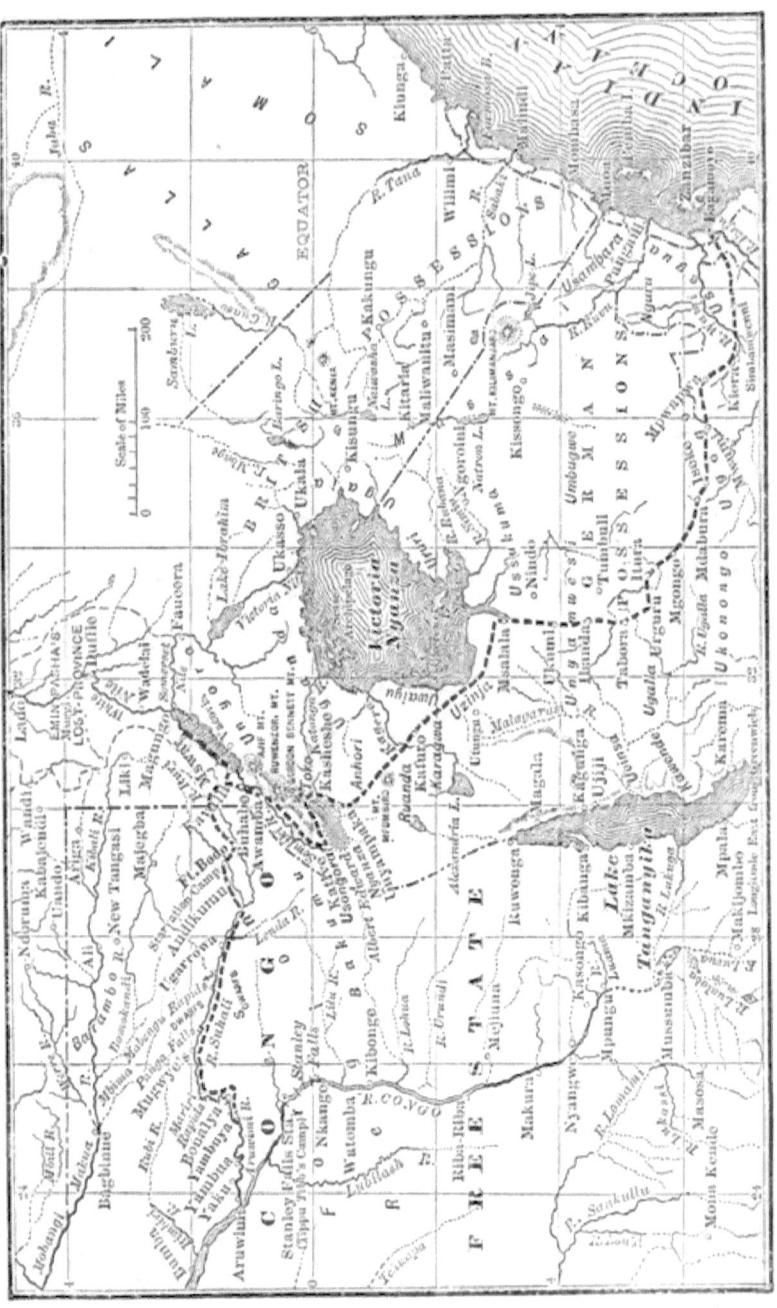

MAP SHOWING STANLEY'S ROUTE FROM THE ARUWIMI TO THE SEA, AND EMIN PASHA'S PROVINCE.

tricts, from what happens every day in Africa, that its fate was sealed."

And the sequel showed too clearly that his silent prophecy was right. Four years passed. The same traveler led his caravan once more across this sylvan country. "As we approached the villages we wondered that no one came out to receive us with rejoicings, that no merry laughter greeted our ears. We entered the deep shade of the mighty palms, and to the right and left were the clearings where our friends had stood. Tall grass had overgrown all that formerly gladdened us. The crops were destroyed ; everything was laid waste. The silence of death breathes over the lofty crowns of the palms waving in the wind. We enter, and it is in vain we look for the happy homesteads and erst peaceful scenes. A charred pole here and there, a few banana trees, are the only evidences that man once dwelt here. Bleached skulls by the road-side, and the skeletons of human hands attached to poles, tell the story of what has happened since our last visit."

Some wretched fugitives from them supplied the
missing links in the story. "People with long
white shirts and wearing cloth round their heads
(the Arabs) had been there with their chief, who
was called Tippoo Tib. He at first came to trade,
then he had stolen and carried away the women.
Those who had opposed him had been cut down
or shot, and the greater part of the natives had
fled to the ravines and forests. The Arabs had
remained in the place in force as long as there
was any chance of hunting and finally capturing
the fugitives in the woods. What they could not
utilize they had destroyed or set fire to—in a
word, everything had been laid waste. Then
they passed on. The fugitives had returned to
their former homes, and had endeavored to culti-
vate and renew their fields, and rebuild what was
possible. After three months Tippoo Tib's hordes
had again appeared, and the same scenes had
been re-enacted, and again, for a third time, three
months later. Famine and the greatest misery
had been thereby produced throughout all the

country of the Beneki. A few of the fugitives escaped to the West, but only an imperceptibly small number.

It has been truly said that, if a traveler lost the way leading from Equatorial Africa to the towns where slaves are sold, he could easily find it again by the skeletons of the negroes with which it is strewed.

Cardinal Lavigerie, as Archbishop of Algiers, knows Africa personally. As Roman Catholic Primate of Africa, he is in ceaseless communication with the missionaries of his Church in the Sahara region, the Upper Congo, and the Great Lakes from the south of Tanganika to the sources of the Nile. "Our missionaries at Tanganika write to us," he says, "that there is not a single day in which they do not see pass caravans of slaves which have been brought from afar as carriers for the ivory, or from the markets of the interior, like human cattle. Never, in any part of the known world, or in pages of its history, has there been such butchery and murder, and such contempt for human life. Already millions of human beings have thus been murdered during the last quarter of a century, but the numbers increase continually, and on the high plateaux of the interior the figures given by our missionaries surpass those given by Cameron for the slave-trade of the Zambesi and Nyassa."

Here is a leaf from Stanley's own experience, during the exploration of the Congo :

"Our guide, Yumbila, was told to question them as to what was the cause of this dismal scene, and an old man stood out and poured forth his tale of grief and woe with an exceeding volu-bility. He told of a sudden and unexpected invasion of their village by a host of leaping, yell-ing men in the darkness, who dinned their ears with murderous fusillades, slaughtering their people as they sprang out of their burning huts into the light of the flames. Not a third of the men had escaped ; the larger number of the women and children had been captured and taken away, they knew not whither. We discovered

that this horde of banditti—for in reality and
without disguise they were nothing else—was
under the leadership of several chiefs, but principally under Karema and Kibunga. They had
started sixteen months previously from Wane-
Kirundu, about thirty miles below Vinya-Njara.
For eleven months the band had been raiding successfully between the Congo and the Lubiranzi,
on the left bank. They had then undertaken to
perform the same cruel work between the Biyerre
and Wane-Kirundu. On looking at my map I find
that such a territory within the area described
would cover superficially 16,200 square geographical miles on the left bank, and 10,500 miles on the
right, all of which in statute mileage would be
equal to 34,700 square miles, just 2,000 square
miles greater than the area of Ireland, inhabited
by about one million people. The band when it
set out from Kirundu numbered three hundred
fighting men, armed with flint-locks, double-
barrelled percussion-guns, and a few breech-
loaders ; their followers, or domestic slaves and

women, doubled this force . . . Within the enclosure was a series of low sheds extending many
lines deep from the immediate edge of the clay
bank island, one hundred yards ; in length the
camp was about three hundred yards ; at the
landing-place below were fifty-four long canoes,
varying in carrying capacity. Each might convey
from ten to one hundred people. The first general
impressions are that the camp is much too densely
peopled for comfort. There are rows upon rows
of dark nakedness, relieved here and there by the
white dresses of the captors. There are lines or
groups of naked forms—upright, standing, or
moving about listlessly ; naked bodies are stretched
under the sheds in all positions ; naked legs
innumerable are seen in the perspective of prostrate sleepers ; there are countless naked children
—many mere infants—forms of boyhood and
girlhood, and occasionally a drove of absolutely
naked old women bending under a basket of fuel,
or cassava-tubers, or bananas, who are driven

through the moving groups by two or three mus-
keteers.

On paying more attention to details, I observe
that mostly all are fettered ; youths with iron
rings around their necks, through which a chain,
like one of our boat anchor-chains, is rove, securing the captives by twenties.   The children over
ten are secured by these copper rings, each ringed
leg brought together by the central ring, which
accounts for the apparent listlessness of movement I observed on first coming in presence of
this curious scene.   The mothers are secured by
shorter chains, around whom their respective
progeny of infants are grouped, hiding the cruel
iron links that fall in loops or festoons on their
mothers' breasts.   There is not an adult man cap-
tive among them.   The slave-traders admit they
have only 2,300 captives in this fold, yet they have
raided through the length and breadth of a country
larger than Ireland, bringing fire and spreading
carnage with lead and iron.   Both banks of the
river show that one hundred and eighteen villages

and forty-three districts have been devastated, out of which is only educed this scanty profit of 2,300 females and children, and about 2,000 tusks of ivory! The spears, swords, bows and the quivers of arrows show that many adults have fallen. Given that one hundred and eighteen villages were peopled by only 1,000 each, we have only a profit of two per cent. and by the time all these captives have been subjected to the accidents of the river voyage to Kirundu and Nangwé, of camp-life and its harsh miseries, to the havoc of small-pox, and the pests which miseries breed, there will only remain a scant one per cent. upon the bloody venture. They tell me, however, that the convoys already arrived at Nyangwé with slaves captured in the interior have been as great as their present band. Five expeditions have come and gone with their booty of ivory and slaves, and these five expeditions have now completely weeded the large territory described above. If each expedition has been as successful as this the slave-traders have been enabled to obtain

5,000 women and children safe to Nyangwé, Kirundu, and Vibondo, above the Stanley Falls. This 5,000 out of an annual million will be at the rate of a half per cent., or five slaves out of 1,000 people. This is poor profit out of such large waste of life, for, originally, we assume the slaves to have mustered about ten thousand in number. To obtain the 2,300 slaves out of the one hundred and eighteen villages they must have shot a round number of 2,500 people, while 1,300 men died by the wayside through scant provisions and the intensity of their hopeless wretchedness. How many are wounded and die in the forest or droop to death through an overwhelming sense of their calamities we do not know ; but if the above figures are trustworthy, then the outcome from the territory with its million of souls is 5,000 slaves, obtained at the cruel expense of 33,000 lives ! And such slaves ! They are females or young children who cannot run away, or who with youthful indifference will soon forget the terrors of their capture ! Yet each of the very smallest infants has cost the life of a father, and perhaps his three stout brothers and three grown-up daughters. An entire family of six souls have been done to death to obtain that small, feeble, useless child! These are my thoughts as I look upon the horrible scene. Every second during which I regard them the clink of fetters and chains strikes upon my ears. My eyes catch sight of that continual lifting of the hand to ease the neck in the collar, or as it displays a manacle exposed through a muscle being irritated by its weight or want of fitness. My nerves are offended with the rancid effluvium of the un-washed herds within this human kennel. The smell of other abominations annoy me in that vitiated atmosphere For how could poor people, bound and riveted together by twenties, do other-wise than wallow in filth? Only the old women are taken out to forage. They dig out the cassava tubers and search for the banana ; while the guard, with musket ready, keenly watches for the coming of the revengeful native. Not much food can be procured in this manner, and what is obtained is flung down in a heap before each gang to at once cause an unseemly scramble. Many of these poor things have been already months fettered in this manner, and their bones stand out in bold relief in the attenuated skin which hangs down in thin wrinkles and puckers."

Stanley started from Yambuga Rapids on the Aruwimi, on June 28, 1887. He had with him about three hundred men, including four English assistants. He carried a large supply of goods for Emin, and ammunition. He had a company of two hundred armed Zanzibaris, and in his portable whale-boat had a repeating Maxim gun. He expected to take a course nearly due east to the southern end of the Albert Nyanza first, in the hope that he might find Emin on one of his scientific expeditions sojourning on the lake. Before leaving Yambuga he left Major Barttelot in charge of a fortified camp there with a force of two hundred and forty-six men, with orders to wait for the arrival of Tippoo Tib's re-enforcements, and with them to follow his line of march, bringing the rest of the ammunition and stores. The tragic fate of the leaders of this camp has been too often told to need repeating here. Stanley went on, proceeding slowly, hoping that Barttelot would overtake him. One of his carriers, returning to Yambuga, reported that he had left Stanley eighteen days' march east of Yambuga, at a river flowing •north into the Aruwimi, and that all the members of the expedition were well. This information, which reported his progress up to July 15, was the last news received from the explorers for many months. Then came the rumors that disaster had overtaken the expedition.

A few deserters reached Yambuga in the following June, whose reports gave rise to numerous views of Stanley's safety. One such report read : "Several deserters from Stanley's expedition have reached Camp Yambuga. They say that after traversing the Upper Aruwimi Stanley struck into a rough, mountainous country, covered with dense forests. The natives, who were excited by reports spread by the Arabs, disputed the passage of the expedition, and there was continuous fighting. Stanley was severely wounded by an arrow. He was compelled several times to construct camps in order to repel attacks, and was obliged to use the reserve provisions that were intended for Emin Pasha. The Soudanese attached to the force had all died or disappeared. The deserters estimate that the caravan lost one-third of its men, and they say that many of those remaining were ill, including the Europeans. Stanley was encamped when the deserters left. He was surrounded by hostiles, and he was unable to *send* news to Emin Pasha or directly to Yambuga."

Before that, indeed, reports had reached the world, *via* Zanzibar, that Stanley had been massacred by natives after having been deserted by his own people. The news, however, turned out to be false. It is useless to recount all the rumors that came from Africa while the explorer was

making his way across the three or four hundred
miles of unknown territory between the Yambuga
and the Albert Nyanza, and while the world was
being startled by the news of the deaths of Bartte
lot and Jamieson and the breaking up of the
Aruwimi camp.

Finally, after months of anxious waiting, Stanley was heard from, after passing through months
of a journey overland, during which he had to
cut his way through dense forests, whose hideous
gloom almost drove him mad, and on many occasions to fight his way step by step among hostile
tribes.   Stanley's advance column followed the
left bank of the Aruwimi, as will be seen by the
chart at pages 337, 338.

On October 18, the expedition entered a settlement occupied by Kilingasongas, a Zanzibar slave,
belonging to Abed-bin-Salim, an old Arab, whose
bloody deeds are recorded in the *Congo and the
Founding of the Free State*.

At Kilingasongas', Stanley came to the country
of a powerful chief, Mazamboni. His villages

were scattered over a great extent of country so thickly that there was no other road except through his villages or fields. "From a long distance the natives sighted us and were prepared. The war cries were terrible from hill to hill, pealing across intervening valleys. People gathered by hundreds from every point; war horns and drums announced that a struggle was about to take place. Such natives as were too bold we checked with little effort. A slight skirmish ended in our capturing a cow, the first fresh beef we had tasted since we left the ocean. Night passed peacefully, both sides preparing for the morrow. On the morning of the 10th an attempt was made to open negotiations. The natives finally accepted cloth and brass rods to show King Mazamboni, and his answer was to be given next day. Meantime hostilities were suspended. The morning of the 11th of December dawned. At 8 A. M. we were startled at hearing a man proclaiming that it was Mazamboni's wish that we should be driven back from the land. The proclamation

was received in the valley around our neighborhood with deafening cheers. Their word 'Kanwana' signifies to make peace : 'Kurwana' signifies war. We were therefore in doubt, or rather
we hoped we had heard wrongly. We sent our
interpreter a little nearer to ask if it was Kanwana
or Kurwana. 'Kurwana' they responded, and to
emphasize the term fired two arrows at him,
which dissipated all doubt. Our position lay
between a lofty range of hills and a lower range.
On one side of us was a narrow valley, two
hundred and fifty yards wide ; on the other side a
valley three miles wide. East and west the valley
broadened to an extensive plain, and a higher
range of hills was lined with hundreds preparing
to descend. The broader valley was already mus-
tering its army. There was no time to lose. A
body of forty men was sent under Lieutenant
Stairs to attack the broader valley. Mr. Jephson
was sent with thirty men east. A choice body of
sharpshooters was sent to test the courage of those
descending the slope of the highest range. Lieu-

tenant Stairs pressed on, crossed a deep, narrow river in the face of the natives, and assaulted the first village and took it. The sharpshooters did their work effectively and drove the descending natives rapidly up the slope until there became a general flight. Jephson was not idle. He marched straight up the valley east, driving the people back, taking villages as we went. At 3 P. M. not a native was visible anywhere, except on one small hill a mile and a-half west. On the morning of the 12th we continued our march. During the day we had four little fights. On the 13th we marched straight east, attacked by new forces every hour till noon, when we halted for refreshments. These we successfully overcame. At 1 P. M. we resumed our march. Fifteen minutes later I cried : ' Prepare for sight of Nyanza.'

" The men murmured and doubted, and said : ' Why does master continually talk this way ? Nyanza, indeed ! Is not this a plain, and can we not see the mountains ?'

" After a four days' march ahead, at 1:30 P. M.,

the Albert Nyanza was sighted. It was now my turn to jeer and scoff at the doubters, but as I was about to ask them what they saw, so many came to kiss my hands and beg pardon that I could not say a word.

"This was my reward.

"While in England considering the best routes open to the Albert Nyanza, I thought I was very liberal in allowing myself two weeks' march to cross the forest region lying between the Congo and the grassland, but you may imagine our feelings when month after month saw us marching, tearing, ploughing, cutting through that same continuous forest. It took one hundred and sixty days before we could say, 'Thank God, we are out of the darkness at last.' At one time we were all—whites and blacks—almost 'done up.' September, October, and half of that month of November, 1887, will be specially memorable for the suffering we endured. Our officers are heartily sick of the forest, but the royal blacks, a band of one hundred and thirty, followed me once again

into the wild, trackless forest, with its hundreds
of inconveniences, to assist their comrades of the
rear column. Take a thick Scottish copse, drip-
ping with rain ; imagine this copse to be a mere
undergrowth, nourished under the impenetrable
shade of ancient trees, ranging from one hundred
to one hundred and eighty feet high ; briers and
thorns abundant, lazy creeks meandering through
the depths of the jungle, and sometimes the deep
affluent of a great river. Imagine this forest and
jungle in all stages of decay and growth—old
trees falling, leaning perilously over, fallen prostrate ; ants and insects of all kinds, sizes and
colors murmuring around, monkeys and chimpan-
zees above, queer noises of birds and animals,
crashes in the jungle as troops of elephants rush
away ; dwarfs with poisoned arrows securely hidden behind some buttress or in some dark recess ;
strong, brown-bodied aborigines with terribly
sharp spears, standing poised, still as dead
stumps ; rain pattering down on you every other
day in the year ; an impure atmosphere, with its

dread consequences, fever and dysentery ; gloom
throughout the day and darkness almost palpable
throughout the night.

"This proved an awful month to us," says
Stanley. "Not one member of our expedition,
white or black, will forget it. Our advance numbered two hundred and sixty-three souls. On
leaving Ugarrowwas, out of the three hundred
and eighty-nine we lost sixty-six men by desertion and death between Yambuga and Ugarrowwas, and had left fifty-six men sick in the Arab
station. On meeting Kilingasongas we discovered he had lost fifty-five men by starvation
and desertion. We had lived principally on wild
fruit, fungi and a large, flat, bean-shaped nut.
Slaves of Abed bin-Salim did their utmost to ruin
the expedition. They purchased rifles, ammunition, and clothing, so that when we left their
station we were beggared and our men absolutely
naked. We were so weak physically that we
were unable to carry the boat and about seventy
loads of goods. We therefore left goods and boats

at Kilingasongas under Surgeon Parke and Captain Nelson, the latter of whom was unable to march. After twelve days' march we arrived at a native settlement, called Ibwiri, between Kilingasongas and Ibwiri. Our condition had not improved.

The Arab devastation had reached within a few miles of Ibwiri, a devastation so complete that not one native hut was standing between Ugarrowwas and Ibwiri, and what had not been destroyed by slaves of Ugarrowwas and Abed-bin-Salim, the elephants destroyed and turned the whole region into a horrible wilderness. "But at Ibwiri we were beyond the utmost reach of destroyers. We were on virgin soil, in a populous region, abounding with food. Our sufferings from hunger, which began on August 31st, terminated on November 12th. Out of three hundred and eighty-nine we now only numbered one hundred and seventy-four, several having no hope of life left. A halt was ordered for the people to recuperate. Hitherto they were sceptical of what

we told them.   The suffering had been so awful,
calamities so numerous, forests so endless, apparently, that they refused to believe that by and by
we should see plains and cattle, and the Nyanza
and the white man, Emin Pasha.   We felt as
though we were dragging them along with a
chain around our necks.

"' Beyond these raiders,' said I, 'lies a country
untouched, where food is abundant and where
you will forget your miseries; so cheer up, boys,
—be men.   Press on a little faster.'

"They were deaf to our prayers and entreaties,
for, driven by hunger and suffering, they sold
their rifles and equipments for a few ears of
Indian corn, deserted with the ammunition, and
were altogether demoralized.   Perceiving that
prayers and entreaties and mild punishments
were of no avail, I then resorted to the death
penalty.   Two of the worst cases were accordingly
taken and hanged in presence of all.

"We halted thirteen days in Ibwiri and
revelled in fowls, goats, bananas, corn, sweet

potatoes, yams, beans, etc. The supplies were inexhaustible and the people glutted themselves. The result was that I had one hundred and seventy-three (one was killed by an arrow) mostly sleek and robust men when I set out for Albert Nyanza on November 24th. There were still one hundred and twenty-six miles to the lake, but with food such a distance seemed nothing. On December 1st we sighted the open country from the top of the ridge connected with Mount Pisgah—so named because it was our first view of the land of promise and plenty. December 5th we entered upon the plains, and the deadly gloomy forest was behind. After one hundred and sixty days' continuous gloom we saw the light of day shining all around, making all things beautiful. We thought we never saw grass so green or country so lovely. The men literally leaped and yelled with joy and raced with their burdens.

" This was the old spirit of former expeditions, successfully completed, and all of a sudden revived. Woe to the native aggressor whom we may meet. However powerful he may be, with such spirit, men will fling themselves like wolves on sheep, numbers not considered. It had been the eternal forest that had made abject and slavish the creatures so brutally plundered by Arab slavers."

After eighteen months of hideous suffering, of marching and countermarching, of endless waiting and constant disappointment, of disease and starvation, Stanley welcomed Emin Pasha, the ruler he had been sent to relieve, near Kavallis, a village on the Albert Nyanza, only to find his guest in new circumstances and displaying a new character. To Stanley's intense disappointment, the ruler of the Equatorial Provinces was accompanied only by some six hundred fugitives, Egyptians and Nubians, of both sexes and all ages—of whom the men were so disaffected that they laid a plot to seize Stanley's rifles, and drive him and his followers naked into the wilderness to perish. This plot was no explosion of mere murmurings.

It was carefully laid, it was favored by the mutinous chiefs at Wadelai, and it might have succeeded but for Stanley's determination and promptitude. He rose to the occasion, summoned Emin Pasha's forces to the great square, surrounded them with his armed Zanzibaris, and told them plainly that mutiny and plotting must cease, or he would extirpate them all.

As usual, under such circumstances, he was instantly saluted as their father, the plots were given up for the time, and Stanley had now no obstacle to overcome except the character of the man he had set out to rescue. Emin Pasha's irresolution was almost invincible. He pleaded inability to "desert" his followers at Wadelai, who had mutinied and imprisoned him ; but there was something more, which Stanley himself calls the fascination of the Soudan, which constantly seizes Europeans, and is probably the charm of an absolute and beneficial authority, unfettered by the galling restrictions of Europe. Emin Pasha to the last moment hoped to regain his followers

and his dominions : he evidently had only an
imperfect knowledge of his own relation to his
people ; he believed that they would leave Wadelai at his summons ; he trusted every letter he
received from a mutinous lieutenant of his own,
named Selim Bey ; and he would apparently have
waited on, vaguely hoping for a turn in affairs,
until the Mahdists descended to attack the whole
party.

   After meeting Emin Pasha, Stanley returned to
the Aruwimi, and reached Yambuga, after an
absence of thirteen months and twenty days, to
learn for himself the story of disaster, desertion
and death.   Major Barttelot had been shot by
the Manyuemas.   Jamieson had gone to Stanley
Falls, and Herbert Ward had gone to Bangala.
Stanley says that, at an officers' mess meeting, it
was proposed that his instructions should be can-
celled.   " The only one who appears to have
dissented was Mr. Bonney.   Accordingly my
personal kit, medicines, soap, candles, and provisions, were sent down the Congo as superfluities.

Thus, after making this immense personal sacrifice to relieve them and cheer them up, I find myself naked and deprived of even the necessaries of life in Africa. But, strange to say, I have kept two hats, four pairs of boots, a flannel jacket, and I propose to go back to Emin Pasha and across Africa with this truly African kit. Livingstone, poor fellow, was all in patches when I met him, but it will be the reliever himself who will be in patches this time. Fortunately, not one of my officers will envy me, for their kits are intact."

Wadelai, with the whole region of the Upper Nile and all the populous territories north of the Lakes, is now abandoned to the fanatical Mohammedan leaders following the Mahdi's standard, as the garrison refused any longer to obey Emin Pasha ; and it was with difficulty that Mounteney Jephson, whom Stanley had deputed to arrange for Emin Pasha's departure, after their meeting in April, 1888, on the shores of Lake Albert Nyanza, was able to get him away.

On emerging into civilization once more, Stanley penned the following letter to his old employer, the *New York Herald :*

"First of all, I am in perfect health and feel like a laborer of a Saturday evening returning home with his week's work done, his week's wages in his pocket and glad that to morrow is Sunday.

" Just about three years ago, while lecturing in New England, a message came from under the sea bidding me to hasten and take a commission to relieve Emin Pasha at Wadelai ; but, as people generally do with their faithful pack-horses, numbers of little trifles, odds and ends, are piled on over and above the proper burden. Twenty various little commissions were added to the principal one, each requiring due care and thought. Well, looking back over what has been accomplished, I see no reason for any heart's discontent. We can say we shirked no task, and that good-will, aided by steady effort, enabled us to complete every little job as well as circumstances permitted.

"Over and above the happy ending of our appointed duties we have not been unfortunate in geographical discoveries. The Aruwimi is now known from its source to its bourne. The great Congo forests, covering as large an area as France and the Iberian peninsula, we can now certify to be an absolute fact. The Mountains of the Moon this time, beyond the least doubt, have been located, and Ruwenzori, 'The Cloud King,' robed in eternal snow, has been seen and its flanks explored and some of its shoulders ascended; Mounts Gordon Bennett and Mackinnon cones being but giant sentries warding off the approach to the inner area of 'The Cloud King.'

"On the south-east of the range the connection between Albert Edward Nyanza and the Albert Nyanza has been discovered, and the extent of the former lake is now known for the first time. Range after range of mountains has been trav-

ersed, separated by such tracts of pasture land as
would make your cowboys out West mad with
envy.

"And right under the burning equator we
have fed on blackberries and bilberries and
quenched our thirst with crystal water fresh
from snow beds. We have also been able to add
nearly six thousand square miles of water to
Victoria Nyanza.

"Our naturalist will expatiate upon the new
species of animals, birds, and plants he has discovered. Our surgeon will tell what he knows of
the climate and its amenities. It will take us all
we know how to say what new store of knowledge has been gathered from this unexpected
field of discoveries.

"I always suspected that in the central regions
between the equatorial lakes something worth
seeing would be found, but I was not prepared
for such a harvest of new facts.

"This has certainly been the most extraordinary expedition I have ever led into Africa. A

veritable divinity seems to have hedged us while we journeyed. I say it with all reverence. It has impelled us whither it would, effected its own will, but nevertheless guided and protected us.

"What can you make of this, for instance? On August 17, 1887, all the officers of the rear column are united at Yambuga. They have my letter of instructions before them, but instead of preparing for the morrow's march, to follow our tracks, they decide to wait at Yambuga, which decision initiates the most awful season any community of men ever endured in Africa or elsewhere.

"The results are that three-quarters of their force die of slow poison. Their commander is murdered and the second officer dies soon after of sickness and grief. Another officer is wasted to a skeleton and obliged to return home. A fourth is sent to wander aimlessly up and down the Congo, and the survivor is found in such a fearful pesthole that we dare not describe its horrors.

"On the same date, one hundred and fifty

miles away, the officer of the day leads three
hundred and thirty-three men of the advanced
column into the bush, loses the path and all con-
sciousness of his whereabouts, and every step he
takes only leads him further astray. His people
become frantic ; his white companions, vexed
and irritated by the sense of the evil around
them, cannot devise any expedient to relieve him.
They are surrounded by cannibals, and poison-
dipped arrows thin their number.

"Meantime, I, in command of the river
column, anxiously searching up and down the
river in four different directions ; through forests
my scouts are seeking for them, but not until
the sixth day was I successful in finding them.

"Taking the same month and date in 1888, a
year later, on August 17, I listen, horror struck,
to the last surviving officer of the rear column at
Banalya, and am told of nothing but death and
disaster, disaster and death, death and disaster.
I see nothing but horrible forms of men smitten
with disease, bloated, disfigured and scarred ;

while the scene in the camp, infamous for the murder of poor Barttelot, barely four weeks before, is simply sickening.

"On the same day, six hundred miles west of this camp, Jamieson, worn out with fatigue, sickness and sorrow, breathes his last. On the next day, August 18, six hundred miles east, Emin Pasha and my officer, Jephson, are suddenly surrounded by infuriate rebels, who menace them with loaded rifles and instant death, but fortunately they relent and only make them prisoners, to be delivered to the Mahdists. Having saved Bonny out of the jaws of death we arrive a second time at Albert Nyanza, to find Emin Pasha and Jephson prisoners in daily expectation of their doom.

"Jephson's own letters will describe his anxiety. Not until both were in my camp and the Egyptian fugitives under our protection did I begin to see that I was only carrying out a higher plan than mine. My own designs were constantly frustrated by unhappy circumstances. I endeav-

ored to steer my courseas direct as possible, but
there was an unaccountable influence at the helm.
I gave as much good-will to my duties as the
strictest honor would compel. My faith that the
purity of my motive deserved success was firm,
but I have been conscious that the issues of every
effort were in other hands.

"Not one officer who was with me will forget
the miseries he has endured, yet every one that
started from his home destined to march with the
advance column and share its wonderful adventures is here to-day safe, sound and well.

" This is not due to me. Lieutenant Stairs was
pierced with a poisoned arrow like others, but
others died and he lives. The poison tip came out
from under his heart eighteen months after he
was pierced. Jephson was four months a prisoner, with guards with loaded rifles around him.
That they did not murder him is not due to me.
These officers have had to wade through as
many as seventeen streams and broad expanses
of mud and swamp in a day. They have endured

a sun that scorched whatever it touched. A
multitude of impediments have ruffled their tem-
pers and harassed their hours. They have been
maddened with the agonies of fierce fevers.
They have lived for months in an atmosphere
that medical authority declared to be deadly.
They have faced dangers every day, and their
diet has been all through what legal serfs would
have declared to be infamous and abominable,
and yet they live.

"This is not due to me any more than the
courage with which they have borne all that was
imposed upon them by their surroundings or the
cheery energy which they bestowed to their work,
or the hopeful voices which rang in the ears of a
deafening multitude of blacks and urged the poor
souls on to their goal.

" The vulgar will call it luck. Unbelievers will
call it chance, but deep down in each heart remains the feeling, that of verity there are more
things in heaven and earth than are dreamed of
in common philosophy.

"I must be brief. Numbers of scenes crowd the memory.

"Could one but sum them into a picture it would have a grand interest. The uncomplaining heroism of our dark followers, the brave manhood latent in uncouth disguise, the tenderness we have seen issuing from nameless entities, the great love animating the ignoble, the sacrifice made by the unfortunate for one more unfortunate, the reverence we have noted in barbarians, who, even as ourselves, were inspired with nobleness and incentives to duty—of all these we could speak if we would, but I leave that to the *Herald* correspondent, who, if he has eyes to see, will see much for himself, and who, with his gifts of composition, may present a very taking outline of what has been done, and is now near ending, thanks be to God for ever and ever !

"Yours faithfully,

"**Henry M. Stanley.**"

CHAPTER VII.

THE MARCH TO THE SEA.

On April 26th, 1888, Stanley reached the Equatorial Province and clasped Emin's hand. He found the latter in a state of uncertainty about the future. The expected attack from the Mahdi had not taken place ; on the whole, Emin was unwilling to abandon his government. Anxious for the safety of his rear-guard, Stanley hurried back over his own trail through the woods to Yambuga. He found that Major Barttelot had been murdered, Ward and Troup had gone home, and Jamieson was in search of Tippoo Tib. Less than a third of his two hundred and fifty men could be found. With these he began once more the march through the forest, and in January, 1889, again reached the Nyanza, after much loss and harassing from Arabs and the Wambutti

dwarfs. At the lake the news reached him that
Emin's Egyptian chief officer had rebelled and
thrown Emin and Jephson, his only European
comrade, in prison. This officer, Selim Bey, now
called himself chief of the Province, and had
made a good stand against the Mahdists, who
were at last advancing from the north. The
prisoners escaped from Wadelai, and joined Stanley.

After describing how he hunted up the missing
rear column Stanley portrays the terrors of the
march back to the Nyanza.

"I have already told you that the rear column
was in a deplorable state; that out of the one
hundred and two members remaining I doubted
whether fifty would live to reach the lake; but
having collected a large number of canoes, the
goods and sick men were transported in these
vessels in such a smooth and expeditious manner
that there were remarkably few casualties in the
remnant of the rear column. But wild natives,
having repeatedly defeated the Ugarrowwas

raiders, and by this discovered the extent of their own strength, gave trouble, and inflicted considerable loss among our best men, who had always to bear the brunt of the fighting and the fatigue of paddling. However, we had no reason to be dissatisfied with the time we had made.

" When progress by river became too tedious and difficult an order to cast off canoes was given. This was four days' journey above the Ugarrowwas station, or about three hundred miles above Banalaya. We decided that, as the south bank of the Ituri River was pretty well known to us, it would be best to try the north bank, although we should have to traverse for some days the despoiled lands which had been a common centre for the Ugarrowwas and the Kilingasongas bands of raiders. We were about one hundred miles from grass-land, which opened up a prospect of future feasts of beef, veal and mutton, and a pleasing variety of vegetables, as well as oil and butter for cooking.

" On October 30, having cast off the canoes, the

land march began in earnest, and we two days
later discovered a large plantain plantation in
charge of the Dwaris. The people flung themselves on the plantains to make as large provision
as possible for the dreaded wilderness ahead.
The most enterprising always secured a fair share,
and twelve hours later would be furnished with a
week's provision of plantain flour. The feeble
and indolent reveled for the time being on an
abundance of roasted fruit, but always neglected
providing for the future, and thus became victims
to famine.

"Ten days passed before we reached another
plantation, during which we lost more men than
we had lost between Banalaya and Ugarrowwas.
Small-pox broke out among the Manyema, and
the mortality was terrible. Our Zanzibaris
escaped the pest, however, owing to the vaccina-
tion they had undergone. We were now about
four days' march above the confluence of the
Ihuru and Ituri Rivers and within about a mile
from Ishuru. As there was no possibility of

crossing this violent tributary of the Aruwimi we had to follow its right bank till a crossing could be discovered. Four days later we stumbled across the principal village of the district, called Andikumu. It was surrounded by the finest plantation of bananas and plantains we had yet seen, which all the Manyemas' habit of spoliation and destruction had been unable to destroy. There, our people, after severe starvation during fourteen days, gorged themselves to such excess that it contributed greatly to lessen our numbers. Every twentieth individual suffered from some complaint which entirely incapacitated him from duty.

"The Ituri River was about four miles S. S. E. from this place, flowing from E. N. E. It was about sixty yards broad and deep, owing to heavy rains. From Andikumu six days' march north-east brought us to another flourishing settlement, called Indeman, situated about four hours' march from a river, supposed to be the Ihuru. Here I was considerably nonplussed by a grievous discrep-

ancy between native accounts and my own observations. The natives called it the Ihuru River,
and my instruments and chronometer made it
very evident it could not be the Ihuru. After
capturing some Dwaris we discovered it was the
right branch of the Ihuru, called the Dui River,
this agreeing with my own view. We searched
and found a place where we could build a bridge
across. Bonny and our Zanzibari chief threw
themselves into the work and in a few hours the
Dui River was safely bridged. We passed from
Indeman into a district entirely unvisited by
Manyema."

Here followed daily conflicts with the Wambutti dwarfs, which were very numerous in this
region. The Wambuttis clung to the north-east
route, which Stanley wanted to take. Accordingly, he went south-east and followed elephant
tracks. But on December 9th we were compelled
to halt for forage in the middle of a vast forest,
at a spot indicated by my chart to be not more
than two or three miles from the Ituri River,

which many of our people had seen while residing at Fort Bodo. I sent one hundred and fifty rifles back to a settlement that was fifteen miles back on the route we had come, while many Manyema followers also undertook to follow them.

Six days passed without news of the foragers. For the first four days the time passed rapidly, almost pleasantly, Stanley being occupied in re-calculating his observations from Ugarrowwas to Lake Albert down to date. This occupation ended, he was left to wonder why the large band of foragers did not return. On the fifth day, having distributed all the stock of flour in camp, and having killed the only goat they possessed, he was compelled to open the officers' provision boxes and take a pound pot of butter with two cupfuls of flour to make an imitation gruel, there being nothing else save tea, coffee, sugar, and a pot of sago in the boxes.

On the afternoon of the same day a boy died, and many of the people were so weak that they could not stand. Before night a Mahdi carrier died, and many of the Soudanese showed signs of collapse. On the morning of the following day Stanley fed his one hundred and thirty people with a broth made of a pot of butter, a can of condensed milk, a cupful of flour, and, as he naïvely remarks, an abundance of water.

The crisis was so alarming that Stanley called Bonny and the chiefs to a council. Fears were expressed that the foraging party of one hundred and fifty men had forgotten their starving comrades and were enjoying themselves in some district well stocked with food. Another supposition was that they had lost their road and were in danger of starvation themselves.

Bonny volunteered to remain in camp with ten men if ten days' food were provided for each person. Stanley managed to scrape together enough to make the usual light gruel for this party, but no provision could be made for the sick and feeble, who would also be left behind in the forest. Twenty-six of these were in camp, and there was no hope for any of them unless food could be found within twenty-four hours.

Stanley then started out on his search for the foragers. He traveled nine miles on the first day, passing several dead bodies on the way. On the second day after, he met the foragers marching easily along, as if there were no reason for them to hurry. He prodded them along so energetically that they all reached Camp Starvation twenty-six hours later, laden down with bananas, plantains, and meat. Twenty persons died in Camp Starvation. It was the nearest approach to absolute famine in the whole of Stanley's African experience.

The story of the rebellion against Emin is best told by Lieutenant Jephson.

"On August 18 a rebellion broke out, and the Pasha and I were made prisoners. The Pasha was a complete prisoner, but I was allowed to go about the station, but my movements were watched. The rebellion was gotten up by some half-dozen Egyptians—officers and clerks—and gradually others joined, some through inclination, but most through fear. The soldiers, with the exception of those at Labore, never took part in it, but quietly gave in to their officers.

" When the Pasha and I were on our way to Regaf two men—one an officer, Abdul Voal Effendi, and the other a clerk—went about and told the people they had seen Stanley, and that he was only an adventurer, and had not come from Egypt ; that the letters he had brought from the Khedive and Nubar were forgeries ; that it was untrue Khartoum had fallen, and that Emin Pasha and Stanley had plotted to take them, their wives and their children, out of the country and hand them over as slaves to the English. Such words in an ignorant, fanatical country like this acted like fire among the people, and the result was a general rebellion and we were made prisoners. The rebels then collected the officers from the different stations and held a large meeting to determine what measures they should take, and all those who did not join the movement were so insulted and abused that they were obliged for their own safety to acquiesce in what was done.

"The Pasha was deposed, and those officers suspected of being friendly to him were removed from their posts, and those friendly to the rebels were put in their place. It was decided to take the Pasha as a prisoner to Regaf, and some of the worst rebels were even in for putting him in irons, but the officers were afraid to put their plans into execution, as the soldiers said they never would permit any one to lay a hand on him. Plans were also made to entrap Stanley when he returned. Things were in this condition when we were startled by the news that the Mahdi's people had arrived at Lado with three steamers and nine sandals and nuggars, and had established themselves on the site of the old station. Omar Sali, their general, sent up three dervishes with a letter to the Pasha demanding the instant surrender of the country. The rebel officers seized them and put them into prison, and decided on war.

After a few days the Mahdists attacked and captured Regaf, killing five officers and numbers of soldiers and taking many women and children prisoners, and all the stores and ammunition in the station were lost. The result of this was a general stampede of the people from the stations of Biddon Kirri and Muggi, who fled with their women and children to Labore, abandoning almost everything. · At Kirri the ammunition was abandoned and was seized by natives."

Writing from the south end of Victoria Nyanza, under date of September 3, 1889, Stanley says :

"The rebels of the Emin government relied upon their craft and on the wiles of the 'Heathen Chinee,' and it is amusing now to look back and note how punishment has fallen on them. Was it Providence or was it luck ? Let those who love to analyze such matters reflect on it. Traitors without camp and traitors within were watched, and the most active conspirator was discovered, tried, and hanged. The traitors without fell foul of one another and ruined themselves. If it is not luck, then it is surely Providence in answer to good men's prayers.

" Far away, our own people, tempted by their extreme wretchedness and misery, sold our rifles and ammunition to our natural enemies, the Manyema, the slave trader's true friends, without the least grace either of bodies or souls. What happy influence was it that restrained me from destroying all concerned in it? Each time I read the story of Nelson and Parker's sufferings I feel vexed at my forbearance, and yet again I feel thankful for a higher power than man's, which severely afflicted them with cold-blooded murders by causing them to fall upon one another a few weeks after the rescue and relief of Nelson and Parke.

" The memory of those days alternately hardens and unmans me. With the rescue of Emin Pasha, poor old Casati and those who preferred Egypt's fleshpots to the coarse plenty of the province near Nyanza, we returned ; and while we were patiently waiting, the doom of the rebels was consummated." After this time of dreadful anxiety Stanley was smitten with fever, and came near dying. The strain had been too much, and for twenty-eight days he lay helpless, tended by the kind and skillful hands of Surgeon Parke. Then little by little he gathered strength and finally gave orders for the march for home.

He again plainly laid before Emin Pasha the object of the expedition, and offered to wait a reasonable time for him. Emin agreed that twenty days was a reasonable time for preparation. The interval was occupied by Surgeon Parke in healing the sick. So devoted and skillful was he that Stanley was able, on April 1, 1889, to turn out two hundred and eighty able-bodied men, whereas in February it would have been difficult to muster two hundred.

Stanley complains of the immense loads of property the refugees brought in, entailing endless work upon his men to bring to the plateau, and which was practically rubbish, because it must be abandoned on the march. On March 1 he ordered the stuff be stopped from being brought to camp. Thirteen hundred and fifty-five loads had already been brought in. A month after Selim's departure a letter arrived from him announcing that rebels, officers and everybody, were unanimous to depart for Egypt under Stanley's escort.

Stanley now finding great delay likely in assembling the refugees called a council of the officers, and stated in detail the position of the case, also the danger of trusting the rebels implicitly, as Emin was inclined to do, when they had already boasted of their intention to entrap Stanley with cajoling words and strip his expedition. Finally, Stanley asked the officers whether he would be justified in waiting beyond April 10. Each officer replied in the negative. "There, Pasha," said Stanley, "you have your answer. We march on the 10th."

"In reply to Emin's question," continues Stanley, "I said we could certainly, in our conscience, acquit him of having abandoned the people."

It was clear that the Pasha no longer had authority. At this time, Stanley discovered conspiracies in the camp. The Egyptians tried to steal the rifles of the Zanzibaris, and the number of malcontents kept increasing. Emin had also received news of a bad state of things at Wadelai. Therefore Stanley decided upon immediate action. Those who refused to come were arrested and placed in irons and some were flogged. All denied any knowledge of a plot.

"I told all who desired to accompany me to stand aside and, through the Pasha, threatened to exterminate them wholly if there were any more rebellious tricks. They promised religious obedience. This muster consisted of about six hundred persons. On the 10th we started, numbering about one thousand five hundred persons, including three hundred and fifty newly-enrolled native carriers. On the 12th we camped at Mazambonis. The march was resumed on May 8, adopting a route skirting the Baregga Mountains, forty miles from Nyanza. Arriving at the southern end of the mountains, a successful encounter with the King of Ungoro cleared the route as far as the Semliki River.

The first week of August found the long caravan at Karagwé, a well-known Missionary Station, on the Nyanza's southern shore, whence the route was south-east through the Usukuma and Unyamwezi countries to the coast.

In one of his letters Stanley says : "We have made the unexpected discovery of real value in Africa of a considerable extension of the Victoria Nyanza to the north-west. The almost southerly reach of this extension is south latitude 2° 48', which brings the Victorian sea within one hundred and fifty five miles only from Lake Tanganika. . . . . On the road here I made a rough sketch of it, and I find that the area of the great lake is now increased by this discovery to 20,900 square miles, which is just about 1,900 square miles larger than the reputed exaggerations of Captain Speke."

Discovery after discovery in this wonderful
region was made—the snowy ranges of the
"Cloud King," or "Rain Creator," the Semliki
River, the Albert Edward Nyanza, the plains of
Noongora, the salt lakes of Kative, the new
peoples of the Wakonju or Great Mountains, the
dwellers of the rich forest region, the Awamba :
the fine-featured Wasonyora, the Wanyora ban-
dits, the tribes and shepherd races of the Eastern
uplands ; then Wanyakori, besides the Wanyaru-
wamba and Wazinja.

Stanley came out of Africa with all the Europeans who were connected with Emin Bey's
efforts in the Equatorial Province. He reached
Mpwapwa November 11, on the fifty-fifth day from
the Victoria Nyanza and the one hundred and
eighty-eighth day from the Albert Nyanza, bringing with him seven hundred and fifty people,
including two hundred and ninety of Emin's
people and the white men. The whites with him
were Lieutenant Stairs, Captain Nelson, Jephson,
Surgeon Parke, William Bonny, Mr. Hoffman,

Emin Pasha and his daughter, Captain Casati, Sig. Marco and a Tunisian, Vitu Hassan, an apothecary, and Péres Girault and Schinze, of the Algerian Mission.

The journey eastward was accomplished in two hundred and two days—a quick passage as compared with the journey from Zanzibar to Emin's Province, which took four hundred and twenty-nine days. The return march lay through the country claimed by the Germans. In this latter part of the march the way had been smoothed by the exertions of Captain Wissman in subduing and placating the natives of that region.

Met by Wissman's forces at some distance from the coast, Stanley was greeted with military honors, escorted to Bagamoyo, where German war-vessels fired salutes, and thence was carried in a man-of-war to Zanzibar, where he received by cable dispatches the congratulations of Emperor William of Germany, and of distinguished personages, noted explorers and learned societies.

The British India Steam Navigation Company

gave a luncheon to the hero on board the steamer *Arawatta*. Stanley made a speech, in which he predicted the rapid growth and prosperity of East Africa.

The Queen sent a cable dispatch, in which she said :

"My thoughts are with you and your brave followers, whose hardships and dangers are at an end. I again congratulate you all, including the Zanzibaris, who displayed such devotion and fortitude during your marvelous expedition."

During the progress of a banquet Emin Pasha, owing to his partial blindness, walked off a balcony, and received severe injuries, from which, however, he apparently recovered, though at this writing he is still a very sick man.

Emin Pasha is a man who has won, under somewhat unpropitious circumstances, a claim to something that is better than fame. He is one of the reformers, one might say one of the regenerators, of the race, and to him and to his public career the apothegm may be ascribed that he has made the world better than he found it.

Like General Gordon, who was his prototype, he defended his position against all the assaults of barbarism. In these days of self-seeking politics nothing reads stranger than Gordon's words: "I re-appoint you for civilization's and progress' sake," and Emin's acceptance of the duties of a sacred obligation in the words: "I remain here, the last of Gordon's lieutenants. It is my bounden duty to follow up the road he showed us."

Emin was no sham leader. He once said in words that will be historical: "These people have trusted me and I cannot desert them." It was with the utmost difficulty that Stanley rescued him. His own people revolted before he could be brought to believe that circumstances were desperate. Even then a sentiment of romantic fidelity toward his rebellious people prevented action on his part which would have been wise and sagacious. It was not until Stanley reached him that he could be persuaded to abandon his place.   His name will go down to posterity as that of " Emin the Faithful."

A glance at some of the results of Stanley's last great spanning of the African continent may be of interest to the reader.

Lieutenant Stairs, in June, 1889, spent two days in an attempt to reach the summit of the snowy Ruwenzori, a name which Stanley says, is identical with the " Mountains of the Moon " of the ancients.   In an article on the subject in the *London Times* it is explained that Lieutenant Stairs " only succeeded in reaching a height of 10,600 feet, further progress being stopped by three deep ravines, covered with dense vegetation, that lay between them and the nearest snowy peak, which rose to a further height of 6,000 feet. But beyond this were other peaks, one of which at least rises even higher, so that Stanley's original conjecture of 18,000 feet may, after all, be correct.   The mountain sides, up to 8,000 feet, are inhabited by a people who have apparently taken refuge there from the raiders in the plains below. They disappeared before Stairs and his party.

"Bamboo forests clothe the lower mountain sides, above which was a dense growth of true heaths rising to a height of twenty feet. Here and there were patches of stunted bamboos, beneath a spongy moss, here and there violets and lichens, and scattered around blueberry and blackberry bushes. Lieutenant Stairs made a large collection of plants. The night spent on the mountain side proved to be bitterly cold, a great contrast to the sweltering valley they had left, and yet the thermometer registered 60° when the party turned in for the night. The upper part of the bare, rocky peak before him, Lieutenant Stairs could see, was devoid of vegetation. The extreme top of the peak is crowned with an irregular mass of jagged and precipitous rock and has a distinct crater-like form. In the distance another peak could be seen having a similar form.

"Lieutenant Stairs has come to the conclusion

that the Ruwenzori range, or rather boss, is really
an extinct volcano ; the jutting pinnacles on the
sides of the mountains are old cones that burned
out after the central vent had been choked up ;
the whole evidently having a strong resemblance
to the mountains of Auvergne. From the central mass spurs jut out in all directions, and
down the valleys below these spurs torrents make
their way from the central snow-clad summit,
many evidently finding their way to the Semliki
River and Lake Albert Edward. The debris of
these moldering volcanoes brought down by the
Semliki River, Stanley points out, is enormous,
and is rapidly filling up the south end of the
Albert Nyanza.

"Of the snow on Mount Ruwenzori the greatest mass lay on the western slope, nearest to the
party, covering the slope wherever its inclination
is not too great. The largest bed of snow would
cover a space measuring about six hundred feet
by three hundred feet and of such depth that

only in two spots did the black rock crop out above its surface. Smaller patches of snow extended down into the ravine. The height from the lowest snow to the summit of the peak is about 1,200 feet. Little animal life was seen on the mountain, but there were numerous signs that animals of various kinds went there.

Many people think the African in Africa is a barbarian, but while some of them are, the majority of them are far from being so. Stanley in his travels visited the very worst classes on the Congo. They are no criterions of the Mahometan negroes, but quite the contrary. Africa contains 130,000,000 negro inhabitants outside of the Moors and people of Arabic descent. When we say negroes, we mean natives with woolly hair Woolly hair is characteristic of the negro, but the flat nose and thick lips are only peculiar to them. One of the finest nations of Africa is the Foulah, which numbers about 30,000,000 souls, and live back of Senegambia, occupying a country 1,000 miles north to south and 1,500 east to west. These people are all Mahometans and write their own language in Arabic characters, also speaking, reading and writing Arabic. They are black, with woolly hair, but have thin, prominent noses and very thin lips. No traveler has ever been in their country since 1870. They make their own guns and gunpowder and fine leather work. In their cities they build houses two and three stories high of adobe and frame. They are governed by a Sultan and each man is entitled to four wives. Their costumes are similar to the Turks. Within their nation they have very large cities, but as they will not allow strangers within the borders all that can be learned of them is from such members of the country as make visits to the coast and elsewhere. On one occasion a French army of seven hundred French and 2,500 mixed soldiers with officers attempted to invade the Foulah country and got one hundred and forty-seven miles. Only seventeen succeeded in getting back These people make pilgrimages to Mecca, a distance of 6,800 miles, to pay their respects to the great shrine of the Mahometans. The most beautiful race of negroes are the Jaloff, from which the beautiful negroes of Louisiana were brought.

In Africa polygamy is the rule, and the proportion of females born is two and one-half to one of males. One African—Men Manna, King of the Eastern Veys—had two hundred and thirty-eight wives, five hundred and eighty-four children and 1,860 slaves, and every one of his children, it is said, resembled him to such an extent that one could not fail to recognize them after once seeing the father.

Stanley gives details of much interest concerning the various tribes among whom he passed, tribes mostly in a state of constant apprehension from the raids of their powerful neighbors. The Wakontu are the only people who dwell upon the mountain ; their villages are found at a height of 8,000 feet above the sea. When the Warasura invade their country they retreat still higher up,

to the edge of the snow.   The lower slopes of the
mountain are extensively cultivated by the
Wakonju, who became very friendly with Stanley
and his people.

, The inhabitants of Usongora are described as a
fine race, but in no way differing from the finer
types of men seen in Karagwé and Ankori, and
the Wahuma shepherds of Uganda.   The natives
of Toro are a mixture of the highest class of
negroes, somewhat like the natives of Uganda.
Stanley maintains that the Ethiopic (Abyssinian)
type is thickly spread through these Central
African uplands.   Wherever, he says, we find a
land that enjoys periods of peace we find the
Wahuma at home, with their herds, and in looking at them one might fancy one's self transported
into the midst of Abyssinia.   In Ankori the
Wahuma race is more numerous than elsewhere.
Many of them have features as regular, fair, and
delicate as Europeans.

The country south of Lake Albert Edward,
Stanley thinks, is still unexplored, but that it must

be very different from what it is represented to be in his own map of the ' Dark Continent.' Ruanda, beyond Lake Albert Edward, is evidently a fine country, with a people quite equal in numbers and strength to those of Uganda.

It is thus evident that the geographical results of this memorable expedition are of equal importance to the results in any other direction. Stanley has been enabled to solve some important puzzles in African geography. He was the discoverer of the Congo, and now he has been able to discover one of the remotest sources of the Nile and lay down the water-parting between the two great rivers. From Yambuga to the Albert Nyanza, and thence to Msalala, he has laid down an immense stretch of what is essentially new country, filled in its great physical features, and collected far more precise information about the varied tribes of people than ever he had before.

Stanley's own notes on the physical geography of the lake region are highly interesting. If, he says, we shall draw a straight line from the

debouchure of the Nile from Lake Albert in a
direction south-west magnetic, we shall have
measured the length of a broad line of subsidence
from twenty to fifty miles wide, that lies between
3° north latitude and 1° south latitude, in the
centre of the African Continent. On the west of
this is a great upland, rising from 1,000 to 3,000
feet above the chasm, to which its eastern face
slopes almost perpendicularly down, and the
western side bears away gently westward to the
Ituri and Louva basins. To the right or east is
another upland, rising from 1,000 to 3,000 feet
above the chasm and trending gently eastward on
the Unyoro plateau. In this section lies the
Albert Nyanza. The central section of the so-
called chasm, ninety miles long, consists of the
Ruwenzori range, from 4,000 to 15,000 feet above
the average level of the trough of the Semliki
River valley. The remaining section of the
upland is from 2.000 to 3,500 feet higher than the
trough, and consists of the plateau of Usongora,
Unyampaka, and Ankori. In the south section,

only fifty miles long, lies Lake Albert Edward and the plains between the lake and the mountain.

Lake Albert Edward is comparatively small, not more than half the length of the north lake. The part of the Semliki Valley which extends from the lake south-westerly is very level, for thirty miles not more than fifty feet above the lake, and, in Mr. Stanley's opinion, of quite recent formation. At some distance south of the lake everything is saturated with moisture. At about seventy-five miles from the Albert Nyanza the valley attains a height of about nine hundred feet above the lake, and then the forest region abruptly ends, and as abruptly a new climate is reached, in its drought a complete contrast to the moisture-laden region in the north.

Stanley came first of all down upon the north-west shore of Lake Albert Edward, where lies the district of Usongora. The great tongues of swamp between this and the mountain show how far the lake must at one time have spread. But the plain is a desert, though at one time there are

evidences that it must have been thickly popu-
lated. The raids of the Waganda and Warasura
have depopulated the land of the Wasongora and
left only a miserable remnant. The Ankori plateau, to the south of Unyampaka, Stanley
describes as a large country, thickly peopled.
The plateau is 5,000 feet above the sea, but the
mountains rise to a height of 6,400 feet.

If we lay a huge triangle across Central Africa,
with the apex between the River Aruwimi and
the Lake Albert Nyanza, and with the two
extremities of the base at the mouth of the Congo on the west and at Zanzibar on the east, we
see that Stanley climbed from west to east by way
of the huge obtuse angle which took him through
forests and marshes never before traversed by
civilized man, and amongst strange and quasi-
fabulous peoples, fierce cannibals, and savage
little dwarfs, who offered every obstacle to his
advance. Nor is that the sum of his achievements. When his work seemed to be half-
accomplished, when he had reached the northern

apex of his triangle, he had to return to pick up
the scattered remnants of his rear-guard, left a
long way in the south west. This done, the intrepid and indefatigable man went back again to his
work. Having reached the Albert Lake once
again, and taken up Emin Pasha and the other
fugitives from Wadelai, he struck a direct line to
the coast. No more important contribution to our
knowledge of African geography has been made
within this generation, and no better hope has
been held out for the ultimate civilization of this
unmanageable continent, than the news that the
extremities of the lakes of Victoria Nyanza and
Tanganika are within a distance of each other
which may easily be traversed by a well-equipped
caravan, and which might in time even be joined
by a line of railway. Not less important, though
less encouraging, is Stanley's boast that he has
changed "the dead white" by which the charto-
grapher has marked the Great Desert, which he
crossed, into "a dead black"—a region covered by
"one great, compact, remorseless, sullen forest,"

swarming at intervals with intractable savages.
But apart from the geographical significance of the
journey, it is memorable as a magnificent victory
of human courage over the resistances of Nature.
Neither famine nor fever, neither marsh or forest,
neither the slackness of disheartened followers,
nor · the violence and treachery of countless
enemies, could turn this indomitable leader of
men from doing what he had pledged his word
that he could and would do.

At first sight it seems remarkable that no one
has hitherto discovered the south-western extension of the Victoria Nyanza, of which Stanley
seems inclined to make so much. It is nearly
thirty years since Speke and Grant passed northward to the west of the Victoria Nyanza, through
a country mountainous and marshy, and discovered that Lake Ujiji, which Stanley tells
us in much more extensive than they made out.
They also heard of Lake Akenyara, which Stanley subsequently extended and baptized the Alex-
andra Nyanza. At first one is inclined to con-

clude that these and other lakes and lakelets, which are so numerous in this region, are really only extensions of the Victoria Nyanza.

But this is not the explanation. Stanley's own route when he marched south from Uganda to Ujiji on his first great journey was to the westward of Speke and Grant's, so that then he had no chance of discovering the extension. But at an earlier period of that journey, it will be remembered, he sailed both north and south pretty close to the south-west coast, but yet too far away to detect any extension, which, as he tells us, would be concealed by the mountainous islands which fringe the shore. At a much later date Mr. Pearson, one of the Uganda missionaries, skirted the whole of the south and west coast, going in and out among the islands, and often quite close to the shore. But just at the south-west corner a very considerable bend is indicated, which neither Mr. Pearson nor any one else has visited, and it may well be this bend which Stanley, coming through a perfectly new country,

has found to extend some seventy miles to the
south-west, just as another arm extends far to
the south in the region in which lies Msalala. If,
then, this arm of the lake reaches to 2° 48' south
latitude, it must bring Tanganika and Victoria
Nyanza within one hundred and fifty miles of
each other, though it should be remembered that
the longitudes, even on our best maps, are most
uncertain in this part of Africa.

As to the future career of Mr. Stanley much
might be said. There is a strong probability that
both he and Emin will lend their services to the
British East Africa Company, the members of
which have been so active in connection with this
expedition, and that not a few of Emin's companions will settle down in the company's territories.

This will probably be Stanley's last great expedition. His achievements as an explorer make him
one of the foremost men of his time. He is
honored by all classes and conditions of men. As
has been well said, it is inspiring to note that this

man, whom kings and princes delight to know and praise, spent his boyhood in obscurity, and that in every sense he has been the architect of his own fortunes.

FINIS.

www.ingramcontent.com/pod-product-compliance
Lightning Source LLC
Chambersburg PA
CBHW020239110726
47898CB00004B/1324